Also by Austin Williams

Misdirection
The Platinum Loop
Crimson Orgy
Straight Whisky (with Erik Quisling)

Diversion Books
A Division of Diversion Publishing Corp.
443 Park Avenue South, Suite 1008
New York, New York 10016
www.DiversionBooks.com

For more information, email info@diversionbooks.com

First Diversion Books edition October 2015.
Print ISBN: 978-1-62681-778-4
eBook ISBN: 978-1-62681-556-8

Connect with Austin Williams on Twitter **@awilliams_books**

BLIND SHUFFLE

A RUSTY DIAMOND MYSTERY

AUSTIN WILLIAMS

DIVERSIONBOOKS

BLIND
SHUFFLE

A

1.

The brunette hadn't said a word the whole flight. Rusty detected an aloof vibe from the moment he took an aisle seat next to her when boarding the 737 in Baltimore. He made a cursory stab at conversation and got only an annoyed shake of the head. From the preflight safety spiel through takeoff and into cruising altitude, his comely seatmate did a fine job of acting like he wasn't there.

It didn't bother Rusty, but it made him curious. He wasn't the easiest guy to ignore, based on appearance alone.

The brunette's refusal to even glance at him rendered an uneasy feeling that he'd somehow become invisible. She looked up from her laptop only twice—both times to tell the flight attendant she'd like another glass of Pinot Grigio.

Maybe it's the tattoos, Rusty thought.

He'd taken off his leather jacket and stuffed it under the seat, wearing a black t-shirt underneath, leaving the snaking vines of symbols and incantations covering both arms from shoulder to wrist open to plain view. His seatmate didn't look like the kind of woman apt to recoil from some well-inked body art, but then it was sometimes hard to tell.

They occupied the two port seats in row 3. First class, the way it ought to be, located in front of the gangway and separated by a curtain from coach. Rusty was no snob, but after shelling out more than a grand to upgrade his ticket, he felt the difference should be noticeable.

He scratched his goatee and pondered draining another glass of scotch. The dimly-lit cabin filled with searingly bright illumination, making him blink. Huge flashes of lightning strobed through the windows, followed by an ominous roll of thunder deep enough to induce vibrations in his seat.

The brunette jerked her head up from her laptop to raise the window shade. Her posture had gone rigid. Rusty turned to look over her shoulder. A menacing mass of dark clouds filled the oval glass partition, pierced by another burst of lightning.

The brunette pulled down the shade and recoiled into her seat. Rusty suddenly understood the source of her withdrawn demeanor.

She's scared out of her wits.

Not an unjustified reaction, on this flight. The first two hours had passed calmly enough, but they ran into the outer rim of a massive cyclonic event shortly after entering Louisiana airspace. The "fasten seat belts" sign came on with a ping as the captain casually intoned over the intercom things might get a bit choppy between here and the tarmac.

That proved to be an understatement. For the past half hour, this 737 felt more like an ill-conceived amusement park ride than an airliner. Rusty had only flown through one serious storm before, years ago, and at the time he was so blasted on muscle relaxants and champagne he'd found it more entertaining than frightening. He was enjoying this flight considerably less.

"Shit!" his seatmate yelped as the plane banked ten degrees to the right, sending a splash of Pinot Grigio onto her laptop. The glass rolled off the tray table as its emptied contents trickled down the computer screen.

"Christ, I hate flying," she said with an embarrassed glance at Rusty. "Did I spill on you?"

"Nah. Just missed me."

He reached down to retrieve the errant glass and set it on her tray table. "Dead soldier, I'm afraid."

"Doesn't make any difference. I could hammer back a whole bottle and I'd still be a wreck."

"It was supposed to be a clear evening, at least when I checked at BWI. Then again, I learned a long time ago not to trust the weather where we're going."

"Do you live in New Orleans?" she asked.

"Used to. This is my first visit in a while."

The plane bucked again, harder than before.

"Oh Jesus," the brunette muttered, gripping the seat divider.

Rusty saw her expending great effort to maintain a polished facade, and failing. He couldn't help but sympathize.

"I'm a little nervous myself," he said, leaning just a bit closer. "But not about getting there safely. That's the least of my worries."

She looked at him with new interest, a trace of the fear removed from her eyes.

"Why's that?"

Rusty paused before answering. He saw no reason to confide in this stranger, other than passing the time a bit faster before they landed.

"I plan to visit some people I haven't seen in a long time. They don't know I'm coming, and I have no reason to think they'll be glad to see me."

"Do they owe you money or something?" she asked, amused by the question.

"Just the opposite. I owe them a hell of a lot, more than I can ever repay. Especially the old man. He taught me my trade, asked for nothing except loyalty."

Rusty paused before adding, "I let him down. His daughter too."

"So you're coming to ask their forgiveness?"

The question hit a nerve. A sense of obligation cutting deeper than common regret had propelled Rusty from his comfortable rented home in coastal Maryland, all the way to the airport in Baltimore and into the first class cabin of this airliner. When he actually reached New Orleans and looked Prosper Lavalle in the eye for the first time in more than half a decade… he had no idea what might happen at that point.

"I just want to clean things up, if possible."

He turned to his seatmate and detected an innate kindness in her face, tucked away beneath the glossy veneer.

"I hope it goes well," she said. "People can forgive a lot if you're sincere in asking for it. Seems like you are."

"I appreciate that," he replied, offering his hand. "My name's Rusty."

She reciprocated with a businesslike shake.

"Erin."

Another jolt to the cabin caused her hand to close tightly on his. Five lacquered nails dug into his skin in a way Rusty didn't entirely dislike.

"God, I fucking *hate* this," Erin said hoarsely. "Last time I ever get on a plane, guaranteed."

"This is a homebound flight, then?"

She nodded.

"I'm a sales rep for Revlon. When I interviewed for the job I told them: no travel. So far they've honored that, but I really felt pressured to make the convention in Baltimore."

"We'll be all right," Rusty said, looking at his watch and noticing she hadn't freed his hand. "Less than an hour, you'll have Louisiana soil beneath your feet."

"I might just kiss it."

A new ping on the intercom claimed their attention.

"Hey folks, this is Captain Thompson. I want to apologize for that last little dip. We ran into a microscale atmospheric gradient, also known as a wind shear. That tends to happen more often during clear air turbulence, but stormy conditions can sometimes produce the same result. Our aircraft is equipped with a reliable on-board detection system, so it's extremely uncommon for us to fly directly into one of these pesky things. That wasn't a very big one, even if it felt like it. Unfortunately the scope and severity of this storm may have confused our system regarding its exact location."

"Very reassuring," Erin said, clutching Rusty's hand tighter.

"I'm guessing that's not part of the airline's approved spiel," he answered.

"Not to worry," Captain Thompson continued. "We're lowering our altitude now as we approach our initial descent. This should cut down on the turbulence signifi—"

The plane banked hard, fifteen degrees to the left. Rusty and Erin tipped toward the window in unison. She cried out briefly before clamping her mouth shut. More than a few startled noises arose within the first class cabin, with one full-out scream emanating from coach.

"Just sit tight, folks," the captain cautioned over the intercom, sounding noticeably less relaxed. "We'll be out of this soon. It might not be the smoothest landing in aviation history, but we'll get you on the ground as quickly and safely as possible."

Erin had released Rusty's hand, both of hers folded tightly in her lap. A trickle of sweat ran from her brow, sending a runny line of mascara down her cheek.

"Shit, shit, shit," she muttered in a strained whisper. "Say something to me, please."

"What would sound good right about now?"

"Anything, doesn't matter. Just take my mind off this."

Rusty considered offering some statistics about the safety of flight as opposed to other forms of transportation, but that wasn't what was called for. What this woman needed was some misdirection.

"Look me in the eye, Erin."

In response to her wary glance, he added:

"Trust me, this is a great distraction."

"OK."

"Good. I want you to think of someone. Someone you know personally. Don't tell me who it is, just form a clear picture of this person in your mind."

She took a deep breath, closing her eyes. Then she opened them and said, "OK, I've got someone."

"All right. Now give me both hands."

She hesitated as he held his own hands out, palms up, then did as he'd asked. Rusty closed his fingers around each hand, pressing gently on the webbed flesh located between her thumbs and forefingers. He felt the inner play of muscles and tendons as her pulse slowed by degrees.

"OK. You're thinking of a man, that's obvious."

She gave a wan nod.

"Fifty-fifty chance of getting that one right."

"I'll try to get a little more specific. Keep looking me

in the eye."

Rusty's thumbs pressed more closely, feeling out the part of her hands known in medical texts as the *thenar eminence*. He picked up on each tiny throb, felt the muscles tense and relax in sequence as his touch grew heavier.

Reading her gaze, he spoke with better than moderate confidence:

"This guy's name begins with an M."

A small spark lit Erin's eye, and he saw her smile for the first time.

"Not bad," she said, "but come on. You had a 1-in-26 chance of getting that right. Probably one of the more common letters in a first name."

Rusty heard the words, but kept his focus on the way she was unconsciously communicating with him. The faint wrinkling of her nose, a tightening of the jawline so minute as to be undetectable by anyone who hadn't spent years studying the vast range of facial and bodily gestures people employ to transmit information without being aware of it.

"It's not Matt," he said. "No, definitely not. And it's not Martin."

Erin replied with a nod, sensing that to speak would offer an unintended clue.

"I won't even bother asking if it's Monty. And Mycroft is a long shot, unless his parents are really into Sherlock Holmes."

"You're just fishing now."

That was partially true, but in replying Erin supplied him with another telling bit of insight—the emphasis she placed on the first syllable of *fish*ing.

"Nope," Rusty answered casually as he released her hands. "I knew his name was Michael all along."

He let that hang there for a moment, clocking her reaction. The smile that grew on Erin's face, free of any tension or anxiety, made up for her earlier standoffishness.

"He goes by Michael, right? Not Mike."

"Michael it is. I'm impressed."

"And he's your…fiancé. Yeah. Probably waiting to greet

you at the airport with a big kiss."

Now the smile changed shape, widening to express something beyond passing amusement.

"Not bad. So you're, what, a magician?"

Rusty was pondering an adequate reply to that question when the 737 hit a massive wind shear at two hundred miles per hour. The plane's nose buckled down sharply like it had been nailed with a gigantic fly swatter.

Erin screamed. A genuine scream, pulled from her lungs with the force of real terror, and hers wasn't the only one.

Multiple bags tumbled from overhead containers jolted open by the drop. A service cart near the flight deck rolled from the galley into the aisle on spinning wheels, its brake set loose. A plump flight attendant fell to her knees trying to stop a heavy roller bag from falling onto an elderly man in 4C. The attendant's head struck the metal edge of an armrest, opening up a deep gash. Blood sprayed from the wound, prompting a fresh volley of screams from the first class cabin. The noise coming from coach sounded like a packed theater in the middle of a particularly intense horror movie.

Another first class attendant ran to assist his partner, yelling for calm over the panicked cries. It was a futile effort, even the captain's voice on the intercom was lost in the din.

Rusty and Erin huddled in their seats, arms wrapped around each other in an instinctive clinch. The cabin trembled and heaved, everything rattling hard enough to loosen hinges and splinter apart.

The 737 kept dropping into a sharp dive for well over a thousand feet. Three thousand. Five. The engine roar overlapped what sounded like a hurricane raging outside the shuddering windows. It seemed to go on and on, as if the ground below kept racing away to delay the inevitable, catastrophic impact.

Finally, Rusty felt the cabin start to level out. He and Erin were shoved back into their seats as the plane's nose pushed upward. Some measure of calm returned to the first class cabin.

"Flight personnel be seated immediately," Captain Thompson resumed on the intercom, his voice hardened to a drill instructor's bark. "Suspend normal cross-check."

The wounded flight attendant lowered herself into a galley seat. She pressed a towel seeped in red to her face and strapped on an over-the-shoulder safety belt. Her partner scrambled into the adjacent seat.

Rusty clutched Erin tightly, feeling her heartbeat hammering against his chest. His eyes blinked shut against another burst of lightning off the plane's port side. He felt no particular fear. He sensed, on a gut level that had nothing to do with logic, this plane would reach the ground safely.

I know it, without knowing why.

Secure in his intuition of momentary safety, Rusty inhaled deeply, allowing oxygen to fill his lungs at a slow controlled pace. He felt completely alive. He felt good. Yet at the same time, he couldn't entirely dismiss an unnerving sense that whatever awaited him down on the Louisiana soil threatened him more gravely than the prospect of crashing to it from high above.

2.

Ninety minutes later, Rusty was alive and on the ground, moving with a purposeful stride down one of the quieter blocks of Bourbon Street, deep in the Quarter and heading for the river. He was still amped from the hairy flight. Too amped. His destination stood barely a hundred paces away, and he didn't want to get there before he felt adequately centered.

Clear your head and calm down, he cautioned himself. *Makes no sense to do this all jacked up on adrenaline.*

Captain Thompson hadn't been lying when he warned his passengers not to expect a cushiony landing. It was the roughest Rusty had ever experienced. By the time they'd taxied to a stop, Erin had grown so pale she looked in need of a transfusion. Soaked in sweat, her nails left a few red divots in Rusty's palm. He didn't complain.

She recovered quickly once the cabin door opened, walking without a wobble up the jetway next to Rusty. They stayed side by side down the escalator to the arrivals level. Her beetle-browed fiancé stood waiting anxiously by baggage claim. He shot Rusty a hostile look when Erin treated him to a thankful hug for helping her get through it. The hug lasted maybe a half-second too long, and Rusty released himself with a quick goodbye.

He rented a Kona Blue Mustang GT at the Hertz desk and navigated light traffic on the eastbound I-10 into New Orleans. The storm had blown over with tropical dispatch, leaving a shimmery slickness on the roads and an unblemished sky turning lavender with sundown. Taking the Esplanade Avenue exit into the French Quarter, Rusty drove to the Cornstalk Hotel on Royal Street, a fabled Victorian monument dating back to the mid-nineteenth century.

His room, a king suite, was appointed in high Southern gothic, replete with an antique canopy bed and a clawfoot tub that pleased him for some reason he couldn't name. It also contained an electronic wall safe, as he'd requested.

Rusty splashed some water on his face and changed into a fresh shirt. He unzipped an inner compartment of his travel bag and pulled out a thick manila envelope. For a long moment he weighed it in one hand, reaching for a decision.

Bring it now or try to break the ice first?

The envelope felt unaccountably heavy in his palm. It contained exactly $124,600. All crisp new hundreds. He had no idea if the money would be accepted or thrown back in his face.

And I'm not ready to find out just yet.

Rusty nodded in affirmation of that decision. He deposited the envelope in the safe and set a four-digit code on the digital screen. A quick tug on the handle confirmed the safe was secure. Then he rode the elevator down and hit the street, feeling the uneven flagstones of the Quarter under his feet for the first time in over a decade.

He walked away from the Cornstalk at a casual pace, forcing himself not to hurry. Stars glimmered in the darkening canopy above Royal's wrought-iron balconies like tiny spotlights over a sprawling stage.

His footsteps halted at the intersection of Bourbon and Toulouse. A one-story, slant-roofed building occupied the northwest corner. The Mystic Arts Emporium.

That grandiose name, spelled out in faded letters above the entrance, stood in contrast to the small size of the place. It was really no more than a hurricane shack, built many decades ago from plaster and aged planks, resting on a foundation two feet above street level to secure against flooding and infestation by vermin.

Rusty took a last measured breath, then stepped through a curtain of multicolored beads.

The sound of those beads rattling yielded a powerful rush

of nostalgia. It was heightened by a dank, musky fragrance filling the air: incense, the same hand-dipped sticks he himself used to make, wrap, and sell by the dozen in this same room. All those different scents came back to him like the names of estranged family members. Black Magic. Gris-Gris. Devil's Bone. Spectral Love. Eau d'Laveau. And the ever-popular Gator's Breath, whose tangy bayou bouquet now pulled him deeper into the Emporium with invisible hands.

Rusty heard the voice before he saw the man who spoke. From the far end of the room, Prosper Lavalle's signature rumble cut through the darkness, sending a shiver up his spine.

"Circle in close now, people. This here magic, she thrives on communal energy."

Rusty stepped deeper into the Emporium, marveling at what an odd hybrid it was—half low-end shop selling souvenirs of dubious value, and half legitimate shrine to the most rarified aspects of conjuring. For every cheap trinket made in Korea, an artifact of colossal import to anyone with the knowledge to recognize its value lay waiting to be discovered on the velvet-lined shelves.

He moved past a rack of plastic magic wands and $3 bags of gris-gris, approaching a small group of people clustered around a glass display case. Behind the case, clad in a black top hat and maroon velvet cloak fraying at the sleeves, stood the most elegant man Rusty had ever known.

Tall and rangy, Prosper carried himself with a studied poise that appeared utterly loose and natural. Simple actions such as laying his hand on a doorknob or scratching his nose assumed a poetic fluidity. His eyes, a shade of brown just slightly darker than his skin, gleamed with secret knowledge and a sense of mirth that could appear benign or malevolent by turns.

Rusty felt a thrill as he inched closer to the display case. But he also felt something else—a sense of shock that he hoped wasn't visible on his face. Prosper appeared to have aged more than a decade in less than half that time since Rusty last saw him. Despite his familiar sartorial trappings, the man was a shell of himself.

That voice, however, rang out with all its former strength.

"I want y'all to pay close attention to the movement of these here bones," Prosper commanded, eyes roving from one audience member to the next as his gloved hands manipulated a pair of large wooden dice, their black sides etched with grinning ivory skulls.

"This ain't no parlor trick. What you're about to see here is straight-up *hoodoo*, taught to me as a boy by my grandaddy out in Terrebonne Parish. He carved these blocks himself, and he set a spell on 'em the last night of his life."

Rusty moved closer to the glass case, standing behind a man clad entirely in denim who watched the demonstration with one arm draped around his wife's freckled shoulder.

Prosper breezed through the illusion with a series of precise motions and expert misdirectional cues. He caused the dice to disappear one at a time, then return to his palm from thin air. The inlaid skulls changed color, from stark white to bayou blue to a deep angry red. In a final flourish, he offered the dice to a young girl who squealed with delighted panic as they dissolved into a plume of gray smoke the instant she touched them.

An appreciative murmur rippled through the audience, augmented by a few claps. Someone dropped a bill in the tip jar.

Then it happened. Rusty's gaze met Prosper's, and for half a tick they were the only people in the room. Prosper broke eye contact first, producing the dice from a pocket and returning them to a leather case. Rusty saw a tiny tremble in his hand, but he doubted anyone else in the room noticed, or had the slightest idea what a disruption his appearance created.

"I'll be needing some assistance for my next illusion," Prosper said, running his eyes over the assemblage in search of a worthy candidate.

A giggly redhead wearing a tanktop with the words "Flotation Device" spelled out in spangles raised a hand to volunteer, nudged by her hulking boyfriend.

Prosper appeared to weigh her worth as a participant, then shaped his right hand into a gun, long forefinger pointing like a barrel directly between Rusty's eyes. Rusty almost flinched, feeling as if the full accusatory weight of that finger could strike him down with an invisible bullet.

"You, sir. Do you think you're capable of assisting me with this ancient and sacred illusion?"

"Do my best," Rusty said, stepping forward and ignoring a nasty look from the disappointed redhead's companion.

"It requires no special skill. Only an honest mind and a small modicum of physical coordination." Prosper rolled his eyes in a pantomime of doubt that his chosen assistant possessed those qualities, drawing a laugh from the audience.

He signaled for Rusty to join him behind the glass case. Rusty did so, his dismay rising as they stood shoulder to shoulder. The last time he'd seen Prosper, they were of virtually identical height. Now, with his wilted stance, the elder magician appeared at least two inches shorter.

"Before we get started," he said, eyes boring into Rusty's with unnerving intensity, "perhaps you'd be willing to empty the left pocket of that fine leather jacket."

Feeling a shiver of almost telepathic anticipation, Rusty slid a hand into the pocket. His fingers touched something that wasn't there mere seconds before.

Son of a bitch.

"Pull it out!" Prosper shouted, voice raw with anger.

Shaking his head, Rusty produced a small folding knife from the jacket. It was oblong in shape, constructed entirely of wood. The handle's smooth surface was inlaid with a complex pattern of arcane symbols. Inside the handle lay a four-inch blade of polished teak that was sharper than any switchblade.

A stunningly unique object. It even had a name, carved in letters so minute as to be unreadable unless seen in bright light: The Marrow Seeker.

Rusty had first held this knife in a tremulous grip at the age of seventeen. That was just a few days after Prosper found him shivering and underfed on the stoop in front of the Emporium and decided for reasons—never fully explained—to take the homeless runaway under his wing.

He didn't feel Prosper planting the Marrow Seeker on him

a moment ago. Rusty himself had performed countless similar plants, either slipping an item into some unwitting person's pocket or liberating it from them. He was supposed to be a pro, and his old mentor just schooled him badly in front of an audience.

"Are you familiar with this establishment's policy regarding thieves?" Prosper asked loudly.

"I'm guessing it's harsh."

"That's an item of incalculable worth. The only one of its kind, also hand-carved by my grandfather and never replicated. You've dishonored the spirit of the Lavalle lineage by trying to steal it."

Murmurs of disapproval arose from the cluster of spectators. Rusty could almost feel waves of contempt floating across the room in his direction.

He gave the Marrow Seeker a last admiring glance, then set it down on the glass case.

"Guess it was a bad idea."

"Bet your life it was a bad idea," the tourist decked out in denim snarled, as if a theft had been attempted on his own property. "This man could throw a curse on you, boy. Ought to, anyhow."

"Hell yes," another voice rose in agreement. "Hex his ass."

Prosper waved away that suggestion, speaking to the lowly thief without favoring him with eye contact. "Doesn't appear you've made any friends here. Should I notify the police?"

The Flotation Device's boyfriend took an aggressive step forward. "Forget the cops," he slurred. "I'll deal with him."

"No need for that," Rusty said, hands raised in a conciliatory posture. The last thing he wanted to do was lay this drunk fool out cold on the floor, but another step in his direction would limit the alternatives.

"I believe a hasty exit is your best course," Prosper said, turning his back on Rusty. "Remaining gone would be a wise decision."

"He means *stay* out," Denim Man offered for clarification.

Rusty was already moving through the beaded curtain and

leaving the Emporium. He stepped out onto the damp sidewalk and just stood for a moment in mute admiration. Despite the deficiencies of advancing age, Prosper Lavalle remained the best magician he'd ever seen.

No question about it. But tonight's not over.

Rusty carried that resolution across the street, leaned against a lamppost, and waited.

3.

Just past midnight, a few last lingerers filed out of the Emporium. Prosper emerged through the bead curtain and turned to close a folding iron gate. The ancient hinges screeched in protest.

Rusty quickly crossed the street to assist him. The gate clanged shut and Prosper locked it.

"Didn't ask for no help. Don't need no help."

He pocketed the key and pulled down the brim of his top hat.

"Nice plant," Rusty said, following him up Bourbon toward Canal Street. "Never saw it coming."

"How *could* you see it, with your eyes glued up high like that? Child's play to make a cross-hand placement, as long as you hold the mark's gaze above the neckline."

"Of course," Rusty nodded. "Misdirection 101."

"I guess you forgot that, along with everything else I taught you."

"Only thing I forgot is how fast your hands are. That was a stupid mistake I'm not apt to repeat."

"Ah, Rusty," Prosper uttered with a shake of the head. "If there's one thing we've learned about you, it's that you're certain to repeat mistakes. Especially the stupid ones."

They walked in silence for twenty paces before Rusty tried again.

"Buy you a drink? Or coffee and a beignet?"

"Thank you, no."

"Where you headed?"

"Storyville. Got a real nice hoochie out there. She's waiting for me with a pitcher of Hurricanes and a feathered whip."

The sardonic spite of those words landed so harshly on Rusty's ears that he didn't offer a reply. He'd expected no better, but it still stung.

"I'm catching a streetcar home," Prosper said, a measure of acid removed from his tone. "Been on my feet for ten hours and barely a hundred in the till to show for it."

"Can you tolerate my company from here to the stop?"

The old man offered no answer, which Rusty chose to interpret as tacit acceptance.

They traversed, without words, the noisiest blocks of Bourbon. Past open doorways filled with blaring music, stumbling tourists, ladies of questionable repute. All of it bathed in a murky neon glow and smelling like last week's spilled beer.

Not until they'd reached the streetcar stop at Canal and Decatur did Prosper speak.

"Why you here, Rusty?"

"Does making up for lost time sound too optimistic?" Answering his own question with a nod, he quickly added, "I came to square things, with you and Marceline both. Really hoping it's not too late for that."

He saw Prosper recoil slightly.

"You don't want to see me," Rusty continued, "that's fine. But the ledger still needs balancing. You two left Vegas in such a hurry, never collected your full pay from Caesars."

Prosper stopped in his tracks. He looked at Rusty with fresh surprise.

"You think some money's gonna patch it up? Make things like they were before that desert turned you into something…"

He didn't finish the sentence, like the memory it alluded to was too distasteful to be spoken aloud.

"For 682 shows," Rusty said, "you and Marcie served as the best backstage assistants I could ever want. You only got paid for 360 of those shows before you bailed on me."

"And it took you two years to figure out we're owed this money?"

"I've known all along. Just didn't know the best way to face you. If this opens a door to getting us back on a good footing, I'd love that. If not, I'm on a plane in two days and won't bother you again."

"Keep your payoff. We're getting along just fine."

"It's not a payoff, damnit. It's simple compensation for the work you both did."

"I said keep it."

"Are you answering on Marceline's behalf? I really don't think that's your call, old man."

Prosper wheeled on him angrily, but Rusty kept talking.

"She's entitled to decide for herself. I don't believe she'll turn it down. Not with a baby on the way."

"How you know about that?"

Rusty paused before answering. He knew he was entering perilous ground but saw no way around it.

"She came to visit me. A few months ago."

Prosper sagged for a moment, as if receiving long-delayed verification of some dreaded suspicion.

"It was entirely her doing, OK? She used the Internet to track me down, showed up on my doorstep without any advance notice."

"In that godawful desert?"

"No. I left Vegas over a year ago. Pretty sure you must've heard about that."

"I heard you vanished, that's all. Everybody asking, 'What happened to the Raven?' Big star magician disappears without a trace, and just when things were going *so well* for you."

The biting disdain of that last utterance was enough to give Rusty pause about his whole purpose in coming to New Orleans.

"I moved back to Maryland," he soldiered on. "Got a house in Ocean Pines, near where I grew up. That's where Marcie found me. We spoke briefly, but the conversation got cut short."

A rattling of unoiled brakes announced the imminent appearance of the next streetcar from around a blind corner.

"She's an adult who can make up her own mind," Prosper grumbled. "What are you bothering me for?"

"I don't have her address, or even a phone number. Hoping

we can all sit down tomorrow and handle this."

Prosper almost replied, then stopped. His upper body trembled as if animated by some inner palsy. Rusty laid a hand on his shoulder, half surprised it didn't get shrugged away.

A streetcar rolled noisily toward them, its bottle-green flank grinding to a halt at the curb. People started filing in. Some with the $1.25 fare handy, others searching their pockets for change.

"What's wrong?" Rusty asked, hand still on the quaking shoulder. "Talk to me, please."

"Won't do no good," Prosper answered, stepping forward to free himself. "Even if I give you the address, you won't find her."

"What are you talking about?"

Prosper eased himself onto the first step leading into the streetcar, then turned. For the first time, Rusty beheld the full grip of misery suffocating his estranged mentor. It wasn't mere age that had carved those hollows in his face, etched those dark circles under his eyes. The man was clearly terrified.

"She's gone, Rusty. Five months pregnant, and my baby girl's gone."

He stood on the step for an agonized moment, backlit by the soft yellow light of the streetcar's interior. Rusty grabbed the hem of his velvet jacket, yanking him around.

"Hold it! What do you mean, gone?"

Prosper brought both gloved hands together as if in prayer, then drew them apart with splayed fingers. It was a familiar performance bit, usually accompanied by a burst of flame from ignited flash paper.

"Disappeared, like smoke. Four days and no trace of her. Tell me, what you gonna do about that?"

Prosper turned away and dropped a handful of coins into the fare box. Rusty remained for a moment on the curb, mind churning incoherently. The sense of disorientation he'd been surfing since the turbulent plane ride reached a dizzying crest.

Gone?

The door started to swing shut with a metallic shudder. Rusty reached one arm in through the gap and lurched up the step. The door clanged hard against his shoulder.

The gray-haired driver, screwed into his pilot's chair with a weary mien that suggested he'd been navigating this route since the first tracks were laid, shot Rusty a dirty look.

"What the hell, man? Ever boarded a streetcar before?"

Prosper sat slumped in an aisle seat, not even glancing up as Rusty bumped past him. The window seat was occupied so he took one two rows behind. He forced himself to stay calm and wait for a chance to ask the question humming in his brain like a maddened wasp.

What the hell happened to Marceline?

• • •

Twenty minutes later, Prosper reached up to pull the cord as the streetcar approached the intersection of St. Charles and Felicity. They'd advanced into the Lower Garden, a largely residential district with a smattering of food and nightlife options adding to the foot traffic.

Rusty rose and followed him out the car's back exit. They walked slowly down Felicity's cracked sidewalk, toward the river.

"Are you gonna tell me what's going on, Prosper?"

"Told you already. I ain't heard from my daughter in going on a week. If you came to see her, I can't tell you where she is 'cause I don't know."

"When was the last time you saw her?"

"Four nights ago, which you wouldn't have to ask if you'd been listening."

"So that was Monday?"

"She stopped by the house to show me one of those... pictures they take inside her belly."

"An ultrasound?"

Prosper grunted in confirmation, then continued. "We were gonna meet for lunch at Two Sisters the next day. She never showed. Didn't return my calls all day and night. So I drive over to her place—"

"Is she still living in the Marigny? She mentioned that, last time I spoke with her."

Prosper directed a glimpse of bottled fury at Rusty, silently telling him one more interruption would bring this conversation to a permanent close.

"Place ain't fit for habitation, I never understood why she chose to live there. Her apartment's not bad but the neighborhood's halfway to a slum. Anyway, she wasn't home. I called the hospital where she works, they ain't seen her. She missed three shifts in a row. They're about ready to fire her."

"Have you talked to the police?"

"Damn right I have. Went straight to the precinct, didn't bother with the phone. Detective there, man named Hubbard, he brushes me off quick."

"He didn't even take a report?" Rusty asked incredulously.

"He took one. I gave him a picture of Marcie and all her information. Next day he calls me back, says they got nothing. Investigated her place, no sign of a crime. Her car's gone so they think she maybe just took off. Like that's something she does all the time."

Rusty mulled in silence for a few paces. It did strike him as wildly out of character for Marceline to take a trip without letting her father know, but how sure could he be of that? Close as he'd once been to these people, years had since passed. He didn't learn much from Marceline's surprise visit to Ocean Pines last fall, except that she was pregnant and employed at a hospital in New Orleans.

In fact, he suddenly remembered, *she never told Prosper she was coming to visit me. Worried it might upset him too much.*

"Is there any reason you think some harm has befallen her?" he asked. "I know it's unlike her to take off without telling you, but is there anything specific that's got you so scared?"

Prosper stopped talking. He stopped walking, too, as if a mental image had just formed that rendered forward movement an impossibility until it cleared his vision.

"No-count son of a bitch. Man's bad news all around, I told her that from the jump."

"Who?"

"Abellard, for Christ's sake. Son of a bitch who knocked her up."

Hawking and spitting on the pavement like the name he'd just uttered left a poisonous taste in his mouth, Prosper resumed his shuffling gait. Rusty followed in silence for a few steps.

"You think this man knows where she is?"

"Course I do. She broke it off with him last month. Said she's had enough of his disrespect, that's what she told me. But there's more to it than that. Man like him, he ain't gonna lay down when a woman shows him the exit. 'Specially not with his seed already planted."

"Abellard, huh. What's his first name?"

"Joseph. First time Marcie brung him around, I said lose this one, he'll bring you nothing but tears. She used to listen to me, same as you did. She says don't worry about it, he's only rough on the outside. Six months later she's pregnant. She wants to break it off, but it's too late. Man ain't gonna let her walk, I know it."

"Where can I find this guy? I want to talk to him."

Without replying, Prosper stopped walking again. For a moment, Rusty thought the old man had expended enough effort to lay down right here on the uneven cement of the sidewalk. Then he saw Prosper reaching in his pants pocket for a key chain, and realized they'd arrived at the Lavalle homestead. Rusty had been so consumed by the disturbing conversation, he hadn't even realized they'd reached the 1400 block of Camp Street.

A 1920s-era shotgun house crouched low behind a ragged row of hedges opposite Coliseum Park. A cluster of palmettos and elephant ears filled the front yard, enclosed by a chain link fence. Under the glow of twin porch lamps, the house grinned at Rusty like an old friend caught by surprise.

I'll be damned. Looks smaller than I remembered it.

A modest domicile by most measures, the significance of this house assumed mountainous heights in his psyche. It had once been more than just a home for a young and wayward Rusty Diamond. It had been his school, his refuge, the inner sanctum where he'd spent untold hours in study of the skills that would later bring him fame.

Looking at the stooped old man trying to find the right key on a rusted brass chain, Rusty saw him unobscured by the ravages of age and the gap in communication that yawned between them. He'd never known a man like Prosper Lavalle. More than a mentor or even a father, during the formative years of Rusty's life he'd been something close to a living god. And his daughter, Marceline, once seemed no less than the embodiment of love itself.

"I'll find her," Rusty said.

"Ain't your problem, son. Police already done what little they're willing to. I'll stay on them, at the end of thirty days maybe they'll get serious and start asking for some DNA samples. Meantime I post flyers around town, call the hospitals and central morgue every night. Bracing myself for the worst. All the while, I'm waiting for her to show up on this stoop, out of the blue with some funny story about where she's been."

"Prosper, I'll find her. I promise."

Those words didn't come easily, reminding Rusty of the last time they'd been together and the wafer-thin basis of trust connecting them.

Prosper shook his head in protest, but it was a meek effort.

"Don't trouble yourself. You got some guilt you wanna pay off from what went down in Vegas, fine. I'll hold the money for her, and if…"

The sentence died unfinished. Rusty knew Prosper had caught himself before saying, *if I ever see her again.*

He'd probably thought those words a hundred times in the past several days. It was Rusty's unannounced appearance out of the past that brought them to his lips. Both men knew it.

"Why don't you invite me in? Make me some of that jasmine tea I remember so well, and we can talk about it."

4.

Rusty leaned against a lamppost by the streetcar stop as his wristwatch ticked over to 1:16 A.M. One hand instinctively reached for the wallet in his hip pocket, to make sure it was still there.

He wasn't worried about losing the thick roll of cash it held, or even his ID. The wallet's most valuable item was a small piece of paper on which he'd scribbled some crucial data while hunched over a battered coffee table in Prosper's living room.

Marceline's home address. Her landline and cell numbers. Her car's make, model, and plate number. Name and address of the hospital where she worked as a maternity ward nurse. Name and number of the Sixth Precinct detective who'd taken the report from Prosper three days ago.

It was a solid list, enough to get him started. He'd strained to think of anything else that might prove valuable but came up with nothing. By that point, Prosper was already ushering him to the door. The old man looked so exhausted that he was moving like a somnambulist, lids drooping heavily over eyes devoid of their usual spark. Rusty said he'd be in touch the minute he learned anything useful.

He glanced down Felicity toward the shotgun house, hoping Prosper was already asleep. Then he started walking. After eight blocks, his legs began to complain so he was relieved to see a cab heading in his direction. He called out for it and gratefully climbed into the back seat.

"Where to, baby?" the heavyset driver asked with a glance in the rearview mirror.

"Cornstalk Hotel."

"Mmhmm," the cabbie hummed, punching the meter. "Fancy joint."

The drive progressed in silence. Rusty stared out the window without taking notice of the darkened cityscape flashing by. Just before they crossed Canal into the French Quarter, he leaned forward in his seat.

"Change of plans," he said, reaching for his wallet.

"Mmhmm. Talk to me."

Rusty unfolded the piece of paper with his handwritten notes.

"1242 Burgundy. That's in the Marigny."

"I know where it is," the cabbie mumbled, easing into the left turn lane. "Sort of a different kind of destination, ain't it?"

A few minutes later, the taxi took a right onto Burgundy. They drove for a dozen blocks into a poorly-lit residential neighborhood, each block less inviting than its predecessor.

When they reached the 1200 block, the cabbie slowed to a crawl. Rusty peered out the window, surprised by the seediness of this street. His memory of the Faubourg-Marigny was a hip district loaded with live music joints and funky shops. This section looked closer to a ghetto.

"Slow down a little," Rusty said.

"That's the place there," the driver said, pointing at a red brick building on the left side of the street. It was a duplex split down the middle into two adjacent units. Lights burned in the windows on the left side, while the right side was entirely dark.

"Just cruise past it, slowly."

The cabbie braked as they reached the end of the block.

"We stopping here, or is this a drive-by only?"

"Tell you what," Rusty said, pulling a twenty from his wallet and handing it through the partition. "There's another fifty in it for you if you'll just hang here for a few minutes. I won't be long."

"I suppose I can do that."

"Pull around the corner, and kill your lights. But keep the engine running."

The cabbie rotated in his seat to face Rusty.

"This gets more interesting all the time, babe. Now I'm not so sure I need that fifty."

"Nothing sketchy going on. I just want to see if a friend's home. If she isn't, we're out of here. If she is, I'll come back and tell you to split. The fifty's yours, either way."

"How come I get the feeling she ain't expecting you at this late hour?"

"'Cause you've been driving this cab long enough to pick up a thing or two," Rusty said, opening the door. "We got a deal?"

The cabbie hummed in contemplation for so long that Rusty started to think he was putting him on.

"Deal," the cabbie finally said. "You don't show in ten, I'm leaving without that fifty."

"Fair enough."

Rusty got out and shut the door softly.

The driver put it in gear and crept around the corner. Rusty waited to make sure he didn't keep driving. The cab came to a stop just out of sight and the taillights died. Satisfied he wasn't getting ditched on this unfriendly street, Rusty started walking toward the duplex.

Each footstep echoed on the pavement with amplified volume. The street appeared utterly empty of pedestrians, not so much as a stray cat on the prowl.

All the buildings were residential and rundown in a way devoid of the elegant decay that gave similarly unkempt parts of the Quarter a sense of charm. Only a few cars parked on the street, none of them recent makes.

Three cement steps got him from the sidewalk to the front stoop of Marceline's apartment. An overhead bulb buzzed and emitted a greenish light. A pair of doors stood before him. Flanking each door was a narrow window. A mailbox next to the right door read "Lavalle."

Rusty peeked through a gap where the inner curtain didn't quite meet the window frame. Darkness inside, and not a sound to be heard. Retreating a few steps, he craned his head back to gaze at two square windows facing the street from the second floor. Both of these were also dark, with the blinds drawn.

The apartment next door was clearly occupied. Dull light seeped through the drapes and the murmur of canned laughter wafted out. Rusty pondered circling around to the rear of the building to see if there was anything to be learned back there. He started to take a step and stopped cold.

He couldn't believe he'd missed it until now. The front door to Marceline's apartment was open. Less than an inch, but clearly ajar. A thin black line of empty space filled the gap between the door and the frame.

Rusty quietly returned to the door and pressed an ear to the crack, straining to hear anything that might tell him what was happening inside. Silence. Another rumble of televised laughter from next door rendered further surveillance from this position futile.

He laid a palm on the door and slowly pressed forward. It swung inward an inch at a time, allowing a dim glow from the outside light to creep across a polished hardwood floor.

Rusty stepped inside, hand still on the door. He took a quick scan of the room, eyes gathering as much information as possible while keeping the door ajar.

He was standing in the entryway of what looked like a living room. A two-seater sofa sat on the right, with a glass-topped coffee table in front. Across the room was a small TV perched atop a wooden cabinet. A stairway in the far left reached up to the second floor. Beyond its narrow bannister, the hardwood floor switched to linoleum tiles leading into a kitchen.

Sealing this information in his mind's eye, he quickly pulled the door back as he'd found it. The room went black. Rusty stood there a moment, adjusting to the darkness.

A tactile sense of place rooted in his mind. He recognized it. During his time as a magician on the Vegas strip, Rusty had performed complex and frequently dangerous acts while deprived of sight. Twelve times a week in the Etruscan Room at Caesars Palace, he did an entire segment of his show blindfolded—throwing and dodging knives, juggling chainsaws, walking a tightrope above a cage filled with live scorpions, and narrowly avoiding dissection from a swinging pendulum.

The countless hours he'd spent developing his senses of hearing and touch to compensate for a lack of vision, they all came back to him now.

Rusty took two and a half steps forward, knowing without seeing how far away the coffee table stood. He stopped just before his shin collided with the glass top. Turning to the left, he took a slow breath. Four more steps got him to the staircase.

He reached out and laid a hand on the bannister as easily as if the room were brightly lit.

That's when he knew there was someone else in the apartment.

It wasn't the sound of breathing, not at first. Rusty sensed rather than heard a corporeal shift in the room. A moving presence he hadn't felt before.

Standing motionless, hand still on the bannister, he waited to hear what he knew must come next. It came—a slow, compressed exhalation. Slightly ragged, it sounded male in origin. Whoever was in here must have been holding his breath ever since Rusty entered the apartment.

He's behind me, Rusty thought, spinning around and raising a protective arm.

Something hard struck him above the left eye. A glancing blow, it yielded only an angry surge of adrenaline.

Rusty swung wildly with his right fist, having a good idea of where the attacker stood, but only guessing at the man's height. He aimed too low, striking what felt like a shoulder before his left ribcage exploded in pain. A heavy boot had drilled him in just the right spot to create a maximum loss of balance. Rusty felt the floor rising to meet him but prevented a bad fall by extending his right arm downward.

Footsteps shuffled away from him, toward the front door.

"Stop, fucker!" Rusty shouted.

Lurching upright, he flailed with both arms to grab the unseen assailant. His fingers briefly grazed a handful of greasy hair, but slipped free as the attacker ran forward. Rusty heard the creak of hinges and the door swung wide.

"Stop!"

Half a second gave Rusty a fleeting view of the escaping man, silhouetted in the doorway. Medium height, thick muscular build. A long tangle of dark untended hair. Rusty bolted after him, but he'd lost the critical moment.

The man bounded off the stoop. He took all three steps in one misplaced jump and landed badly, falling to one knee on the sidewalk.

Rusty charged through the doorway, onto the porch. The man was just pulling himself upright, gripping his ankle in pain. Rusty knew he could catch him with a flying tackle.

Knees bending to propel himself with maximum velocity, Rusty never saw the length of chain swinging at his head. It struck just behind his right ear, raising a cluster of stars in his vision. The stars faded into a white glare and he was down again before he realized he'd been hit.

"Just stay right there, asshole."

Those words came from behind him. Rusty decided to do as he was told, feeling the back of his head roar.

He just barely registered the sound of a car door slamming, followed by an engine coming to life. When he heard a squeal of tires, he knew the man inside Marceline's apartment had gotten away.

5.

"Don't do anything stupid now," the voice behind him cautioned, sounding as calm as if reciting the ingredients for buttermilk pancakes. "Your fun's all used up for the night."

Rusty rotated to the right and saw an XXL pair of dirty blue jeans positioned a few feet away. He raised his eyes to get a fuller picture of the man who'd just knocked him senseless. Well over six feet tall, with a closely cropped head and handlebar mustache, this able citizen was glowering down at him and holding a two-foot length of heavy chain.

"That's what you belted me with? Christ, you could've killed me."

"Never happen, pal. I got me some real good control. Just looking to incapacitate you long enough to get 911 on the horn."

The big man added in a gentler tone, "Why don't you do that, peach. Tell 'em we got a break-in suspect neutralized and ready for pickup."

Rusty turned and saw a woman standing in the doorway of the apartment next to Marceline's. She held a sleepy-eyed toddler to her breast. The child toyed with the belt of her robe and didn't seem at all bothered by the late night disturbance.

"Don't worry about it," the big man continued. "This fool ain't going nowhere."

The woman disappeared from view into the apartment. Rusty again tried to raise himself, but a brisk rattle of the chain made him think better of it.

"I'm a friend of the woman who lives next to you," he said, his tongue feeling a bit thick.

"Sure. That's why you come busting out the door in the middle of the night, with the place all closed up. Makes plenty of sense."

"You may have noticed I was chasing someone. What happened to him?"

"Dove into a shit-ugly Pontiac parked at the curb and tore off. I could only take down one of y'all. You were closest."

"Great. I don't suppose you got a plate number."

"How the hell am I gonna read a plate from this distance?"

"Look," Rusty said, "I told you I'm a friend of Marceline Lavalle. If you'll let me stand the fuck up I can show you a picture to prove it."

The neighbor pondered that suggestion for a tick, then nodded. "Just take care to do it slow."

Rusty rose to his feet, employing the most non-confrontational body language he could muster.

"You can put down that chain. Doubt you'd need it anyway."

"Let's just see the photo."

The woman reappeared in the doorway. She clutched a phone in place of the toddler.

"They got me on hold again, Pete," she said with a yawn.

"Goddamn emergency response ain't worth shit around here," the big man uttered, shaking his head.

"It's on my cell phone," Rusty said quickly. "The photo of me and Marceline."

He wanted to derail any police involvement fast. If the cops showed up, someone would be getting a free ride to the station to sort this out, and he was the only guy around who qualified.

"Listen to me, Pete," he said, trying to claim the neighbor's attention. "I gotta get it from my pocket."

Pete eyed him closely as Rusty pulled his mobile phone from a front pocket of his pants. He turned it on, swiped the security code and opened up an album of images.

"About time," he heard Pete's woman mutter to the 911 dispatcher. "We got a burglar trapped on our porch."

Rusty scrolled rapidly through a collection of photos taken over the last several years. He double-tapped a thumbnail to enlarge it, then held out the phone to Pete.

"Tell her to hang up, man. That's me and Marcie in Vegas."

Pete craned his head to examine the image on the screen, then glanced up for a comparison.

"It's a few years old," Rusty said, sensing his skepticism.

"We're in the Marigny," the woman continued impatiently to the dispatcher. "You oughta recognize this number by now. Been out here enough times."

"Come on," Rusty pleaded. "She really is a good friend of mine. Her middle name is Hart. She works at the Bon Coeur maternity ward. Her favorite color is purple, for Christ's sake."

"Well," Pete mumbled, fondling the chain with his thick fingers. "I guess so."

He spoke over his shoulder to his companion.

"You can cancel that roller, doll."

"You sure, Pete?" she asked, squinting through the doorway at Rusty with an expression of distaste.

"Yeah. Seems this fella knows Marcie. He chased off some other guy lurking in her pad."

Shaking her head as if the whole matter wearied her beyond description, the woman told the 911 dispatcher not to bother. False alarm. Then she disappeared back inside the apartment, letting the screen door slam.

The two men stood facing each other awkwardly on the porch. The initial numbness behind Rusty's ear was seeping into a sharp pain that wrapped itself all the way around his skull.

"So what exactly happened in there?" Pete asked, letting one end of the chain dangle loosely by his ankles.

Feeling more secure with the weapon lowered, Rusty described how he'd let himself into the apartment when he noticed the door was open. He gave a quick account of spotting the other man and trying to apprehend him before Pete's chain put a stop to that.

"Didn't get a decent look at him, huh?"

"Too dark," Rusty answered. "I know he's got a beard, longish brown hair. Maybe 5'10" or so. That match up with what you saw?"

"Close enough."

After a pause, Pete said, "Sorry about that tap on the dome. Don't hurt too bad, does it?"

"Nah," Rusty lied. He didn't want to be invited inside for some homespun first aid.

"So you and Marcie go back a ways, huh?"

"Since we were teenagers. I lived in NOLA for about five years."

"She's a doll. Hell of a lot nicer than the old lady used to be in that unit."

"Her father says it's been almost a week since he saw her. That's why I came over. Thought I'd check to see if she's alright."

A dubious aspect returned to Pete's swarthy face.

"Picked an odd hour to drop by."

"Just got in town tonight. The old man's really worried. I was hoping to put his mind at ease as soon as possible."

Pete seemed to buy that, his features settling back into a friendlier arrangement.

"Ain't seen Marcie myself, come to think of it. I figured maybe she'd gone to pop out that baby. But she ain't due for a few months yet, is she?"

"Not until May, I've heard. Do you see her often?"

"Just to say hi on the stoop. She made some kickass jambalaya for us once. Did some other favors when my lady was laid up in bed with a busted toe. Sweet girl, she really is."

"Ever see any rough-looking dudes around here? I'm not prying into her personal business, just trying to figure out where she might be."

"She keeps to herself, mostly. I never saw that bastard in the Pontiac before."

"It's weird. If he was a burglar, why didn't he carry anything out of the place?"

"Maybe we should call the cops back, report it. I can give 'em a description of the vehicle, if nothing else."

Rusty thought about it for a moment. A wave of crushing fatigue was settling into his bones as the adrenaline of the past few minutes receded. His phone's screen read a few minutes before two. The last thing he wanted to do right now was repeat this conversation with a cop.

"Tell you what. I'm heading over to the Sixth Precinct in the morning. Gonna see a detective who took the missing person's report from Marcie's dad. I'll fill him in on what happened here. And I'll leave you out of it, if you want."

"Hell, you can mention me. I got a stake in this thing too. Technically the man broke into my home, seeing as we share a common wall. Tell him he can talk to Pete Banning if he needs any more info."

"Thanks, I'll do that."

Rusty made his way onto the street and heard the door of the Banning household slam shut again. Each step yielded a fresh wave of painful dizziness, but he concluded from lengthy experience he hadn't suffered a full-blown concussion. Back in the crazy Vegas days, he'd racked up enough of those to become intimately familiar with the symptoms.

Too wired to mentally process the events of this bizarre night in any kind of orderly fashion, Rusty kept one thought primary in his mind as he approached the street corner.

Christ, I hope my cab is still there.

It was.

6.

The JAX brewery towered over the riverbend like a monument to some fabled industrial boom time. Its iconic neon sign spelled out the name of the South's second oldest beer in three red letters the size of eighteen-wheelers turned on their ends.

The parking lot behind the brewery lay almost empty at a few minutes before three in the morning. Claude Sherman had no problem finding a free spot.

Claude parked his two-toned Pontiac station wagon in a row close to the brewery's back exit. He doused the lights. The wagon, with over 150,000 miles on the odometer, had served him well since he'd acquired it from a used car dealer who owed Mr. Abellard a favor. Claude found it a comfortable ride, with ample room in the back for hauling, but the shitty two-toned paint job bugged him. He was due for a vehicular upgrade, and he intended to remind Mr. Abellard of that when the proper moment arose.

Claude couldn't worry about that right now. He needed to get this phone call over with, and keep it brief. His left ankle still throbbed from the bad landing he'd taken on the sidewalk after his leap off the front porch, but it didn't feel worse than a minor sprain.

What a fucked-up night. Claude almost couldn't believe he'd been ordered to break into the girl's apartment, but that's what Mr. Abellard wanted. And Mr. Abellard got what he wanted.

It was a strange thing, being instructed to look for clues in a crime Claude himself had committed. Like a rabid dog sent out to track down his own scent. But what choice did he have?

It started out well enough. Claude had parked his wagon across from the apartment shortly after eleven. He patiently sat there for more than two hours, waiting for her next door neighbors to turn off their lights and go to bed.

When midnight passed with no sign of that happening, Claude made the calculated risk of breaking in while they were still awake. It turned out to be a good decision. The murmur of their television stifled the sound of him picking the lock. He was inside in less than a minute, leaving the door open just a small gap so he could exit the apartment with total silence after searching the place.

All smooth enough. A hell of a lot smoother than when he'd broken in the first time. Claude found it much simpler to unlawfully enter a person's home without having to carry an inert body in a duffel bag on the way out.

Claude shook that image from his mind and dialed the number in Vacherie.

"You're late," he heard after the first ring. "Start talking."

"I went through the whole place, the way you told me. Every room with a penlight. Desk, drawers, closet, cabinets, all of it."

"And you saw nothing like we talked about? No sign of a break-in?"

"No. Everything looked, uh, normal. Just some chick's pad."

A short silence ensued, and Claude realized it probably wasn't a great idea to refer to Marceline Lavalle in such a casual way. Not to Joseph Abellard. Not in light of recent events.

"I guess I gotta believe you, Claude."

"I don't see why you wouldn't. Even if this was about the hospital, my neck's stuck out a lot farther than yours."

A lengthier silence met those words. Claude shrank into the driver's seat. Silence from Joseph Abellard could inspire more dread than the most unhinged tirade, and he was a man capable of unleashing an apocalypse of verbal abuse when prompted.

"I'm glad you mentioned that," Abellard said calmly. "Spares me the trouble. You *are* in this shit deeper than me. Deal turns sideways, who's the first motherfucker going toes-up?"

"You've made that clear, Mr. Abellard. Many times."

"Better hope it sunk in."

Jangled by the threat, Claude almost opened his mouth to mention the dude who jumped him inside the apartment. That qualified as the most unexpected turn of the night, though he badly wanted to dismiss it as sheer coincidence. Why not? Random guy sees an open door and ducks in for something to steal. Either that or just another drunk on a Frenchman Street bender, too hammered to find his way home to the right address.

Wasn't that possible? Claude wanted to believe it, so he kept his mouth shut.

"OK fine," Abellard said gruffly. "It was worth a look. You didn't find anything, tough shit. We got bigger priorities right now. Professor Bitch needs that new batch, pronto."

"I don't see how we can make that happen. Told you already—"

"Never heard her so wound up," Abellard interrupted, "spouting some crazy noise about what's goin' down if we don't deliver on schedule."

"What do you want me to do?" Claude asked with a note of annoyance that he'd never let slip if speaking to his boss in person.

"I want you to *stalk* that motherfucker at the clinic tomorrow. Don't let him leave until he knows our business is the only priority he needs to worry about."

"I already talked to Roque, more than once. He gives me the same answer each time."

"Sounds like talk ain't getting it done."

"Cash will. He wants a bigger bite, says his end's worth twenty percent."

"I don't need to hear any of that, Claude. My deal got done months ago, nobody said shit about negotiation. All I want to know is you're delivering the next batch, harvested and viable, by Tuesday morning. If you gotta lean on the fucking doc to make that happen, lean on him."

"Why not meet him halfway? Offer ten and he'll probably take it."

"Fine, if it comes out of your cut. Split it up any damn way you want, long as he delivers."

"Look, Roque's the only source we got. He knows it. Goddamn maternity ward's out."

"And who's fault is that?"

Claude silently cursed himself, unable to believe he'd just made the mistake of broaching that particular topic.

"Forget I mentioned it. Bottom line, Roque thinks he's holding the cards. That's the problem."

"It's your job to make him see the situation otherwise. Fail to do that, you fail to be of any use to me. And by now, Claude, I think you've pieced together a pretty clear picture of how I handle deadweight."

7.

The head nurse at the Bon Coeur maternity ward kept Rusty hanging for six minutes before glancing up from her computer to acknowledge his presence. It was just past nine in the morning. Rusty's head still thrummed from Pete Banning's blindsided blow despite the four Advils he'd swallowed before going to sleep, and another four upon awakening. The head nurse didn't know about that, and probably wouldn't care if he told her.

"I only need a moment of your time," he said as the minute count ticked up to seven.

"With you just as soon as I can, sir."

She delivered those words without averting her eyes from the computer screen. Something utterly fascinating must have kept her gaze so focused.

Probably a white-hot game of Solitaire, Rusty mused.

Bon Coeur was an impressive medical establishment. Located a block off St. Charles in the leafy Upper Garden, Rusty figured it must cater to a well-heeled segment of the New Orleans populous.

He didn't know how Marceline had landed a job here, but her motive for seeking this kind of work didn't escape him. She'd been a natural caregiver since he'd met her at the age of fifteen.

During his long apprenticeship with Prosper, Marceline had devoted almost as much time to magic as he did. The two teens served as trusted assistants to her father. A coy off-stage romance developed during countless twilight performances on the corner of Royal and Dumaine.

Remember all those nights? Rusty asked himself as he waited to speak with the head nurse. *Crouching behind that black velvet tent… rattling the tip jar after every show?*

He didn't truthfully remember it in any great detail. That five-year stretch lived in his memory only as a happy blur, so far removed from his current life that it might have been someone else's experience.

Trying to keep both eyes on the old man, tracking the movement of his hands…but never looking away from her for very long. Christ, I loved her.

Back then, Marceline devoted many free afternoons to visiting sick children and elderly patients at the Touro Infirmary. She'd read to them, often dragging Rusty along to perform some of the rudimentary illusions he'd mastered.

So when she made an unannounced visit to Rusty's home in Ocean Pines last October, after having broken contact with him in Vegas more than a year before, it didn't come as a surprise to learn she'd chosen to pursue nursing as a vocation. The bump in her belly did surprise him, though he had no reason to feel jealous after all the time that had passed since their romantic union was still active—not to mention his own many missteps that had led to its dissolution.

"Did I hear you say you have no relation to any newborns under our care?" the head nurse asked with a dubious squint, yanking him from his reverie.

"That's right. I'm here about one of your nurses. Marceline Lavalle."

"What about her?"

"I'm hoping to find out where she is. Understand she hasn't shown up for work in a few days."

"It's not this hospital's policy to disclose the work history of its employees. I'm sure you can imagine what kind of headaches that would bring on."

"Not really, no."

"Litigation, for one." The head nurse looked ready to start counting off reasons on her plump fingers but restrained herself. "Fraudulent insurance claims, for another. On top of which, we respect the privacy of our medical staff and don't go handing out their schedules to anyone who might walk in the door."

"Look, I'm a friend, OK? I'm concerned about Marceline because she seems to have gone missing. I talked to her father last night, he's out of his mind with worry and I can't blame him. Given her condition, it seems more than a little urgent to find out where she's keeping herself."

A wordless moment elapsed. Just as Rusty was convinced he'd get nothing from the head nurse except directions to the nearest exit, her expression softened.

"I'll be honest with you, Mister…"

"Diamond."

"Honestly, Mr. Diamond, I'm disappointed. Nurse Lavalle has performed splendidly since we took her on last fall. I know she's taking a leave of absence in May, and that certainly isn't a problem. She's been very conscientious about providing a specific timeframe."

"Is it a temporary leave? Does she plan on returning to work?"

"She's given no reason to expect otherwise, at least not to me." The head nurse frowned, then continued. "It's, well, quite out of character for her to act in such an irresponsible manner."

"That's why we're so worried. Me and her father."

"Do you have reason to think something *untoward* may have happened?"

"Really don't know. The NOPD's been notified. I'll be following up with them soon as I leave here. Just hoping maybe there's some personal insight I can pick up from the people she works with. Something I can tell the cops they might not already know."

Rusty expected the mention of police involvement to instill a deeper sense of cooperation within the head nurse. Just the opposite occurred—she retracted in her seat, a distrustful look returning to her face. The flicker of compassion Rusty had spotted a moment before evaporated like a drop of water on a heated stove. She looked angry, as if Marceline's disappearance hit her as some kind of personal slight.

"As I said, we all knew she'd be taking a leave shortly, which makes her failure to appear all the more disappointing.

We're shorthanded as is, the last thing this ward needs is a no-show caregiver."

"Is there anyone on the staff she might confide in? Another nurse or doctor she's particularly close with?"

The head nurse paused a moment, seeming to assess the merit of his question.

"There's one girl, works part time. She and Nurse Lavalle take lunch together more often than not."

"I'd love to speak with her. Is she on duty now?"

Another weighted pause, which the head nurse broke by reaching for the phone mounted next to her computer.

"I'll call for Monday."

Rusty's brow furrowed.

"You want me to come back Monday? Can't we do it now?"

"Her *name* is Monday," the head nurse said with an exasperated sigh, as if that should be obvious even to a dimwit like Rusty.

"Oh. That's unusual."

"It's real, printed right on her ID when she interviewed for the job. Don't ask me why. Druggies for parents, probably."

"Maybe she was born on a Monday," Rusty said.

Dialing 9, the head nurse cleared her throat and said, "Nurse Reed, please report to the admin desk. Paging Nurse Reed to the admin desk."

The phone landed on its cradle harder than necessary, telling Rusty he'd enjoyed as much of her attention as he was going to get. He stood near the elevators, gazing at a glass partition in front of the nursery. An anxious-looking young man, barely out of his teens, pressed his face against the glass and waved timidly.

Rusty heard footsteps. A woman emerged from the nursery and he knew it was the one who'd been paged.

With just a bit of exaggeration in a few key areas, she might resemble a vintage pinup fantasy version of a nurse, the kind that kept the blood of wounded soldiers warm and flowing during times of war. Her hair, pomegranate red tinged with raven tones, was wrapped tightly beneath a prim white cap. Rusty had an intuition it might reach the small of her back when set free to fall unbound.

As she spoke quietly to the head nurse, casting a quick glance his way, he detected the tip of a tattoo peeking above the starched collar of her uniform. The dark ink stood out in bold contrast to the pale skin of her neck.

Let's focus here, he reprimanded himself as she turned away from the admin desk and approached him. The white shoes on her small feet squeaked softly on the polished floor.

"Let me guess," she said, her tone flat and notably lacking in warmth. "You're the magician."

Rusty required a half-beat to conjure an adequate response.

"Good guess. I'll hazard one of my own. Marcie must have mentioned me once or twice."

Nurse Reed nodded a few centimeters in assent. Rusty noticed a delicate cleft in her chin. A small imperfection that somehow perfected her face, whose dominant feature was a pair of large green eyes the shade of spring grass.

"My name's Rusty."

"I've heard."

"Well, you know what a sweet girl Marceline is. So don't believe all the good things she had to say about me."

"That won't be a challenge."

A pause followed that well-aimed jab.

"I'll get to the point, Nurse Reed. Do you have any idea where she is?"

"No," Monday answered, and for the first time Rusty heard concern in her voice. "I'm truly sorry to say I have no idea."

"Is anyone around here worried about her? I didn't get a sense of that from your supervisor."

"I'm worried, yeah. Talked to a few of the other nurses about getting a search party together. Her father dropped off some flyers, I've been putting them up around here and where I live."

"I told Prosper I'd do what I can to track her down."

"Is that something you're qualified to do? Are you sure she even wants you looking?"

"No. But this feels wrong, and if there's any way I can

give the police some incentive to take her disappearance more seriously, I'm in."

Monday didn't reply to that, but the skepticism on her face spoke clearly enough.

"Look," Rusty said, "you probably know things ended badly between us."

"She never got too specific about what happened in Vegas. But, yeah, I know you fucked up somehow."

"What you might not know is she paid me a visit a few months back. It was a shock, believe me. Never expected to see her again, she just showed up out of thin air."

"I guess a magician should appreciate that," Monday said with a wry grin.

"We didn't get much time to talk. And now…Christ, no one knows where she is."

Monday studied him for a long moment. Rusty sensed she was weighing his sincerity.

"What can I do to help?" she asked.

"Could we just talk for a few minutes? I understand you and Marcie are pretty tight."

"Yeah, I mean we're not super close or anything. We take lunch together most days. I'm only here part-time."

"Anything you can share would be helpful. What's been going on with her lately…what's her state of mind…is she worried or excited about the baby? Anything at all."

Monday cast a brief glance over her shoulder at the admin desk. Rusty followed her gaze. The head nurse stared intently at her computer, but something about her posture made it obvious she was monitoring their conversation.

"I can't really talk now," Monday said, turning back to hit him with the full wattage of those green eyes. "Meet me at my other job tonight. It's a little looser there."

"Sure thing. Whatever's best for you."

"You know Temptations? My shift starts at ten."

Rusty realized too late he'd failed not to raise a reflexive eyebrow.

"On Bourbon?"

"If he can't be trusted not to butcher the seasonals, he can stick to cutting grass."

Waiting for the call to end, Rusty's mind flashed to the last building of this kind he'd occupied. The Ocean City Police Central Station, near his current home in coastal Maryland. He wondered what his old friend Jim Biddison was doing right now. An OCPD lieutenant he'd known since grade school, Biddison played a central role in an ugly multiple homicide case Rusty found himself wrapped up in several months ago. It all got resolved more or less satisfactorily in the end, thanks to some wholly unauthorized measures Rusty had employed to help the OCPD lock up the men responsible for the murders.

He'd surprised himself by discovering a knack for assisting in the investigation while flagrantly ignoring any police warnings that hindered his efforts. Even more surprising was the satisfaction he derived from inflicting his own brand of punishment on some genuinely bad dudes who deserved it.

"Rose, he's your nephew," Detective Hubbard droned into the phone. "I'd just as soon hire a competent gardener than toss him the job. All right, you know best. Gotta go."

He placed the phone on its cradle and stared at the pockmarked ceiling, as if picturing the damage being wreaked on his beloved backyard garden this very moment.

"Sorry about that. American dream, my ass. Home ownership's more like one long headache spilling right into the next."

Rusty was about to reply that he didn't give a shit about home ownership headaches, but Hubbard cut him off by reaching for a manila folder lying open on his desk.

"Man runs a magic shop on Bourbon, right? The father?"

"That's right. The Mystic Arts Emporium."

"Seemed like a nice old guy. Something of a local institution, I gather. He was all kinds of worked up about his daughter."

"Imagine that."

Hubbard looked up from the report in his hands.

"Still no sign of her?"

"No sign. Today I went over to the hospital where she works.

She's missed four consecutive shifts, which her supervisor says is highly out of character."

"Well, here's the thing with missing persons complaints, Mister..."

"Diamond," Rusty told him, for the second time.

"Here's the thing, Diamond. People go missing all the time. We get calls to this precinct on a constant basis. Reports of someone who didn't come home, failed to show up for work, left the kids waiting after practice, what have you. What do we do about it? Not a damn thing, most of the time. That's because the majority of these cases don't involve any criminal activity."

"I understand. But in a case like this, when it's totally out of character for someone to just disappear—"

"People behave out of character six days a week and twice on Sundays, Diamond. It's not against the law to take a trip without telling anyone in advance. Rude? OK. Inconsiderate? Sure, but you'd be surprised how often it happens. And you're looking at me like I just lit a fart in here."

"Just surprised the NOPD takes such a laid-back approach to someone vanishing. A pregnant woman, no less."

"Oh, we get plenty involved, any time there's evidence pointing to a crime. Doesn't take much to get this department moving, which is more than we've got concerning Miss Lavalle."

"Can you be a little specific about what it *would* take?"

Hubbard lowered the folder onto his desk.

"We didn't just blow this off, like you're thinking. I personally went over to the apartment on Burgundy. No indications of forced entry, all the lights turned off, no sign of her car near the building. In other words, everything to suggest she left the premises of her own free will."

"So that's as far as it goes? No further investigation?"

"Her name's been added to the NCIC database. Vehicle information, too. That means every cop in the nation will see she's been reported missing, if they happen to pick her up somewhere. You want my advice? Try to be patient."

"Great. Maybe I'll look for a needle in the nearest haystack while I'm at it."

Hubbard leaned back in his chair, producing a squeak from its abused hinges.

"You might take comfort from the fact that the numbers are on your side. Vast majority of people who end up in the database return home of their own will. Most often within four days."

"She's been gone five days."

"It's not a damn science. I'm talking about averages. Some folks take longer to rejoin their normal routine. And, yes, some never do—for reasons that don't intersect with criminality on even a passing level. Maybe Ms. Lavalle just decided she's had it and wants to start fresh."

"When she's due to give birth for the first time? Does that seem likely, Detective?"

"I don't know the woman," Hubbard answered with a shrug. "Far as being pregnant, that doesn't tamp down the possibility of her doing a runner. Just the opposite, in my experience. A woman in her shoes might easily make some erratic decisions."

Rusty didn't respond, allowing the detective to continue his line of reasoning.

"Look at it, man. Here she is, about to become a single mother. Apparently on bad terms with the man who, well…"

"I'm glad you mentioned that," Rusty said. "Have you talked to this guy?"

Again Hubbard reached for the report. He flipped a few pages, his finger tracking down a single-spaced sheet.

"Abellard, Joseph. Resident of Vacherie, St. James Parish. No record."

"Her father says she broke it off with him last month. Seems he's got a mean temper, not the kind of man who'd respond passively to being dumped by the woman carrying his child. Isn't he the first person you'd want to interrogate in a case like this?"

Hubbard glanced up to give Rusty a hard look.

"First off, I don't know what kind of case this is, or if it can even be called that. Second, Vacherie's in St. James Parish. Well beyond this department's jurisdiction."

Rusty opened his mouth to voice a complaint but Hubbard cut him off.

"Hold on. I forwarded Abellard's info to the Sheriff's Department in St. James. They sent a deputy over to his place of business…when was it…Wednesday, the 17th."

"Good," Rusty said, easing back into the uncomfortable chair. "What did they find out?"

"Nothing to go on. Abellard claimed he hasn't seen the woman in over a month. That matches what the father says, right? The deputy noted that he seemed genuinely distressed to hear Miss Lavalle's whereabouts are unknown."

"Sure. What else is he gonna say, if he knows where she is and maybe doesn't feel like sharing that knowledge?"

"He admitted they're estranged. Said he wasn't mad, intends to provide for the child even if they don't get back together. Straightforward enough for you?"

"I don't know," Rusty mumbled irritably. "Better if they'd taken him in for a formal questioning, don't you think?"

"On what grounds?" Hubbard let the file drop from his hands in such a way as to suggest he wouldn't be picking it up again.

Rusty paused before speaking. All morning, he'd debated how much to tell the detective about his late night visit to Marceline's apartment. Reporting the stranger who'd attacked him seemed eminently sensible, even if he could only offer a scant description. It wasn't much, but it would bolster Rusty's assertion that something bad may well have befallen Marceline.

A sense of caution froze the words on his tongue. How exactly could he explain his decision to enter the darkened apartment uninvited at one in the morning? Since he'd first sat down in Hubbard's office, the detective tossed a series of appraising glances his way that didn't suggest any positive impressions were taking hold.

But Rusty knew he couldn't worry about that right now. So he told Hubbard what happened last night, including as many details as he could recall. Once he got to the part about being jumped inside the apartment, the detective picked up a legal pad and started jotting down notes.

"So you broke into the place?" he asked when Rusty finished his account.

"No. Like I said, the front door was unlocked. The guy who broke in left it ajar, probably so he could get out with as little noise as possible."

"Maybe he had a key."

"I doubt it."

"Any signs of a break-in? Was the lock disabled, anything like that?"

"To be honest, I didn't think to look. It was late."

"So it's possible this person was there with Ms. Lavalle's knowledge, isn't it?"

"What the hell was he doing, sitting there in the dark? And why'd he jump me?"

"Could be he thought *you* were a burglar."

"You should talk to her neighbor. Pete Banning, he got a look at the guy and the car he drove off in. Said it was a Pontiac, that's all he knew last night but maybe he can remember something else."

Hubbard scribbled some more notes, then nodded.

"I'll talk to the neighbor."

Rusty pulled a piece of paper from his pocket with his cell phone number written on it. He placed it on Hubbard's desk and said, "I'll be checking in regularly, if that's alright."

"We keep the lights on all night around here. How long do you plan to be in town?"

"As long as it takes to bring her home."

He rose and reached across the desk to offer his hand. The detective looked mildly surprised by the gesture, but met him with a firm shake.

Rusty was halfway out of the office when Hubbard spoke again.

"You didn't seem to care for my first piece of advice. Want another one?"

"Sure."

"You're really worried about this woman? Hire a private

detective. I could dig up a reference, if you want to go that way."

Rusty gave a small nod. It wasn't quite the nugget of professional insight he had hoped to hear. If this was the best Dan Hubbard had to offer, Rusty felt more than ever like he was on his own.

"I'll call you about that," he said, stepping away to free himself from the sun-starved confines of the Sixth as quickly as he could without looking like a man on the run.

9.

Dr. Philip Roque leaned back in the padded leather chair behind his desk, a look of studied compassion etched across his handsome if fleshy face. His eyes, a placid shade of blue that had long aided him in both personal and professional affairs, drifted left to right and back again. Roque paused his gaze to meet that of the young woman seated across from his desk, hands folded nervously in her lap.

I know, his expression told her. *This is an uncomfortable and, yes, sad situation. But you've done nothing wrong and I help people like you every day. Together, we'll find the best possible resolution.*

Roque's eyes rotated to the opposite position. Here those sky blue corneas expressed manly commiseration toward the twitchy young fellow seated in a matching chair.

Feel ya, dude. I know it's a drag but you're doing the right thing. Lot of guys in your shoes, they'd let her handle it all by herself. Good on you, bro.

Back and forth, Roque imbued a two-tiered sense of trust in this anxious couple from the suburban enclave of Kenner. They felt good about bringing their troubles to someone who treated them both with discretion and respect. In all of Orleans Parish, no medical professional could possess more empathy than Philip Roque, MD.

"Well," the young woman said, dabbing at her eyes. "We have a big decision to make."

"You certainly do. This isn't something to be undertaken on a whim. You'd be surprised how many young people come in here with that outlook. I'm glad you folks have an appropriately mature view of the matter."

Roque resisted an urge to glance at his Rolex. It had to be almost five o'clock.

The sign in front of his office on the third floor of this swank medical plaza just off Magazine Street read "Uptown Family Planning." That sounded a whole lot friendlier than "Uptown Abortion Clinic," but the latter would have been more accurate. Very little in the way of family planning ever transpired here. If pressed, Roque would find himself challenged to conjure an adequate description for that term. Stocking up on diapers was probably a big part of it.

Philip Roque had no children. He had an aggravated soon-to-be-ex-wife who retained an uncanny ability to emasculate him with a few choice words, even though they mostly communicated through lawyers these days. And he had a mistress already angling toward a five-carat marquis engagement ring, who drained his bank account with a rapacious determination that made her bedroom attentions seem demure by comparison.

Most of all, he had expenses. The two houses—both of them situated on coveted Uptown streets within walking distance of the bridle paths in Audobon Park—one of them soon to be forfeited as part of the divorce settlement. And the yacht, moored on Lake Ponchartrain. Christ, what a windblown fancy of middle-aged insecurity that acquisition had proved to be. All because Yvonne, his mistress, convinced him with honeyed words that sex afloat the waves left its landlocked counterpart in the dust.

And those were just the big outlays. Roque also had the Jaguar, requiring near-constant repair. The time-share condo in Orlando, which hardly ever got used. And the membership dues at Riverside—that galled Roque to ponder more than any of his other looming obligations. Because the club is where he wanted to be right now, instead of inside his office which adjoined the examination and operating rooms.

Roque felt pretty certain this youthful couple had not yet reached a point where they were ready to terminate their unplanned pregnancy. Today's consultation was quite possibly

...o more than preamble to a procedure that never happened, and or which Roque wouldn't receive a dime. Which seemed pretty unfair—a man's time ought to be worth something.

"You've given us a lot to think about, doc," the father-to-be said.

"Yeah," the pregnant girl nodded. "I'm even less sure now than before."

"Don't let that trouble you," Roque said. "My advice is to let the matter sit for now. Talk it over, consult your friends, family, clergy…anyone whose opinion you hold in high regard."

"That rules out *your* family," the young man uttered with a sideways grin at his partner. The humorless look he got in return to that witticism knocked the smile off his face as efficiently as a right hook.

"However you wish to proceed," Roque said, allowing a tone of avuncular wisdom to indicate this conversation was about over, "please know I'm here to answer any questions."

"Thank you, Doctor Roque," the girl uttered quietly.

"Yeah, thanks," the young man said, rising from the chair with a velocity that betrayed his intense desire to vacate his clinic.

"Call any time," Roque said, standing himself. "If you decide to proceed with what we've discussed, I'm here to make it as pleasant and pain-free as possible."

The couple murmured more thanks and turned for the door. Roque opened it for them and they stepped into a carpeted hallway leading to the waiting room. Margaret, the silver-haired receptionist who'd been in his employ since he opened the clinic more than a decade before, looked up from her copy of *Redbook*.

"Will we be scheduling a follow-up?" she asked, glancing first at the couple and then at the doctor.

"Not today, Maggie."

Roque handed each of them a card from the front desk and waved goodbye as they exited the clinic.

It was only after the door swung shut that Roque noticed the waiting room's other occupant. Solidly built and of medium height, with a scruffy beard and a thick torso that leant him an almost anthropoid aspect of brute strength, Claude Sherman sat in a leather chair closest to the door. He wore a custodian' uniform. An upright vacuum cleaner stood next to him, it rubber neck clenched in one knuckled hand.

Roque locked eyes with him for a tense moment, then turned to address Margaret.

"Last appointment for the day, I think?"

"That's right. We had a cancellation, the Grahams."

"Very well," Roque murmured, casually leaning against th counter in front of Margaret's desk.

"What's he doing here?" he whispered.

"Beats me," the receptionist responded quietly. "Asked i he could clean up now instead of waiting for the overnight. Say he has plans he can't break."

Raising his voice, Roque said, "Why don't you knock of Maggie. I'll close up."

Margaret didn't need to hear that twice. It took her less than a minute to shut down her computer, gather up a leather purs from beneath her desk and waddle out of the clinic with hurrie wishes for the doctor to have a good Sunday.

"What the hell are you doing here?" Roque demanded afte the door clicked shut.

"We gotta talk. It's important."

"I told you never to show your face during business hours Now I realize you're not concealing an excess of gray matte under that greasy mop, but don't tell me you're actually dumbe than you look."

Claude's only response was a rippling of the muscles in hi shoulder and neck. Just enough to tell the doctor he was making an effort to restrain himself.

"Fine," Roque sighed. "My office."

Claude followed him down the hallway. Inside the office Roque started briskly packing up his briefcase.

"We need a new batch," Claude said. "We need it now."

"Afraid I can't help you. I haven't performed any procedure since we last spoke."

"Gettin' a lot of heat on this, doc. Abellard's crawling up m

ss and I don't even want to know what the Professor's telling
im. We need to deliver, tonight."

"Look around, Claude. Do you see any patients lining up
o volunteer?"

"What about them that just left?"

It took a beat for Roque to comprehend he was referring to
ie young couple from Kenner.

"What about them?"

"Are they gonna have it done?"

"They haven't decided."

"Did you *tell* them to have it done?"

Roque almost laughed at the blunt naiveté of that question
s it related to his role as a family planning physician.

"I don't tell people to do anything, Claude. Whether they
hoose to terminate a pregnancy or see it through is entirely
ieir decision. I simply offer the best counsel I can."

"You could at least suggest it," Claude grumbled in a louder
oice. "We need *more*, for Christ's sake."

Roque took a half step closer to his desk, weighing his next
vords with considerable care.

"You know, this is all academic. Until we clarify the matter
f equity I mentioned in our last conversation, any new material
s out of the question."

Claude inched closer, just enough to telegraph some
atent hostility.

"What're you talking about?"

Roque retracted a full step, slowly.

"Don't pretend I have to remind you. I want a larger taste
f whatever Abellard's seeing on the back end."

"Yeah, I remember. He says forget it. A deal's a deal."

"Look, whoever you're supplying is paying a hell of a—"

"Hold on there, doc. You don't want to know nothing about
vhat happens after you hand over a package. Ain't that right?"

"That's right," Roque agreed with a swift nod. "Where the
naterial goes, who the ultimate buyer is and to what use the
ells are put…I want no knowledge of that. As far as price,
lat's a different issue. I want twenty percent of whatever

Abellard is getting from his client. Either that, or a flat fee c
$10,000 per batch. Since I don't know what the final sale pric
is, I can't determine which option is better from his point o
view. However he wishes to meet my fee, that's his busines
Until we settle this, don't expect any more material coming fro
this office."

"He's not gonna like that."

"Then he can look for another source."

"You ain't the only scraper in town, doc."

Roque flinched at the word 'scraper' and saw Sherma
smile at his reaction. It was infuriating, but he forced a cal
tone into his reply.

"Correct, Claude. I'm not the only family plannin
specialist in New Orleans. You and Mr. Abellard are free to sho
around for an alternate connection. Finding someone with m
discretion, that's your challenge. And that's why you're going t
meet my terms for continuing this arrangement."

Feeling emboldened, Roque snapped his briefcase shut. H
stepped out of his office, hoping the conversation was over. I
disturbed him to see Claude following closely behind, all the wa
into the waiting room.

"Try to do a better job with the dusting from now on," th
doctor said over his shoulder. "This facade won't hold up i
you're not a convincing custodian."

Roque opened the door, then added, "And don't forget t
turn the lights out. Goddamn Louisiana Power's worse tha
a vampire."

With that, he stepped out of the clinic and pulled the doc
closed behind him.

• • •

Claude Sherman badly wanted to smash something. He scanne
the silent office for a likely target. Margaret's gooosenecked des
lamp. Ceramic bowl filled with pens. Glass-covered wall paintin
of Lake Ponchartrain at sunset. Claude didn't care. Anythin
would suffice. He'd struggled hard to maintain his composur

or the last several minutes. Releasing some measure of his
uppressed fury felt really important right now.

He resisted the urge, knowing he'd have to clean up any
ness made by such a pointless outburst.

Christ, he hated coming to this place. Taking the part-
me overnight custodial gig was degrading enough, though it
rovided a sensible cover for his frequent visits. What he really
ated was having to interact with the man who called the shots
ere. Forced to look at that shit-eating smirk, those artificially
vhitened teeth glistening every time he opened his mouth,
tretching the spray-on tan covering that overgrown infant's
ace. It was almost too much to bear.

Claude had despised Philip Roque on a gut level since the
lay four months ago when the abortionist had driven out to
Vacherie for a sit-down. The whiff of superiority that oozed
off him like a sickly cologne rankled Claude in a serious way.
Ie wasn't alone in this reaction. All the guys at the casino felt it.

He'd complained to Mr. Abellard numerous times that he
lidn't want to deal with Roque directly. Those protests fell on
leaf ears. Abellard insisted he be the one to handle transport
of their contraband from the clinic to a refrigerated safe in
Vacherie. No arguments.

Well, Mr. Abellard had a few surprises coming his way. All
n due time.

Grabbing a feather duster from a pouch sewn into the
ide of his vacuum cleaner, Claude violently rubbed it over the
urfaces closest at hand. The receptionist's desk, the phone, the
omputer. He scrubbed and swiped and slashed with the duster,
lmost knocking a lamp to the floor before catching it with his
ree hand.

Do a better fucking job with the dusting? Is that what the
on of a bitch said to him?

Claude would do a fine job of dusting, all right. When
he doctor had outlived his usefulness, Claude would dust
hat fucking arrogant smile right off his overfed face. And he
vouldn't use a feather to do it.

Oh, yes. Abellard. Roque. Even Professor Guillory. Claude

would be squaring all accounts, when the time was right.

That was a pleasing thought, but it did nothing to help him right now. He'd come here with a very specific purpose—obtain a fresh batch of material. Deliver it to Vacherie within twenty four hours, without fail. Dire consequences awaited, should that deadline not be met.

Now the doctor was gone. With the clinic closed tomorrow, Monday was the earliest possible day to deliver, and that would be too late. Claude had miserably struck out in persuading Roque of the matter's urgency. He'd fallen short, and he had no alternative but to report his failure to Mr. Abellard.

Claude walked down the hallway and through a side door into the operating room. He flicked on the overhead light and continued waving the duster around with only scant awareness of what he was doing. Every corner of his conscious mind turned itself to the same pressing dilemma.

More material. Tomorrow. Whatever means necessary.

Deadweight.

That last word echoed louder than the others. He knew what it meant, having seen firsthand the way Abellard dealt with individuals who by bad luck or gross incompetence failed to prove their usefulness.

Claude had been pushed to the edge of a cliff, by no fault of his own. This was survival, plain and simple. He didn't want to do anything bad. He wasn't warped. He only did bad things when someone made him. Someone he wasn't strong enough to say no to.

A plunge over the cliff. That was the only alternative to delivering what Mr. Abellard expected. Claude consoled himself with the knowledge that he had no real choice at all.

He stepped over to a glass case mounted on the wall adjacent to the operating table. Inside, lined up with careful precision, lay a collection of surgical knives. Many different shapes and sizes, with blades ranging from a curved hook barely an inch long to a straight cutting edge the size of a nail file. All of them gleaming with polished perfection.

Claude pulled a rubber glove from the open vent of a box

n the counter to his left. He slid it onto his right hand and
eached for the knob of the case. The glass door opened silently.

Whatever it takes.

He would do what had to be done, like always. And he'd do
with one of the doctor's own instruments. That was the best
art. He even giggled a bit pondering the beauty of it.

After the bad thing was done, he'd walk back into this clinic
ith one hell of a shock for Philip Roque. And then he'd see
ow easily the son of a bitch smiled through that.

Feeling like he was in control of events for the first time
ince his tense phone call with Abellard last night, Claude pulled
four-inch straight blade from the case.

10.

Bourbon Street pulsed under a cloud-bloated sky. A short-live
downpour around ten o'clock had left a glossy veneer ove
everything. The damp flagstones reflected a smeared rainbo
of neon.

Rusty kept a slow pace along the sidewalk. A glance at hi
watch told him it was six minutes before midnight. He'd kille
the past few hours idly canvassing the Quarter, sitting out th
brief storm over a ruminative drink at the Old Absinthe House

Even with his thoughts consumed by Marceline, it was har
not to stray into a nostalgic fugue. The nine years since he'
last seen the Quarter felt like a tick of the clock too miniscul
to measure.

This place had once constituted his entire world. It hel
everything he could ever want. He'd had the greatest mento
a fledgling illusionist could ever hope to study under. Nightl
crowds of spectators in front of whom he could practice hi
trade, making small but essential improvements with eac
sidewalk performance. Most of all, he had Marceline, the perfec
companion for his first clumsy forays into the realms of lov
and sex.

When exactly did I decide this wasn't enough? Rusty wondered a
he walked.

He concluded it had occurred right after his twenty-firs
birthday, when he'd announced to Prosper and Marceline tha
the time had come to abandon NOLA for a bigger and brighte
stage. Las Vegas beckoned, and he'd been convinced that
where his ultimate destiny lay waiting.

Father and daughter had accompanied him on that starry-eyed westward pilgrimage, despite their reservations. Abandoned everything they'd called home out of love and loyalty for him.

Yeah. And I sure as shit paid them back.

Rusty shook off that familiar stab of self-reproach and quickened his pace, reignited with purpose.

Hold on, Marcie. Please. Wherever you are, I'm coming for you.

At Bourbon and Conti he reached his destination. A red neon apple the size of a satellite dish hovered over the entrance to Temptations.

Inside, a musky black-lit darkness enveloped him like an invisible cloak. It was a small place, nowhere near the cavernous strip clubs he'd frequented with almost nightly regularity when living high in Vegas. One narrow stage stretched down the far wall, a single smudged pole rising from the middle.

Twisting around the pole was a diminutive blonde, clad only in high heels and everything she was born with. A thumping hip-hop bassline guided her movements, which were energetic if less than polished. A cluster of men huddled over their drinks in the glare of the footlights. Based on the paltry sprinkling of bills Rusty spotted on the grooved floor of the stage, it was a stingy crowd.

He scanned the room, looking for Monday Reed. No sign. He took the end seat in front of the stage to make himself as visible as possible.

The blonde dancer fluidly sashayed his way, dropping to all fours when she got close enough to offer a personalized view. She seemed grateful to have some fresh attention, and threw herself into a series of contortive gyrations that left Rusty impressed.

A napkin materialized in front of him. He looked up to see Monday standing with a cocktail tray in hand. Her wardrobe consisted of a pink tanktop revealing plenty of midriff and some sprayed-on black tights. The glimpse of ink Rusty had noticed beneath the collar of her nurse's uniform revealed itself as a well-rendered rose tattoo, complete with thorns from which a single drop of painted blood tricked onto her clavicle.

"You're punctual," she said.

"One of my few redeeming qualities."

"So I've heard. What are you drinking?"

"Scotch, rocks."

"Dewar's all right?"

"Unless there's any Glenlivet 18 hiding back there."

"I'll see what I can rustle up. You're buying me a Captai and Coke, too."

She turned away, then stopped.

"And show Tiffany some love. It's her first night, the gi could use some encouragement."

Rusty dropped two twenties on the stage just as the hip ho track ended. The blonde picked them up with a childlike smil then collected a few other bills from the stage.

Three minutes later, Rusty and Monday occupied a table i the back corner. They each had a drink in front of them that sa ignored on its leather coaster. There was a break in the actio on stage, with some brass band jazz playing over the PA at subdued level.

"OK, hold up," Monday said, interrupting a question abou Marceline's recent state of mind. "I get that you're worried, an you seem sincere enough. This just feels a little weird."

"What does?"

"The timing. Marceline goes missing, then a few days late her old flame shows up out of nowhere?"

"I admit the timing's odd. Before I got here, all I wa worried about was an awkward reunion with her and her fathe Then I find out she's fucking vanished."

"You used to be pretty tight with the family, huh?"

"For a long time, they were practically *my* family."

"What happened?"

"Long story. I'm hoping you can fill me in on what's bee going on these past few months."

"Well, she's excited about the baby. Not worried or anxiou far as I can tell. She seems to be in a good state of mind, overall.

"But not entirely."

"Let's face it, she's not in an ideal situation for a expectant mother."

"Trouble with the baby's father, you mean."

Monday made a sour face. "I take it you're not acquainted with Joseph Abellard?"

"Haven't had the pleasure of his company."

"I really don't know that much about him," she said, her expression darkening further. "So I don't want to give any false ideas, OK? I just know I don't like him."

"Don't hold back. Prosper hates his guts, that much is clear. What's the story with this guy?"

"I only met him a couple times. The last time, it wasn't pretty. I've been telling Marcie for months she should break it off. Even if she's carrying his child, she doesn't have to put up with…whatever he made her put up with."

"Did he abuse her?"

The question yielded a pause.

"Talk straight with me, Monday." Catching the interrogative tone in his voice, he added, "Please."

"He never abused her, that I know of. At least not physically. But he's got a mean temper. I saw that for myself."

"When?"

Monday inhaled and took her time expelling the air, as if surveying a bridge and mulling whether or not to cross.

"He came by the hospital two weeks ago. They had an argument, right in front of the nursery. It didn't get physical, but he was totally out of his mind. Like, *foaming*. Took two security guards to haul him out of there."

"Did they call the cops?"

Monday shook her head, diverting her eyes.

"No one got hurt, so…"

"Jesus. Did this incident at least get reported after she went missing?"

"I honestly don't know."

"That's something the NOPD needs to hear about, for Christ's sake. Pretty hard to believe you don't understand that."

She glanced up at him sharply, any trace of hesitancy vaporizing.

"Watch how you talk to me, asshole. Who are you to stick

your nose into this, anyway?"

A waitress emerged from the darkness with fresh drink though they'd barely touched the first round. Rusty almost wave her off, then figured it was probably a two-drink minimum. H paid the waitress, using the brief interval to regain his cool an hope Monday was doing the same.

"Just help me understand this," he said in a calmer voice "Abellard came to the ward two weeks ago, right? Prosper sai it's been more than a month since she broke it off with him."

"That's true. I was thrilled when she told me. Like, finally."

"You think he was trying to get her back?"

"I don't think he ever believed she'd left him. Doesn't strik me as the kind of man who'd just accept it. But that's not wha they were arguing about. There was something else. Somethin about the hospital, I think. I only heard bits and pieces befor the guards dragged him off."

"Did you ask her what it was all about?"

"Sure. She wouldn't say, just made it clear she was don with him and not to worry about it. I'd tell you if I knew more."

"Fair enough. What else is there to know about this guy What's his line?"

"He owns the Carnival Casino, out in Vacherie. Knov where that is?"

Rusty nodded, though he only had a vague impression "Cajun Country, right? To the east?"

"About eighty miles, but it might as well be off the map Vacherie is half swamp, half plantation land. Whole lot o nothing in every direction. Really poor country, aside from th tourists who bus in to see what it was like in Old Dixie."

"Seems like an odd place for a casino. Pretty out of the way."

"I agree, which makes me think they got more going or than blackjack. Being in the sticks probably gives Abellard a lo of breathing room. To do exactly what, I wouldn't try to guess."

"Ever been out there?" Rusty asked.

She nodded, wrinkling her nose with distaste.

"It's a shithole. Makes the riverside casinos in Shrevepor look like Monte Carlo. I went one time with Marceline, bacl efore she called it quits with Abellard. We didn't stay long, just ad a drink and I made her drive me back."

"How'd she get hooked up with him in the first place?"

"Some charity event at Tulane. I gather he's involved with arious do-gooder things. Probably to whitewash his image, vhich I'm sure needs it."

"You saying he's a crook?"

"He's a casino boss in the middle of Cajun Country," Monday answered with a shrug, as if that was a distinction vithout a difference. "Got a few other businesses out there, too. Couple of car washes, shrimp and po' boy shack on the old River Road, stuff like that. Fronts, I'm guessing."

"Hard to see her getting involved with someone like that. Granted, we parted ways quite a while back, but it seems out of character."

"Maybe she just has poor taste in men."

Monday gave Rusty a blunt look to drive home that observation. He didn't offer a retort.

"Abellard probably has his charms," she continued after draining her drink. "I tried to steer Marcie away, but didn't make a dent. She kept insisting he's a respectable member of the legal gaming industry. Finally, she got wise."

"Yeah, maybe too late for her own good," Rusty uttered. He took a swallow of scotch, fighting off a tide of unease that swelled with each new detail Monday provided about the man whose baby Marceline was carrying.

"I gotta get back on the clock. Hope I've been able to help a little."

"You have. Really, I appreciate the time. Especially since Marcie hasn't given you much reason to think I was worth it."

Monday started to step away but paused. Rusty didn't need to employ any mentalism techniques to read the unasked question on her lips.

"What are you wondering about?"

"I was going to ask what went wrong with you two, out n Vegas."

"Like I said, long story. You can hear it chapter and verse, once I know she's safe."

Monday shook her head, a long amber curl falling over th
rose tattoo.

"None of my business, and I don't need to hear another sac
story in that department. That's why I tried not to give Marci
too much grief about Abellard. With my track record, it'd mak
me a bigtime hypocrite."

"The cops questioned him, you know. Not the NOPD, th
Sheriff out in Vacherie."

Monday's brows arched with what looked like surprise.

"No shit. What did he say?"

"Doesn't know where she is, and he claims to be worried.
don't know anything more specific than that."

"Maybe it's the truth. I'd like to think so."

"Not good enough for me. I'll be dropping by the Carniva
Casino tomorrow, and I won't be leaving till I get a little fac
time with Joseph Abellard."

Rusty delivered those words without raising his voice to b
heard over a blaring metal track that heralded the next dancer's
appearance on stage. Monday heard him clearly enough. She
appraised him for a moment, her face taking on a warmer aspect

"Let me see your phone," she said, reaching out with ar
upturned palm.

Rusty handed her his mobile and watched as she dialed a
ten digit number with a 504 prefix.

"Call me when you learn something. I'd really like to know
our girl's all right."

She turned and disappeared into the hazy neon gloom of
Temptations. Rusty cast a quick glance at the stage, where a
curvy Latina was stepping out of a white lace thong. With a def
flick of her foot, she launched it airborne toward a drunken tric
hunched below her.

Rusty watched the guy in the middle snatch it from the ai
with a triumphant leer and decided he'd had enough of this
place. He rose without bothering to finish his drink and cut a
straight path for the exit.

11.

The fetid air outside Temptations didn't offer much relief. Rusty drew in a lungful of what passed for fresh air on Bourbon, then cut a quick left onto St. Luis. His pace accelerated, fueled by a craving for the king bed in his suite. It had been a frustrating day, and tomorrow's trip to Vacherie loomed tall in his thoughts.

His cell phone vibrated as soon as he reached Royal Street. A 504 area code showed on the screen, but it wasn't the number Monday had given him.

"Diamond," a gruff male voice intoned. "Dan Hubbard, NOPD."

The hairs on the back of Rusty's neck rose, responding like sonar to an invisible threat.

"What is it, Detective?"

"There's…well, there's a body for you to identify. At the coroner's. I just came from there."

Rusty's feet kept moving, but he had no awareness of forward motion.

"Turned up about an hour ago," Hubbard continued. "Busboy found her in a dumpster behind the Crescent City Oyster House. Fits the description we have for Ms. Lavalle. Black female, average height. Looks to be in her twenties."

Rusty swallowed before asking, "Was she—"

"I thought it best to call you," Hubbard interrupted, "instead of the father. Figured this might be too much for the old guy."

"You made the right decision. Was this woman pregnant, Detective?"

Hubbard gave what sounded like a sigh before answering.

"We think so. Given the condition of the body, it's hard to say for sure."

"What are you telling me?"

"Look, you should know what to expect before you walk in there."

A brief pause elapsed. Rusty felt the heat of his phone pressed against his ear, a sense of dread seeping in through every pore.

"The coroner's initial examination suggests she was carrying," Hubbard continued. "That hasn't been verified yet. A proper autopsy will tell us, but that'll be a few days."

"Did you see the body yourself?"

"I did."

"So how can you not know?"

"She's cut up bad, OK?" Hubbard paused before adding, "Bad as anything I've seen in twenty-two years."

Rusty barely registered the last few words Hubbard had spoken. He froze on the sidewalk, drilled to the damp ground in front of the show window of an art gallery selling framed lithograph prints of historic New Orleans.

"Jesus Christ," he said shakily.

"Yeah. Like I said, thought you should know before walking in there. We normally don't call people in to do a formal identification, but I know you've been worried about Ms. Lavalle I thought you'd want to know soon as possible."

The potential reality of what he was hearing sunk in. Rusty felt the flagstones start to swim beneath his feet.

"Where do I go?"

"2116 Earhart Drive, off Claiborne. Technically they're closed right now, but I told them to expect you. There's an attendant waiting with the body."

"I'm on my way."

"Call me at this number, soon as you make an ID. Don't worry about the hour."

"I will."

Rusty thought Hubbard had hung up, then heard the creak

of a wooden chair over the line. He pictured the detective leaning back from the cluttered desk in his cramped office.

"I hope it's not your friend, Diamond."

The call went dead.

"So do I," Rusty uttered to the empty street around him. Snapping into focus, he started to run back toward Bourbon where it would be easier to flag down a cab. Then he remembered how close he was to the Cornstalk. His rental car waited in the parking lot.

Turning on a heel, Rusty didn't stop moving until the Mustang's gearshift was in reverse. He backed out of the lot with a screech of rubber and without bothering to see if the road was clear.

• • •

Nineteen minutes later, Rusty pulled the Mustang into a parking space in front of a gleaming marble building that occupied an entire block of Earhart Avenue, less than a stone's throw from the I-10 overpass. He'd barely tapped the brake during the drive, blowing multiple red lights through some of midtown's busiest intersections.

He killed the engine and got out on rubbery legs. The lot lay mostly empty. He forced a measure of composure upon himself, then climbed a broad set of concrete stairs leading to the main entrance of the Orleans Parish Forensic Center.

Rusty crossed the expansive breezeway in five hurried steps, finding a pair of glass doors locked. He pressed an intercom buzzer built into the marble edifice, hearing a faint digital ring emanate from inside.

The front desk, visible through the smoked pane of the door, appeared to be unoccupied. Rusty kept his thumb on the buzzer until he noticed the top of a bald head rise from behind the desk, followed by a formidable pair of shoulders cloaked in a dark blue night watchman's uniform.

The watchman blinked away sleep as he rose from his napping position. He punched in a security code while giving an unfriendly scowl through the glass, then pushed open the door.

"I'm here to ID a body," Rusty said, hearing a quiver in his voice that sounded alien, like it belonged to someone he didn't know and didn't want to meet.

"Uh huh," grunted the watchman.

"Detective Hubbard of the Sixth Precinct called me. He said you were notified I'd be coming."

"Uh huh," the watchman repeated. "We been notified."

"Gonna let me in?" Rusty asked after a weighted pause. "I'd like to get this over with."

The watchman stepped aside to let him enter, then closed the front door. Rusty heard an automatic metal lock click into place.

Returning to his post at the front desk, the night watchman sunk into a padded chair behind a bank of computer screens. He tilted his head toward the far end of the lobby.

"Take the stairs, one floor down. Room 013."

Rusty nodded and brushed past the front desk. A haze of humming electricity burned down from the high ceiling above. It struck him as surreal. The lobby was overlit and elegantly designed in a style that felt inappropriate to this building's grim purpose.

Every surface gleamed—from the polished floor, to the curved brass sconces holding two symmetrical lines of overhead lights, to the steel handrail along a set of stairs leading to the subterranean examination rooms.

Rusty descended on leaden feet, fighting off the fear that built within him. Each step brought him closer to answers he wasn't prepared to face.

Is it her? Can it possibly be her? What will I tell Prosper? What will I tell myself?

Reaching the bottom of the stairs, a narrow hallway stretched off in two directions.

Rusty turned left, his pace slowing by degrees. After the manic crosstown drive, he suddenly felt less hurried to reach his destination.

As he passed three closed doors, a band of cold sweat

formed along his brow. He reached an open doorway on the right side of the hall. Room 013. A beam of faded white light stretched out into the hallway, creating a parallelogram on the buffed cement by his feet.

He stepped inside.

On first glimpse, the examination room appeared devoid of the living. One side of the room contained row after row of dull gray lockers, built into the wall and reaching from floor to ceiling. How many of them held the newly dead? Rusty had no way of knowing, and didn't want to ponder it.

"Hello?" he called out. "Anyone here?"

A muffled cough sounded from a darkened corner of the room. Rusty saw a dull green lab coat emerge from behind a column of lacquered wood file cabinets. It hung loosely on the frame of a gaunt man with a bloodless pallor that could have easily belonged to one of the lockers' inhabitants.

The attendant coughed again, covering his mouth with a balled fist.

"Here for the Jane Doe, I assume."

"That's right."

"Must have some powerful friends in the department."

"No. I don't."

When Rusty didn't elaborate, the attendant continued, "They hardly ever let civilians down here. Not once at this time of night, far as I can recall."

"Just show me the body," Rusty said tersely. He wasn't about to give any explanation for his appearance here tonight, not that he had any to offer. He really didn't know why Hubbard had shown him the courtesy, except possibly out of respect for Prosper.

Shrugging as if he'd expected no more than a quick rebuff to his query, the attendant shuffled over to the wall of lockers. He opened a chest-high lateral door marked 2104-A. The door squeaked softly.

The attendant reached inside and grabbed the steel handles of a slab placed on rollers. Bending slightly at the knee, he pulled with a grunt. The slab shuddered out, extending for two feet before halting with a clang.

A body lay there. Visible in outline from the top of the head to the ribcage, the rest hidden within the locker. It was covered in a white sheet pulled up almost to the hairline, totally obscuring the facial features. Rusty could just make out a thin strip of mocha-colored skin between the top of the sheet and the long tufts of wavy black hair spilling out onto the slab.

Was he looking at the remains of Marceline Lavallee? Absolutely impossible to tell.

He could be. He most definitely could be.

"If you're ready," the attendant coughed, his face forming an expression that could have been either aloof or sympathetic.

He reached for the sheet, placing his fingers on the edge just below the corpse's hairline.

"Wait!" Rusty ordered. He laid a restrictive hand on the shoulder of the attendant, who looked at him with alarm.

"Hey, buddy. I can't let you touch—"

"Just hold on, for Christ's sake."

The attendant released his grip on the sheet and retreated half a pace. He casually repositioned himself closer to a security callbox.

"Relax," Rusty said in a calmer voice. "I won't cause any problems. Just give me a second, OK?"

The attendant nodded, keeping the callbox within reach.

Rusty leaned closer to the slab. He squinted, trying to pick up some clue that would give him an answer to the mystery of this body's identity before confirming it with his eyes.

The thin sliver of flesh visible above the top of the sheet looked very much as Marceline's complexion appeared in his memory. Both the shade and the smooth, unblemished texture struck him as horrifyingly familiar.

He couldn't recognize any telling clues in the dark, curled tresses spread across the slab. Hell, he didn't even know what kind of hairstyle Marceline had worn recently. This woman's hair appeared damp and furiously tangled, as if some terrible struggle had consumed the final moments of her life.

A sick tightness filled Rusty's chest, constricting his breath.

o a shallow ebb. Eyes traveling down the sheet, over twin mounds indicating the woman's breasts, he flinched like he'd been stuck with an electric needle. Clearly visible just where the lab disappeared into the locker, a dark stain spotted the sheet. A complex pattern of dried gore, covering as much of the dead woman's stomach as he could discern from where he stood.

Hubbard's voice rang in his head. *Worst I've ever seen.*

Rusty tried in vain to steel himself. He abandoned the effort and gave a terse nod.

"Do it."

The attendant paused for half a second before he again reached for the sheet. He looked down at the floor, as if rendered unable to behold either the cadaver or the man who'd been summoned at this terrible hour to identify her.

"Do it!" Rusty shouted.

The attendant pulled down the sheet.

12.

It wasn't Marceline.

Rusty required several seconds before he could process tha information. For a protracted moment, he didn't know what h was seeing. The data did not compute. He stood there, lookin down at a face peacefully composed in grotesque contrast to th violence inflicted on the rest of the body.

It's not her.

He heard those words, and understood their meaning. Bu he wasn't sure if he'd verbalized or merely thought them.

Even as reluctant relief flooded his system on a wave o uncorked adrenaline, Rusty wasn't ready to avert his gaze jus yet. It seemed indecent to pay only a moment's respect to th nameless human being in front of him. A sense of decorun peppered with morbid fascination compelled him to look further

She bore little resemblance to Marcie. Thicker facia features, a wider jaw and fuller lips. Broader in the shoulders The concealing sheet had created a false impression in his mind He forced himself to turn away. The attendant was eyeing hin with an expectant look.

"Cover her back up," Rusty said.

"Positive ID?"

"Never seen her before."

"Good news for you, then."

Not bothering to reply, Rusty made for the door. He needed to remove himself from this room as quickly as possible.

He was only semi-aware of traversing the hallway and climbing the staircase. In a kind of waking trance, he reemerged from the gloom of the subterranean level into the overly bright lobby.

He barely registered the presence of the night watchman, who rose with a grumble from his comfortable chair at the front desk to dial the security code and release Rusty from the building.

Restored to the outside night's muggy air, Rusty allowed his sense of equilibrium to resettle. He crossed the breezeway, sorting out what had just happened, and how it related to his purpose in this town.

A growing sense of relief fought against a stubborn impulse to deny it. Nudging up against his gratitude for that unfortunate woman not being Marceline Lavalle, a larger reality sunk in.

I'm still no closer to finding her than I was twenty-four hours ago.

He made his way toward the parking lot and pulled out his phone to dial the most recent number on the call log. Hubbard answered on the second ring.

"What can you tell me, Diamond?"

"It's not her. I don't know that woman."

"Well," the detective said with a deep exhalation, "glad to hear it, for your sake. Sorry for the false alarm."

"That's OK. I'm glad you called me instead of Prosper. You spared him a terrible moment, and I appreciate it."

When Hubbard didn't offer any response, Rusty added, "I really hope you catch the motherfucker who did that."

"We're working on it."

"She was found in a dumpster, you said? Behind the Oyster House?"

"That's right," Hubbard answered, an audible reticence sinking into his voice.

"That's on Decatur, isn't it? Just a block or so from Jackson Square?"

"Uh huh. Why do you ask?"

"No reason. Just thinking."

"Thinking about what?"

"That's a public spot. Very public, even late at night. You'd have to be unbelievably reckless to dump a body there, don't you think? Or just stone crazy."

"Don't concern yourself with it, Diamond. Just tell Mr Lavalle to notify us when his daughter turns up."

"I'll notify you myself, Detective. I'm not going anywhere till I know she's safe."

Hubbard grumbled softly, sounding like that information didn't necessarily please him.

"Give any more thought to a private eye?" he asked. "I go a name for you. Good man, he knows the Quarter and Uptown as well as anyone. The Marigny, too."

Rusty hesitated before answering. An ill-defined sense of reservation stopped him. He couldn't help but suspect that hiring a private detective would render Marceline's disappearance even less of a priority to the New Orleans Police Department.

"Reasonable rates," Hubbard continued. "And I'll vouch for his effectiveness."

"I appreciate it, really. Can I call you on that tomorrow?"

"Whatever you want, Diamond."

Hubbard ended the call, sounding annoyed. Rusty figured he probably felt like he'd gone above and beyond by digging up a reference, and was irked to get no appreciation for his efforts.

Hell, I'm probably being stupid about this. Why not call in a professional?

No logical answer arose to that question. Only a strong gut sense that he'd be better off pursuing this himself. At least for the time being, until he'd had a chance to speak with Joseph Abellard in Vacherie. If tomorrow's effort yielded nothing productive, he would ask Hubbard for the private detective's number.

Satisfied with that resolution, Rusty hustled down the stone steps in front of the Orleans Parish Forensic Center, offering a whispered plea to whatever deity may be willing to listen that he never lay eyes on this place again.

• • •

At the exact moment Rusty's rented Mustang roared away from the Forensic Center, another vehicle entered a deserted parking lot behind the JAX brewery. Claude Sherman's Pontiac station wagon, that of the crappy two-toned paint job he so despised, rolled into a free space in the lot's southwest corner.

Claude wasn't sure if he found the exact spot where he had parked in the wee hours two nights ago. He hoped not, because now he needed to make another phone call. To the same man. To impart new information unlikely to generate anything less than fiery disapproval. The previous call hadn't gone well, and Claude hoped that by placing this one from a different parking spot he might improve his chances.

A stupid notion, he realized. Beyond just stupid, it was flat-out ridiculous. Quite possibly insane.

But Claude wasn't insane. Now more than ever, it was imperative to keep that clear in his mind. Forget what the faceless shrinks at the psych ward had murmured about him during those five nightmarish years as a teenager. Claude knew he wasn't crazy. He only did crazy things when left with no other alternative.

Like tonight. He had no choice, so he did was what was necessary. He needed to make Mr. Abellard understand that. Mr. Abellard was the one who'd pushed him up to the cliff's edge, and he should bear some responsibility for all this.

Claude had spent the past four hours piloting the Pontiac with no purpose or destination. Canvassing large swaths of the city, simply to stay in motion. To create distance from the terrible mess he'd left in the alley behind Decatur.

About an hour ago, he'd stopped at an Esso station in Metarie to fill the tank and realized he couldn't keep driving aimlessly all night. Mr. Abellard was expecting an update, and Claude couldn't wait until morning to give it. Daylight would render the details far too vivid and detailed in his memory. He needed to get it all out in the darkness, and then do his best to forget it.

So he'd driven straight from Metarie to this spot. The decision to park within the brewery's shadow was not random. He felt drawn here by a kind of gravitational force. For reasons unclear, this felt like a safe place.

Retrieving his phone from the glove box, he suddenly

understood why. A crystalline shard of long-discarded memory lit up his mind.

Claude's father, a case-a-day JAX drinker and monstrously abusive felon, brought him here once as a kid. The old man figured a tour of the brewery, complete with plenty of free tasters, would make for a swell outing to celebrate Claude's twelfth birthday. It was one of the few times he'd felt safe in his father's company, and the last pleasant recollection he could claim from childhood.

Shortly after that brewery tour, his old man had turned up on a gurney in the downtown morgue, stabbed in the throat by an unknown assailant in the Saturn Bar. Less than a year later, Claude had developed a ravenous taste for arson.

He'd started small—just heaps of twigs and such—but quickly graduated to structure fires. Caught setting a tumbledown shack ablaze and almost killing two sleeping transients inside, he was sent to the state juvenile ward for psychiatric observation. There he'd remained until his eighteenth birthday, when the overcrowded and understaffed facility had to let him go. He'd presented a convincing edifice of conquering the demons that fueled his exploits as an adolescent firebug.

But Claude was far from free of his demons. A quick peek into the Pontiac's trunk would prove as much. That bloody bundle, and what it signified.

He dialed Abellard's number with a shaky hand, and didn't have to wait long for an answer.

"You know what time it is, Claude?"

"Yeah. I mean, no. I know it's late."

"Tell me you're calling with good news."

Claude's stomach seized up slightly. Could he possibly describe the events of this night as good? Yes, that was possible, if assessed from his employer's point of view.

"Uh, yeah. We got a fresh batch."

"Good man, Claude. I knew you'd find a way to deliver, with the right motivation."

"Yeah, yeah. I delivered."

"You gonna drive it on out now, or in the morning?"

"I, uh…I can't do it right now."

"Alright, you earned some sleep. Get to the casino by eight A.M. sharp. I'll call Professor Bitch, tell her she can expect a package by noon."

"No. I need more time than that."

Claude could hear Abellard breathing hard into the phone as he waited for some clarification.

"The, uh, material," Claude stammered, "it's not ready for delivery yet. I gotta see the doc first."

"What are you saying, man? You didn't get the package from Roque?"

"No," Claude said, shaking his head from side to side, trying to dislodge the ugly truth he struggled to articulate. "Roque wasn't involved. I did it myself."

Another passage of silence, this one unmarked by the sound of breathing.

"Jesus Fucking Christ."

Abellard may have said more than that, but Claude didn't hear him. In his mind, he was occupying a street corner across from the free clinic on Saint Peter, just as he had five hours ago.

He'd watched her leave the clinic, alone, quite possibly the last patient of the day. Long dark hair, wearing a pretty summer dress and attractively plump around the waist. Had to be at least four or five months along, which created complications on the harvesting side of things. But Claude couldn't afford to be choosy.

He'd followed her for many blocks, away from the busier sections of the Quarter and up towards Congo Square. Each block grew progressively darker, less populated. Waiting beneath a street lamp as he watched her fumble in her pocketbook for a set of keys, he'd struck.

Claude couldn't bear to think about what happened after that. The surgical knife he'd lifted from Roque's examination room proved too short for an efficient job. He'd needed to jab and slash many more times than anticipated, and she remained conscious for far too long. Sounds escaped her throat too terrible to recall, though he knew they'd reach out for him from the depths of his nightmares.

Then it was finally over. A last fluttering breath escaped he lungs, and he continued with the necessary work. After that, h faced the task of disposal. If he hadn't been in such a derange rush, he might have taken greater care to select a less visibl spot. But it worked out fine. Nobody saw him as he hoisted th plastic-wrapped body into a dumpster in the alley behind som seafood place on Decatur. Engine still running, the Pontia had sped away almost before the dumpster's heavy plastic li slammed shut.

Then came the empty, enervating hours. The hours spen driving in an aimless pattern around greater New Orleans Steering the wagon in a series of pointless loops, hoping in vai that each mile added to the odometer would create some kin of meaningful distance from the shameful, unforgivable crim he'd committed.

"You said any means necessary," he stuttered into th phone. "That's what you told me. You said I was deadweigh unless I delivered."

Abellard took so long to respond that Claude started t think he'd terminated the call.

"So I did, Claude. Seems you know how to listen, so liste now. I don't want to hear one goddamn thing about where thi package came from. Not a word. You need to see the doc befor you can deliver, see him. Then get your ass out here so we ca close this deal."

"Tomorrow's Sunday," Claude protested. "I mean today Anyway, the clinic won't be open."

"Fuck that! Call him first thing and tell him to meet yo there. Then get out here pronto."

"I don't know how much time it takes. I mean…I don' know what he needs to do to get it ready."

"That's why you're gonna be all over him come sunup Don't let that motherfucker out of your sight till it's done. I' stall Professor Bitch."

"Joseph, you know I didn't want to do this. If there wa more time, if we could still use the ward—"

"What did I tell you, Claude? Not one goddamn word! I don't want to know. Call me from the doc's and give me an ETA."

"I will. But, just…I didn't want to do this!"

Claude waited for another angry admonishment. He knew how reckless it was to ignore a direct order, but he couldn't stop himself. He had to let someone, anyone, understand his hand had been forced. He wasn't the deviant they'd said he was at the psych ward. He was his father's son, but that didn't mean he'd inherited the worst of the man's qualities.

Claude wanted to say all these things. But the phone was dead in his hand.

There was no one to talk to. Abellard wouldn't listen. Tomorrow, he'd make the doctor listen. Yes. Claude Sherman wasn't the only one who'd dirtied his hands in this operation, even if he was called upon to do the worst of it.

Oh, yes. He'd have plenty to say tomorrow, once he'd impressed upon Roque the urgency of harvesting the material so they could make a viable delivery. He would make Philip Roque understand. And when the time came, after Professor Guillory got what she wanted and the deadline was met, Claude would force Joseph Fucking Abellard to listen as well. And wouldn't *he* be surprised to learn what Claude had been up to behind his back!

All of that would happen in due time. But right now, Claude had no one to confide in other than the impassive neon letters high above. And no one to distract his thoughts from that terrible bloody bundle in the trunk.

13.

Rusty kept a boot on the gas and the AC blasting as he powered the Mustang westward along the interstate. It was a smashingly bright Sunday morning, the sun burning with such unyielding intensity he felt glad not to be among the sizable portion of the French Quarter's inhabitants to awaken with a hangover.

The humidity had kicked in shortly after sunrise and showed no sign of abating. The Mustang's temperature gauge read eighty-eight, and it was barely ten o'clock.

He'd arisen from his bed at the Cornstalk feeling no more rested than when he'd set his head on the pillow six hours before. After fortifying himself with some chicory coffee at Cafe du Monde, he called Prosper just as the elder magician was leaving home to open up the Emporium.

Rusty walked him through yesterday's events—excluding any mention of the unidentified corpse—and tried to spin his contact with Dan Hubbard in an optimistic light. Prosper sounded more weary than disappointed to hear that no tangible clues had surfaced. Rusty promised to check in again tonight, after he'd spoken with Joseph Abellard. The call ended on a sour note, doing little to brighten his mood.

So today's excursion to Vacherie felt like just the ticket. Get out of the city for a few hours, inhale some pungent bayou air, and at the very least lay eyes on the one person most likely to shed some meaningful information on Marceline's whereabouts.

Just don't walk in there pegging him as a suspect, Rusty cautioned himself, watching a chain of faded yellow dashes on the pavement disappear beneath the Mustang's hood. *For all I know, the man is just as worried as I am. Let him help, if he can.*

That felt like a prudent approach. It was only fair to take Monday's disdain for Abellard with a grain of salt. Prosper's too, for that matter.

Give him the benefit of the doubt. If he proves unworthy of it, go on the offensive.

This strategic line of thinking occupied Rusty as he kept racking up miles away from the NOLA city limit and sped closer to his destination. Little else competed for his attention. He wasn't driving through an especially picturesque part of Louisiana. Countless acres of green emptiness stretched out in all directions, with an occasional spit of brown muddy water snaking through the flattened landscape.

Rusty didn't know exactly when he'd entered into the region designated as Cajun Country. Five miles back he'd gotten off the westbound I-10, moving south and crossing the Mississippi on an arched suspension bridge before turning west again on a two lane byway. The few dwellings he spotted from his mobile vantage point appeared little more than embellished lean-tos occupying bits of grassy land at a safe distance from the road.

A faded sign overgrown with moss welcomed him to Vacherie. Stopping at an intersection, Rusty soaked up the vista of Southern rural poverty all around him.

On the roadside to his left was a crumbling red brick edifice with three smashed windows and a hand-painted sign reading "Sabur Barber Shop" tilting at a defeated angle toward a haggard plot of grass by the entrance. Across the street stood a metallic shed, its front door blocked by a forlorn three-seater couch whose leather cushions had been slashed in too many spots to count. Another blocky structure stood catty-corner to the barber shop, so covered with weeds and vines only a few random patches of cinderblock remained visible.

Despite the obvious economic blight, Rusty didn't find this a particularly depressing environment. Within an urban setting, the same tableau would have been overpoweringly downbeat. But out in these swampy reaches, Vacherie held a kind of eerie mystique. It was like an inverted Atlantis arisen from the muck, long ago abandoned by whoever had once called it home. The sole inhabitants were mosquitoes, floating in tiny black clouds through the still morning air.

If this is the kingdom Joseph Abellard rules over, how much of a threat can he be?

Buoyed by that encouraging thought, Rusty drove through the intersection and into Vacherie.

• • •

The Carnival Casino wasn't hard to find. Two steel columns reached into the sun-scorched air, well over a hundred feet tall. Atop them sat a rectangular white sign with bold red letters advertising the only legal gaming operations within a twenty mile radius.

Rusty pulled into the Carnival's gravel parking lot, assessing the layout. On the lot's far side stood a gas station no longer in operation. The marquee above the cashier's booth had long ago been demolished by weather or vandalism. Two rows of pumps stood abandoned, their hoses torn away and reserves of unsold gasoline probably siphoned off years ago.

The rest of the lot lay mostly empty. A trio of eighteen-wheelers filled out one corner, with a handful of smaller vehicles parked in haphazard formation.

Rusty backed into the spot closest to the casino's entrance, figuring a quick getaway might prove desirable. The digital clock on the Mercedes' dash read 10:43. He killed the engine and got out, taking a moment to stretch his legs and size up his surroundings.

Like its grander counterparts in the Nevada desert, the Carnival had no windows. That's where the similarities to Vegas ended. The Carnival made no attempt at enticing customers with a flashy facade. It was a steel and concrete block with all the charm of a machine shop, hunkered low over the parking lot without a single touch of neon to attract the eye of passing motorists.

Rusty noticed a surveillance camera pointed down at him

from an archway above the entrance. The lens turned with an audible whirr.

Not running on auto, he thought. *Someone's operating it, and getting a good close look at me.*

That thought rattled him until he remembered no one was expecting him here today. The camera was a standard security precaution, quite possibly for show purposes only. For all he knew, the man he'd come to see wasn't even on the premises right now.

Rusty pulled open the door and stepped inside.

The first sensory impression to take hold was an overpowering smell of cigarette smoke and discarded butts. It was like stepping into a massive ashtray that hadn't been dumped out since Huey Long occupied the governor's mansion. A central air conditioning system was pumping full blast, lowering the temperature to meat locker levels but accomplishing little in the way of filtration.

Rusty stepped through a metal detector, watching an overhead light go green. He kept walking into the darkened foyer. A mountainous security guard planted on a stool gave him a cold stare. Whether that look communicated hostility or a dearth of cognitive function, Rusty couldn't say. He kept walking, turning a corner onto the casino floor.

The entire space throbbed within a murky crimson glow. A bar stretched along the wall to his immediate right. The bartender stood with his back to the stools, engrossed in a dog race being broadcast on a flatscreen TV screwed into the wall.

Rusty moved into the gaming area. The Carnival offered limited options. Two blackjack tables, a third for poker. A row of slot machines blinked and bleeped against the wall opposite the bar. Several zombie-like silhouettes shimmered before them, relentlessly feeding coins. Bobby Womack crooned on the PA.

A glassy-eyed gentleman in a CAT Diesel cap was playing blackjack by himself at the nearest table, slumped over third base with an expression that bespoke many hours without sleep. Rusty joined the game, seating himself at first base. The dealer, a black youth whose wispy mustache didn't quite succeed in making him look old enough to order a drink, swept up his twenty dollar bill from the felt and replaced it with ten yellow chips.

Winning the first hand, Rusty quickly lost the next three in a row. Mr. CAT Diesel wasn't faring much better. It was a single deck game, something not found in any but the most bargain basement gaming houses. Counting cards was childishly easy with one deck, and Rusty wondered why the Carnival offered the option.

Rusty played a half dozen hands before he realized the dealer was cheating. It wasn't the most sophisticated job of card manipulation he had ever witnessed, by a long shot. He'd seen some of the very best in the world during his time in Vegas, and had himself mastered a broad range of card tricks under Prosper's tutelage.

The wispy-mustached dealer was employing a basic blind shuffle. At the end of every third hand, he gathered up all the cards and performed four standard riffle shuffles. Then he offered the deck to either of the two players for them to cut it. Taking the cards back into his possession, he proceeded with two more riffle shuffles before dealing out the next hand.

All standard enough, but Rusty noticed how the dealer allowed a bed of about ten cards to fall from his hand prior to each riffle. Using his ring fingers and thumbs, the dealer separated the cards into two discrete sections and then laid them back together in such a way as to give the impression they'd been properly shuffled.

Except they hadn't. The deck retained the exact same order as during the previous hand, telling the dealer where all the Aces and face cards lay.

The average player probably wouldn't notice this cheat, despite the clumsiness of its execution. It was a wonder Mr. CAT Diesel could read the cards in his own hand, given the glazed sheen of his bloodshot orbs. But Rusty saw it plain as day, and stuck around long enough to lose a few more hands just so he could witness it one more time.

Who taught you your trade, junior? I wouldn't try that in Vegas, if you ever get there. Hard to shuffle with two broken hands.

Rusty flipped his remaining $2 chip to the dealer and stepped away from the table. He ambled over to the bar and cleared his throat loudly to wrest the bartender's attention away from the dog races.

"Abita Amber. In the bottle, if you got it."

The bartender, impeccably dressed in a champagne tux and sporting silver wings of hair above each ear giving him a hawklike aspect, served up a mug of Abita Amber from the tap. He took Rusty's five-spot from the bar and offered no change.

"Mr. Abellard in?"

The bartender's tufted brows, also silver, lifted high enough to bring some animation to his face.

"Who's that now?" he asked in a pack-a-day rasp.

"Joseph Abellard. You must know him, I understand he's the proprietor of this fine establishment."

The bartender grabbed a rag and started wiping down a glass that did not appear in need of cleaning.

"Now why would you be asking?"

"I'd like to have a word with him, that's all."

"Uh huh. And what is it you want to talk about?"

"A mutual friend."

The bartender chuckled softly, working the rag over another spotless glass.

"Something funny about that?"

"You and Mr. Abellard having any mutual friends, man. That's good for my first laugh of the day."

"It's no joke. I've come quite a way to talk to him. Won't take much of his time, but if he's here I think I'll stick around till he sees me."

The bartender's eyes flashed upward, past Rusty's shoulder. An almost tactile silence took over as the juke switched to "Cry Cry Cry" by Bobby Blue Bland. Rusty felt but couldn't see a presence just behind him. He knew the colossal security guard had walked over from his stool.

"Will I have better luck with him?" Rusty asked the bartender, who laughed again.

"I doubt it. Antoine don't play."

Rusty turned and looked up into the guard's impassive face. "Tell Abellard I want to see him, Antoine."

No reply came from the guard other than a quiver in one cheek. Rusty felt the bartender's hand on his shoulder but didn't turn back to acknowledge it.

"Tell him it's about Marceline Lavalle. I'm pretty sure that will get his attention."

The hand on his shoulder tightened momentarily, then pulled away. The bartender gave a small nod to the guard. Rusty watched Antoine exhale through both nostrils like he'd smelled something bad, then turn and stomp away. He disappeared into the darkened hallway behind the poker tables.

"See?" Rusty said, swiveling around. "I told you we had a friend in common."

The bartender didn't reply, standing with his gaze directed away from where Rusty sat. Like he no longer existed, or soon wouldn't.

Rusty shrugged, deciding he wasn't in the mood for more idle chitchat anyway. He settled in to nip at his beer, figuring whatever was going to happen next would probably take some time.

He was wrong. Less than three sips later the guard lumbered back over to the bar. He jerked his head a few centimeters to the left, indicating that's where Rusty should direct himself.

"Is he pointing me toward Mr. Abellard's office or the exit?" Rusty asked the bartender.

"Does it make a damn difference, far as what you're gonna do?"

"Guess not. Thanks for the beer."

Rusty followed the guard across the casino toward the hallway, feeling every eye in the room on his back. The bartender, the cheating dealer, even Mr. CAT Diesel—they were all clocking his progress. What they were thinking, he couldn't guess.

He didn't have much time to ponder it before stepping into a narrow hallway lit only by strings of Christmas tree lights along both sides of the floor. Barely discerning the security guard's bulk as he followed in the darkness, Rusty almost bumped into him when they reached the end of the hall.

Another door stood on the right, open just a crack to allow a thin vertical line of light to spill through.

The guard knocked three times, almost inaudibly. The juke wasn't nearly as loud on this side of the building. Rusty figured some serious sound insulation had been installed into the walls surrounding the gaming area.

He doubted anyone on the other side could hear the knock. But the guard must have picked up some reply, because he pushed the door open and moved aside to allow entrance.

Rusty stepped into the back office, wincing slightly at the brightness of the overhead track lighting.

Seated in a plush leather chair behind a long steel desk resembling a prison mess hall table, Joseph Abellard glanced up from a stack of money nearly two feet tall.

"Start talking, motherfucker."

14.

"I'm looking for Marceline Lavalle. I think you know where she is."

Those words left Rusty's mouth reflexively, before he had time to appraise this room and the man staring him down.

The office was a simple affair, as unadorned as the rest of the Carnival. Square room, twenty feet by twenty. Walls covered with dull wood paneling. Two cheap black lamps straight from the Ikea catalog, both burning but superfluous under the glare of the overhead fluorescent lights. A bulky metal safe with a combination lock took up an entire corner.

Though seated, Joseph Abellard filled the room with a kind of heft most men could only achieve when standing at full height. Large head crowned with short-cropped graying curls, virtually no neck connected it to the brawny torso of an aging prizefighter. His complexion was a light mocha shade suggesting a long ancestral history of mixed race, common among families of Creole lineage.

Abellard's hands, which looked like they could hold five baseballs apiece, were both filled with stacks of cash secured with rubber ties. The right moved one approved stack to a small pile on the side of the desk closest to the safe, while the left pulled a fresh stack from a larger pile for inspection.

Abellard nodded to the security guard. Rusty heard the door close softly behind him, but he couldn't tell if Antoine had left the room or not.

"Here to talk about my woman, huh?"

"I'm here to talk about Marceline Lavalle."

"No shit. That's what Antoine told me. Know what I said to him?"

Rusty didn't hazard a guess. Abellard leaned back in his chair, showing as much concern for the money as a pile of old newspapers.

"I said he had to be outta his motherfucking mind, interrupt my count with nonsense like that."

"I'm not sure he's smart enough to be crazy," Rusty said, taking another step. The insult elicited a dull grunt from behind, telling him what he'd intended to learn without turning around to look. Antoine was still in the room.

Abellard smiled broadly, and Rusty saw in an instant how this man might easily attract a woman whose better sense told her to stay a mile away. The smile completely altered the landscape of his roughhewn face.

"I won't fight you on that," Abellard said, "but the boy does make himself useful. And you done come close enough, so stop moving."

The smile vanished with that command. Rusty stood several feet in front of the desk. He was hoping he'd created just enough distance from Antoine to buy himself some added reaction time, if needed.

"Look, I appreciate you seeing me. I'm an old friend of Marcie's and I'm worried about her. Figure you must be too, considering the circumstances."

Abellard looked bored, like what he was hearing had no connection to him whatsoever.

"Circumstances," he muttered. "What the hell you know about my circumstances, as they relate to Marcie or any other damn thing?"

"I know she took a little vacation without telling anyone, and I know her well enough to know it wasn't by choice. I'm here to find out where she is, make sure she's OK."

"And who exactly are you to be taking such an interest in her welfare?"

"Just what I said, an old friend."

"Girl's got a lot of friends. So what?"

"I'm a friend of the whole family."

"Bully for you, man. How come she never mentioned you being so close?"

"Maybe she did. You don't know my name. I'm Rusty Diamond."

"That supposed to mean something? She never mentioned you, chump."

"That's not really the point, is it?"

More silence. Rusty motioned to a metal folding chair positioned in front of the desk.

"Mind if I sit? I'm not looking to waste your time."

A brusque nod and Rusty seated himself. It seemed like a workable position. He was close enough to the desk to use it for leverage with his feet, in the event that launching backward in attack or self defense became useful.

Abellard retrieved a dead cigar, half smoked, from a crystal ashtray on the desk. He revived it with a lighter, taking his time to get an even burn.

"I'm guessing you don't know much about me," he said between puffs.

"That's true. And I really don't care to find out."

"If you *did* know the first thing about me," Abellard continued, "you'd play this all different. From the jump, it'd be a whole 'nother game."

"I won't argue with that. If I knew a better way to make contact, I'd go that way. Time doesn't give me the luxury of mapping out alternatives. A pregnant woman's been missing for almost a week. Not the kind of situation that lends itself to a leisurely approach. So I came to you direct."

Rusty noticed a slight flinch at the word *pregnant*. This reference to Abellard's unborn child elicited the first reaction suggesting that the man might feel slightly off-guard.

"Fuck all that. You still ain't explained why it's your damn business. I ain't saying Marcie's gone, or sitting easy in our sun room waiting for me to come home. I'm asking why my woman's on your goddamn radar?"

"I did explain it. We go way back, she's important to me."

Feeling only icy disinterest and wanting to puncture it, Rusty added, "From what I heard, she ain't your woman no more."

Abellard's right hand clenched, but he quickly relaxed as if realizing too late he'd conceded a point. He placidly withdrew the cigar from his mouth and tapped an ash into the tray.

"Look," Rusty said, "you might try thinking of me as an asset instead of a threat."

That striking face rearranged itself again, this time into an expression of pure charismatic mirth. Rusty heard a low chuckle from Antoine. Apparently both men found the notion of being threatened by him pretty amusing.

"I've been doing a fair amount of legwork," he pressed on. "Asking around, racking up some names to talk to. No one has a fucking clue where she is, and I'm running out of names. You're not of any particular concern to me, Joseph. You're just the next one on my list."

"Well, ain't that a motherfucking relief."

"I'm asking you straight. Do you know where she is? Is there anything you can tell me?"

"Anything I can tell you? No, no. Let's start talking about what you can tell me. See, there ain't nothing about Marcie that don't concern me. Girl catches a sniffle, I'm all over it with the best goddamn doctor in the state."

"I get it. You care about her. So if you don't know where she is, you must be just as scared as I am."

Abellard pointed a thick finger in his direction.

"Put you and me in the same shoes one more time, you gonna regret it. You ain't shit to her, understand? I don't care if you used to know her or what the fuck. I'm doing everything I can to bring the girl home safe and sound."

Rusty felt a heavy stillness settle over the room. He thought he heard a small gasp from behind him. Joseph Abellard had just revealed he knew Marceline was missing. A mistake yielded by anger, or a calculated admission?

"Back home with you, Joseph? From what I've heard, she doesn't want any part of you. Not anymore."

Rather than bristle at this claim, Abellard went a shade

melancholy. Rusty found himself captivated by the man's expressiveness. The emotional landscape conveyed by his face was remarkable not just for its range but for the swiftness with which it changed. He saw worry written on that face. A genuine worry that told Rusty he wasn't the only one in this room concerned for Marceline's well-being.

"Look, who she lives with," Rusty said, "that's her business. I'm not trying to butt in, and I know she wouldn't want me to. I'm trying to put her father's mind at ease, as much as my own. He's about half-crazy with worry. I'm sure you can understand that."

Abellard stiffened at the reference to Prosper. Rusty counted this as the third sore nerve he'd struck since the conversation started.

"I don't want to hear about that old bastard, understand?"

"He doesn't like you too much, does he? I can relate, believe me. Got plenty of personal experience with what a hardass he can be."

"Motherfucker turned the police on me. Sheriff come out here, spent a damn hour asking the same questions."

"I heard."

"Oh, you heard, did you?"

Rusty nodded.

"From the NOPD. They're tracking this thing along with the Vacherie Sheriff."

In the silence that followed, Rusty saw something new creep into Abellard's earth-toned eyes. Not the dismissive hostility, nor the breezy charm he'd glimpsed once or twice. Abellard was looking at him with a kind of sober appraisal, indicating he was being taken seriously for the first time.

"You told the Sheriff you haven't seen her in, what, a month?"

Rusty wasn't expecting a reply to that, and he got none.

"Look," he continued, "whatever the situation is with Marcie and you, it's none of my concern."

"You're goddamn right it—"

"I mean, it's gotta be rough losing the woman who's carrying your child."

"Listen to me real good. Only reason we're talking is I figured maybe you know something I don't. Seeing as that ain't the case—"

"Don't be so sure," Rusty broke in, throwing out the last arrow in his quiver. "That ugly scene at the hospital? I heard a thing or two about it. And that was a lot less than a month ago, wasn't it?"

Silence held for a solid five-count, other than the muted sound of the juke through the walls. Abellard's face assumed an expression Rusty hadn't seen before, something of a mix between ashen shock and molten rage.

"What the fuck did you say?"

"I haven't mentioned it to the NOPD. Not yet. Don't see any reason to, as long as I know Marceline's alright. Seems the hospital staff wanted to keep it quiet, but that may not be possible now. It's up to you."

With a kind of measured deliberation, Abellard ground out the cigar in the ashtray. He rubbed his fingers together, brushing away a few flecks of tobacco leaf.

"This detective I'm talking to, Hubbard. He seems to think you're in the clear. Who knows, Joseph? He finds out a pair of security guards had to physically remove you when you started screaming at Marcie, just a couple days before she drops off the face of the Earth…he may just take a keener interest in you. You're out of his jurisdiction, but all he needs to do is call the St. James Sheriff. You may want to set aside some time for more question—"

Rusty saw it happen, barely. But it happened way too fast, and he failed to react.

With a velocity unlikely for such a large man, Abellard launched himself across the desk, both arms outreached. Rusty pushed against the desk with his feet as hard as he could, tilting back his chair, but he was a fraction of a second too slow.

Abellard's momentum carried him forward like a cannonball. All ten fingers reached Rusty's throat at the same instant.

The chair toppled over on its hind legs, both men falling hard. Rusty took the full force of Abellard's body weight driving him into the floor. He barely registered the concussive impact of his head against the tiles. It was overwhelmed by the pain in his lower back as the metal edge of the chair dug in.

Everything went white for a beat. He almost passed out. Then the chokehold on his windpipe yanked him back to consciousness.

"What'd you say, motherfucker?" Abellard shrieked, the words landing on Rusty's face in a shower of spittle. "What you gonna do? Huh?"

Thrashing to no avail, legs kicking wildly, Rusty couldn't speak. He didn't try. All his efforts lay in wrenching those brawny fingers from their constrictive vise around his neck. He made no headway, feeling his oxygen supply nosedive to zero.

From the corner of one eye, Rusty saw Antoine back up against the office door. The guard bore an expression of silent shock at the scene unfolding before him.

The color of Rusty's face deepened from red to purple, eyes bulging. A fiery hold constricted tighter around his throat.

"I…want to…help…"

"You ain't doing nothin, punk!" Abellard roared, slamming his head against the floor in synch with each word. "You done said your last words up in here!"

Rusty barely heard him. His windpipe screamed in choking pain, eyes pouring tears that blinded him in the glare of the fluorescent lights above. The hammering of his heart grew more frantic, and he knew a blackout was only seconds away.

"Find…her…"

The plea died, strangled before he could complete it. A black veil passed over Rusty's eyes as consciousness left him.

15.

Only not quite. The pain screaming across Rusty's lower back kept him from passing out. His vision constricted like a tightened aperture and then flared wide. Squeezing his eyes shut, he went still and strained to summon a last reserve of energy to break loose.

Then he heard the security guard speak.

"He's out," Antoine said from his position by the door. "You choked the man out, boss."

With those words, Rusty felt the grip on his throat retract. Oxygen filtered in slowly, but he remained still. Playing possum, at least for as long as it took to restore some semblance of normal respiration, struck him as wise.

He watched through slitted eyes as Joseph Abellard staggered upright. The casino boss leaned against his desk, breathing hard.

"Motherfuck," he uttered in a half-whisper, staring at the outsized hands that almost squeezed the life out of the man at his feet. "Fetch Robert and Bones."

Antoine didn't require a reprise of that command. He quickly vacated the office, closing the door behind him.

Rusty tracked the motions of Abellard's legs as he stepped around the desk and dropped into the leather chair like someone had severed a rope holding him upright. He sat for a long moment, motionless except for the heaving of his chest.

A mobile phone on the desk started ringing. Rusty heard what sounded like a displeased grunt before Abellard spoke.

"Professor. Wasn't expecting we'd talk till this evening."

From his prone position, Rusty fought against the numbing allure of slipping into unconsciousness. Only the pain in his lower back where the chair's edge dug in prevented a total blackout. Vying for a close second with his back's misery was the scalding of his throat.

"We've had this conversation before. I understand the urgency. We're delivering tomorrow night, Tuesday noon at the latest."

A series of muted agreements followed, as if Abellard was responding to a laundry list of commands.

"You're worrying too much, Professor. I told you we're good. Sherman's on it."

A pause elapsed, well over a minute. Rusty could hear Abellard's breath growing more strained, as if he was experiencing physical pain. Figuring this was his best shot to free himself, he planted both palms on the floor in preparation to launch toward the door.

Abellard kicked the chair away from the desk and stood.

"Say that again. No, say those words again, Professor Guillory."

He stepped around the desk and started pacing the office, forcing Rusty to lay flat.

"No, no, no...I need to hear it again, 'cause I know damn well I didn't hear you right!"

Professor Guillory, Rusty thought, struck by the new tone in the big man's voice—both outraged and pleading. *I won't have a hard time remembering that one.*

The pacing gained speed. Abellard's feet pounded the tiles and almost kicked Rusty in the face.

"I want to talk to her. Now! Put her on the damn phone!"

Abellard stopped talking abruptly, his large head nodding as he listened to what was being said on the other end of the call. He coughed out a few more muted grunts, then slammed the phone onto his desk with a curse.

Rusty took a last girding breath and prepared to rise in attack.

Three knocks on the door froze him in place.

"Get in here!" Abellard yelled.

Rusty saw the bottom of the door swing inward. Three pairs of legs stepped briskly inside, then it slammed shut. He recognized Antoine's tree-trunk thighs and black leather shoes. The neat cuffs of some champagne slacks told him the bartender was one of the other two men. A pair of jeans over heavy work boots didn't tell him much about the third.

"Damn," the bartender rasped. "Didn't take long, did it?"

"Listen up," Abellard snapped. "This needs to go down quick. Bones, run over to the storage shed. Grab some heavy rope, plenty of it. And some fishing tackle. Load the skiff on the trailer and hook it up to my ride."

"Who's minding the bar?"

"Man, fuck the damn bar. Anybody still at the tables, show their asses to the exit."

The bartender's shiny wing tips rotated toward the door. Rusty heard the knob turn.

"And fetch a bottle," Abellard said.

"Anything in particular?"

"Just grab something, motherfucker! I ain't drinking the shit."

The door opened and closed again.

One down, three to go, Rusty thought, deciding he wouldn't make a move until the odds shifted further in his favor. His breath and heartbeat had returned to normal levels, and aside from his screaming back he was starting to feel significantly more pissed off than wounded.

"Robert, turn out his pockets," Abellard said.

Rusty forced himself not to move as the man in work boots lowered himself to a crouch. He got a brief view of a broad bearded face, then felt himself being rolled over onto his stomach. Strong hands pulled his wallet from his back pocket before liberating his keys from the front.

The man named Robert tossed the wallet to Abellard, who flipped it open and emptied its contents. He examined Rusty's Nevada ID with a curious scowl.

"What's he driving?"

"Mustang," Robert said, hefting the keys. "Hertz rental."

"Find out which one, then pull it around back and meet Bones by the shed. Go with him, Antoine, and make sure all them suckers hit the door. We're closing early."

Antoine paused before asking, "What're we doing with him, boss?"

"Homeboy's getting an up close and personal view of Barataria Bay."

A weighty silence greeted those words, followed by a low whistle from Robert.

"Damn," he muttered, opening the door.

Abellard tossed the wallet to Antoine and said, "Put it back in his pants. No need for this to look like a robbery."

"Hey, boss," Antoine muttered uneasily. "You sure he's out?"

"He is now," Abellard replied.

Rusty sensed it coming a half-second before it happened. The toe of Abellard's right foot swung at his temple like a wrecking ball. He braced himself, to no great gain, and never felt the blow that knocked him unconscious.

16.

A blinding wash of sunlight brought him back around. It was either that or the bumpiness of the unpaved road they were traveling. Rusty's eyes blinked open. For several excruciating seconds all he could focus on was pain. His lumbar region burned like a hot poker was held against it. With some gratitude he concluded his breathing was coming more easily now than in the casino office.

The vehicle jostled again, front tires falling into a shallow gully. Rusty suppressed a wail and centered himself with a few deep breaths. He was in the backseat of what appeared to be a luxury SUV. A wreathed logo sewn into the fabric of the seatback in front of him told him it was a Cadillac. Most likely an Escalade, judging from the size.

It was moving at brisk speed, bouncing over such rough terrain that even the best German-made shocks did little to smooth out the ride.

Not very promising. We must be in the middle of nowhere, even by Vacherie standards.

Peering out a tinted window, he saw nothing but thick clusters of mangroves and the occasional sunbaked palm. Whoever was driving this vehicle was steering deep into swamp country.

"I'm saying it's rash, that's all."

That voice came from his left. It belonged to the bartender, seated next to him.

"I told you this is how it's going down," Abellard answered from the front seat. "So you can just stop fretting like a bitch and get with it."

Rusty silently assessed his position. He was in the back of the SUV, strapped in with a seatbelt. Hands bound at the wrists behind him. Testing the mobility of his legs, he found both ankles similarly lashed.

The bristles on his wrists felt like hemp or flax. That was good. Metal cuffs or plastic zipties would present a greater challenge. If this was the type of rope he suspected it to be, he stood a decent chance of freeing himself—assuming he was granted a few minutes to work on the knots, and whoever tied them wasn't an expert.

Bones spoke again, addressing the back of Abellard's head. "I'm not saying it can't be done. I'm just wondering about some of the particulars."

"Shit ain't complicated. When nobody claims that sweet ride from the public lot, it's gonna attract attention. Probably take a day or two, maybe more. Rangers may do a search, but they won't be looking in the right place. And homeboy's gonna be about two hundred feet below, regardless."

The Escalade slowed and turned left. Rusty caught a glimpse of a roadside sign that read: Barataria Natural Preserve—23,000 Acres of Beauty.

"Now listen up," Abellard continued to Bones. "On the slight chance someone gets *real* interested in finding out who rented that Mustang, and they start dragging the bay, we got to accept the possibility they might find him. What's left of him. But that possibility's fuckin' slim. Too slim to get all uptight about. We're taking him out where there ain't no kind of traffic."

"Good enough," the bartender replied. "Assuming he stays down below."

"I know what you're worried about, Bones. Some little fishies gonna chew through them ropes and he'll float up on his own. Let's say it happens. Someone finds the carcass in the shallows, calls the rangers and they do an autopsy. What are they gonna find? A bellyful of hooch, and that'll tell the tale. Just another dumb cracker out for some trout, all tanked up and got himself drowned. Real sad, but it happens now and again. Does that satisfy you, motherfucker?"

"Still seems rash," Bones muttered under his breath.

"Man, wake his ass up. I'm tired of debating this."

Rusty felt a hard elbow dig into his ribs, and he knew the time for laying low had passed.

"Rise and shine!" Bones yelled into his ear.

Rusty turned to face him. Bones spun the cap off a fifth of Southern Comfort and held the rim to his mouth.

"Drink up, baby. Clock's ticking."

Rusty pushed the bottle away with his chin.

"I ain't asking," Bones said. "Down the hatch."

"Eat shit."

"Wrong attitude, son."

The Escalade came to an abrupt halt. Up front, Abellard reached over the console to swat Antoine's bulbous head.

"Who the fuck taught you to drive, fat boy?"

"Sorry, boss," the security guard mumbled, his frame spilling out beyond the perimeter of the driver's seat.

Abellard turned around to look at Rusty, his expression more curious than hostile.

"Just tell me you're in on it," he said softly. "I know you are, and it's too late to save your ass. So you might as well spill."

Rusty didn't reply, looking at the man with a new level of hatred. He should have taken the words of Prosper and Monday more seriously. Should have walked into the casino prepared to threaten him with death—and follow up on the threat—unless Abellard told what he knew about Marceline.

"It stretches my belief," Abellard continued, "that you ain't working with Professor Bitch on this deal. Look me in the eye and tell me otherwise."

"Professor Bitch? That's who you were on the phone with...Guillory?"

Abellard appeared mildly jolted that Rusty had overheard the conversation in his office, but he brushed it off.

"We're heading into twenty thousand acres of shit here. No one's gonna find you, understand? And if they do, it'll be about a month too late to do you any good. So come clean with me now, and I'll make this go a whole lot easier."

"I don't know what the hell you're talking about," Rusty said. "I never heard of this Guillory till today. I told you, I'm a friend trying to help. That's all."

Abellard studied him a moment longer. When he spoke again, it was to Bones.

"Get that up in him. Do it quick, and bring the bottle. We'll leave it in his ride."

With that, he got out of the Escalade. Antoine followed, both of them slamming the doors. Rusty could hear them walking around to the back of the SUV and unlatching what sounded like a metal hitch. A moment later, he heard something heavy being pulled off the trailer and landing with a thud on the muddy ground.

A rumble of tires caught his ears. Craning his head to look out the window, he saw his rented Mustang pull to a stop next to the Escalade. The man in the work boots stepped out and helped Antoine drag a flat-bottom skiff across the dusty lot toward a patch of sawgrass as Abellard barked orders.

Rusty turned back to Bones, remembering the note of caution he'd heard in the man's voice a few minutes earlier.

"You don't want to do this," he said quietly.

"Look at the bright side, babe. You'll be down way too low for them gators to get at you."

Chuckling at his own wit, Bones proffered the liquor bottle. "Bottoms up."

"Why?" Rusty asked. He knew the reason but wanted to buy a few more seconds. "What's the point of getting me loaded?"

"Just drink it."

"Fuck you."

Rusty nudged the bottle away. Bones shoved it back, hard enough to crack him on the teeth with the rim.

"I said *drink*. I'm losing patience with you."

"Not thirsty, asshole. What are you gonna do about it?"

A stabbing pain bit into his midsection, just below the ribcage.

"Feel that?" Bones asked. "You feel it, don't you?"

Rusty glanced down and saw Bones' other hand clutching

the handle of what appeared to be a box cutter. He could all too easily feel the tip of the blade poking through the fabric of his shirt.

"Christ. You think this'll look like an accident with a knife wound in my gut?"

The bartender chuckled again.

"Oh, them bottom-feeders got real sharp teeth. Just like little razors, some of 'em. What's one more gash, by the time they get done feeding on you?"

Rusty saw no good options, but gagging down some liquor was preferable to an abdominal stab wound. He nodded tersely. Bones raised the bottle to his lips.

"Atta boy. I'm in your shoes, I'd want to be getting good and sauced."

Rusty opened up the back of his throat and took down a healthy swallow. Coughing slightly at the burn, he glared at Bones and steeled himself for another gulp.

"Not so bad, huh? I brung you some top shelf shit. You could be drinking rail gin right now."

A third long draught triggered a gag reflex but Rusty managed to keep it down.

"Don't be pukin' in here," Bones uttered with a disdainful glance.

After one more taste, Rusty could feel the booze going to work.

"That's fucking enough," he sputtered.

"I'll tell you when it's enough," Bones said, jamming the bottle in his face.

• • • •

The skiff moved almost silently through brackish waters on a southwesterly course through Barataria Bay. Only the rhythmic splash of two wooden oars gave any indication of its progress. If another craft happened to pass within close range, its occupants would see two male figures huddled in the skiff. Just a couple of fishermen or clammers out on a Sunday jaunt in a rather unlikely part of the bay.

Rusty lay on his back in the flat hull, wrists and ankles still bound, with Abellard's feet pressed heavily on his sternum. He'd been in this uncomfortable position far too long, the overhead sun frying his skin and forcing his eyes shut.

They'd spotted no other vessels since entering the water. The closest land mass of any significance, Isle Grande Terre, lay more than three miles to the south. This region was heavily populated by birds, fish, insects and reptiles, but offered little to attract human intrusion.

Risking a brief upward glance into the sun's glare, Rusty saw nothing but blue sky dotted with high clouds. A pair of gulls had circled the skiff curiously for several minutes as it left the shallows and moved into deeper water, but lost interest and flew away some time ago.

Save your strength, Rusty told himself. *Don't do anything but breathe, until there's a chance to do something else.*

He'd choked down more than a third of the SoCo bottle before flatly refusing to take any more. Figuring he'd ingested enough, Bones dragged him out of the Escalade with Antoine's help.

Abellard instructed Bones to drive the rented Mustang to a free public lot in the nearby town of Moreno, and for Antoine to follow. Told them to leave the Mustang there with the half-drained bottle inside. Then come back to this same spot in the Escalade and wait until the skiff returned, minus one passenger.

Rusty had tried screaming for help when they yanked him out of the SUV. Abellard shut him up with several crisp backhands, and Rusty abandoned the effort. He knew they'd driven to a place so remote that no amount of prolonged cries would reach a helpful ear. He was better off conserving his energy until they made their next move. With that admonition, he'd lowered himself into the hull and lay still as they pushed off from the shore.

Robert was working the oars skillfully, guiding them into some of the most isolated reaches of these vast primordial wetlands. A waterbound galaxy of bayous, swamps, forests, and marshes scattered farther than the eye could see.

They traveled into waters seldom used by fishermen or tour guides. Rusty figured the skiff had been moving for close to an hour. Despite a blood alcohol level way past the legal limit for operating a vehicle, he didn't feel clouded. There was too much adrenaline coursing through his system for the liquor to take full effect. Other than a throbbing headache and a mild case of nausea, he felt little worse for wear. If anything, the booze had numbed the pain in his lower back.

"Gotta be getting close, huh?" Robert muttered.

Rusty heard a hesitant complaint in his voice, most likely the result of sore shoulders from all the rowing. Robert declined to say more, head bowed as if realizing how foolish it was to voice discontent within the boss man's earshot.

"See that little bunch of mangroves to the right?" Abellard replied after a prolonged interval of silence. "Take us about a hundred yards past 'em. That'll do."

"Aye aye, skip."

"Almost there, chump," Abellard said to Rusty, then gathered up a length of rope in his large hands. Attached to one end was a cast iron "mushroom" anchor, designed to sink deeply into soft sediment. The rope was hooked securely through the anchor's eyelet. Abellard took the other end and started looping it through the binds around Rusty's ankles.

With his head flat against the hull, Rusty couldn't determine what type of knot he was tying. It felt like a basic Double Fisherman's hitch, which was marginally good news. He was familiar with that kind of bind and could likely free himself, if given the chance. But Rusty didn't think he was going to get much of a chance.

Deeming the hitch sufficiently snug, Abellard let the rope fall from his fingers. He looked down at his captive.

"I'm guessing any last little feeling of hope you might've been clinging to just flew away. That's a twenty-pound weight you're tethered to, dig?"

"Joseph," Rusty said quietly, "I'm not sure you've thought this through. How's it gonna look like an accident with a goddamn anchor tied to my legs?"

Abellard didn't answer, sitting back in the prow as Robert continued rowing. After another twenty strokes, he told him to stop.

The sun was burning down from directly overhead, stinging Rusty's eyes. Sweat poured from his forehead, further obscuring his vision. The glare disappeared as Abellard stood, casting him in shadow.

Rusty felt strong hands grab his ankles, while another pair of hands slipped under his arms and clenched tightly. Then the anchor dropped onto his stomach with enough force to rob him of his breath.

"We doin' this on three or what?" Robert asked.

"Fuck that. When I say heave, take him over portway."

Rusty stifled the urge to speak or cry out. The brief pain in his stomach from the anchor's impact had mercifully receded.

Stop resisting, he heard himself say. *You're going in. Maximize the breath and relax the muscles.*

Heeding that inner caution, his body went slack. His eyes closed. All the tension in his frame dissipated through sheer force of will.

Robert frowned at the sudden lack of resistance.

"Feels like he gave up already."

One more second of silence passed, then Rusty heard Abellard shout:

"Heave!"

Both men swung their arms across the skiff's port side, stretching as far as they could without pulling themselves overboard. Their hands unlocked at the same time.

For the briefest of moments, Rusty felt the misleading liberation of being airborne. The anchor broke the water first, accelerating gravity's pull on his body.

His lungs sealed up like an airlock, trapping as much oxygen as he could hold. Then the warm, muddy water consumed him with a rippling splash, and he vanished from the world.

17.

For several frantic seconds, Rusty saw nothing but a stream of bubbles rising before his eyes. It quickly faded as he sank beyond the sunlight's reach. Inky blackness took over, stretching to infinity in all directions. Less than twenty feet from the surface, he was in the abyss.

His body reacted on sheer survival impulse. Legs kicking and straining against the downward pull of the anchor. Back arching to keep his chin up and head raised as high as possible. It was futile, an ill-advised waste of energy to fight the gravitational descent.

Rusty forced himself to stop. His only chance was to wait until he reached bottom, then see what could be done about getting out of the ropes that bound him. To attempt liberating himself while rapidly submerging was impossible. He'd need the ballast of solid ground if he had any hope of loosening the knots.

He kept sinking, farther and farther away from even a memory of sunlight. The possibility of giving in to full-blown panic was very real. Rusty did the only thing he could think of to stave it off.

He started counting.

One.

Two.

Three.

Keep it up. You've got plenty of time.

Which might actually be true, depending on how long it took for him to touch bottom. Rusty had far more experience with holding his breath for extended periods than the average person. In the not so distant past, he'd trained himself to go as long as six minutes before requiring oxygen. It was an essential component of performing two shows daily in the Etruscan Room at Caesars.

One of the show's most popular tricks was his patented "sunken coffin escape." An elaborate variation on Houdini's legendary Chinese Water Torture Cell, Rusty had spent months developing it despite Prosper's warning that it was too dangerous to perform even under controlled conditions.

The setup was basic: Rusty laid himself into a steel coffin punctured with a series of bullet-sized holes that allowed in both oxygen and water. His ankles and wrists were bound with handcuffs far more restrictive than the ropes now securing them. Two shapely assistants worked a chain-operated pulley to lower the coffin into a massive glass tank on the stage in full view of the audience, containing five hundred gallons of chlorinated water.

The most difficult aspect of the trick was holding his breath long enough to get out of the cuffs so he could force the casket's heavy lid open against the pressure of the water bearing down on it. On a good night, he could free both ankles and wrists in less than three minutes, but it sometimes took as long as four and a half. To prepare for the eventuality of a more difficult unbinding, Rusty had developed his lung capacity to the point where he could go six minutes without taking a breath, even when engaged in strenuous physical activity.

The key to pulling it off was to remain calm. To sustain maximum stillness of both body and mind, conserving the oxygen in his lungs and the strength in his limbs.

Six minutes. Three hundred and sixty seconds. He always used to count each one of them, as he was doing now.

Thirty-eight.

Thirty-nine.

Having not practiced this kind of maneuver in many months, he held no delusion of still being able to hold his breath for as long as he could when in peak physical condition. He estimated five minutes, tops. Three hundred seconds. Maybe.

Sixty-three.

Sixty-four.

Of course, in Vegas he had a reliable escape route handy. At the first sign of trouble, he only had to rap his knuckles against the inside of the coffin's lid in a prearranged sequence. Three quick taps, a pause, two slows taps and then three more quick ones. Hearing that eight-note tattoo, an off-stage technician would flip a switch, sending an electric current into the hinge of the coffin's lid and forcing it open. Rusty could then swim to the top of the tank and emerge for applause from an audience that had been duped into thinking he'd escaped of his own wiles.

It was a source of great professional pride that he'd never needed to employ that cheat of an escape route. Not once over the course of hundreds of performances.

Yeah, some achievement. Which does precisely fuck-all for me right now. Keep counting.

Seventy-nine.

Eighty.

He kept sinking, with the mad hope that he'd make contact with land before reaching a hundred and twenty. That would give him, at best, about three minutes to shake out of the weighted ropes and swim all the way back to the surface.

Down, down, down. The water stretched ever deeper into a canvas of endless black. No hint of life or light. Impossible to track the pace of his progress. He no longer trusted the count, but kept hearing the numbers in his mind's ear as if they possessed a life outside his thoughts. Stretching his legs to their furthest, praying to feel the contact of muddy ground beneath.

A hundred and two.

A hundred and three.

He was going to die down here. Drowned like a rat, with his corpse serving as a buffet for an unimaginable range of finned and gilled bottom-feeders. He might float back to the surface in time, if the fish chewed through the binds as Abellard had suggested may happen. Abellard might not even get away with it. The anchor might be discovered. The St. James Sheriff may take an interest in the owner of the abandoned rental car. Maybe even Dan Hubbard would be brought into the investigation when the car was traced back to the Hertz office and Rusty's name showed up on the computer. Hubbard might actually embrace the possibility then that something bad had befallen Marceline Lavalle. He might initiate a real investigation focusing on Abellard and the Carnival.

Yes, all that could happen. There could even be enough left of Rusty's body for a proper burial once they'd dragged the bay. But he would have accomplished nothing. Marceline would still be missing. Prosper would never see her, or his grandchild.

Even as this bleak panorama of possible outcomes painted itself across Rusty's thoughts, a disciplined corner of his brain kept counting.

One twenty-five.

One twenty-six.

His boots sank into soft mud at a hundred and seventy.

He curled his body into a tight ball, bringing his feet within reach of his hands. The sudden movement may have cost him a few seconds of oxygen but he couldn't worry about it. Even bound at the wrists, his fingers had enough freedom of movement to work on the weighted ties at his ankles. Doing a quick tactile scan of the knots, he determined it was a standard anchor hitch, tied with marginal proficiency. The long end of the rope wrapped itself around the metal anchor that had already disappeared into the powdery sediment bed.

Fortunately the rope was only 3/8" thick, a good diameter for getting a quick handle on the loops of the knot. Rusty kept counting as his fingers acted on pure muscle memory.

Two hundred and one.

Two hundred and two.

If any fish swam by closely enough to leave a wake or give him a curious nibble, he had no awareness of it. He pulled on a freshly loosened end of the knot and the weighted rope fell away.

It happened with such unexpected ease, Rusty almost thought he imagined it. Maybe he hadn't freed himself at all. Maybe his oxygen-starved brain was starting to hallucinate, creating a false vision of freedom before a surge of rancid water filled his lungs.

But no, he was still awake and free. Both legs shook loose like uncaged animals. He could feel a buoyancy lifting him from the muddy surface. Eyes open but sightless, he could only tell which direction was up by an instinctive guess.

Rusty had no way of knowing he deep he was. Or how many seconds it would take him to kick back to the surface. Or if his body still had enough strength to perform the task.

He started kicking. Pushing both legs in tight measured strokes, creating maximum wake. And he kept counting.

Two twenty-two.

Two twenty-three.

After a dozen strokes, he realized with dismay just how drained he was. Each kick seemed to push him forward by mere centimeters. It was so dark that he had no way of monitoring his progress. He didn't know if he was swimming directly toward the surface or in a lateral direction that brought him no closer to escape.

When his internal count reached two-fifty, he knew he wasn't going to make it. His lungs reached that decision before his brain did. The message didn't rely on logic or factual evidence, but a leaden stasis of tendon and muscle that said he simply could not keep moving. His very cells were telling him to quit. That it wasn't so bad. That it would all be over quickly.

With a jolt, he realized he'd abandoned the count. He'd lost track. The numbers had grown too discouraging, then terrifying, and then ultimately meaningless. He could only count to one, over and over. Just a single abandoned digit. A mantra that wouldn't save him but which he kept repeating in time with the movement of his near-useless legs.

One more kick.

One more kick.

Why hadn't he lost consciousness yet, or swallowed half the damn bay? It hardly seemed possible. He'd certainly passed the three hundred mark. Despite the sensory evidence of being in motion, Rusty felt quite sure his lungs had opened by now. No other scenario seemed plausible. He must have expended his limit for constricting his breath long ago. Oxygen supply down to zero, and beyond.

One more kick.

One more kick.

Wait.

Above him—or was it off to the side?—a faint glimmer in the water. A shimmery oval of light, barely the size of a coin. He tried to focus on it, to steer himself toward it. No good. It dissolved as quickly as it appeared, then came back slightly stronger but for an even briefer glimpse.

Rusty didn't let himself believe he'd seen the sun rippling across the bay's surface. It was eminently possibly he wasn't even swimming in the right direction. Hell, he couldn't be sure if his eyes were open or shut. The blackness was the same, lids up or down.

One more kick.

That distant glimmer, there it was again. No doubt this time. But the mere act of seeing it hardly guaranteed its reality. Could very well be the result of an exploded capillary somewhere behind his optic nerve. A tiny vein bursting with the inexorable pressure on his lungs. Fool's gold for an overtaxed body not quite ready to quit out of evolutionary stubbornness.

He no longer felt pain, or even panic. A sense of detaching from his own corpse came over him, and it was a relief. The only thing that bothered him was Marceline. Knowing he'd failed her. But even that started to feel like more of an abstraction than a reality. Maybe she was fine, just taking a little break someplace nice, awaiting her admission to the world of motherhood.

No! I heard Abellard on the phone, asking for her...

Rusty clung to that unclear memory as the glimmer appeared once again. A little brighter this time, its layered golden dimples imprinted themselves on his retinas for a fraction of a second longer.

Rusty allowed that it might belong to the sun, or just as easily his own dying brain. Some kind of synaptic misfire. What did it matter, really? He felt fairly certain he was already dead, and it wasn't so bad.

It was freedom. Release. He knew it, and felt as calmly submissive to that fate as he did when waiting for the plane to crash with Erin's arms wrapped around his neck.

His mind gave in, but his legs had other ideas. Beyond anything resembling simple exhaustion, they kept the pace.

One more kick.

• • •

Captain Dave Thibodeaux—founder, owner, and chief skipper of the Barataria Tour Company—leaned against the helm of his fifty-foot flatboat, *The Swamp Thing*. The wheel turned easily in his hand, moving away from a mossy embankment and into deeper waters. Today's afternoon tour was rounding third and heading for home.

Dave watched an orange sunsplash dance across the bay's placid surface. A pelican skimmed low in search of an easy catch. The Captain never tired of such sights.

It had been a good day, as profitable as could be hoped for at the tail end of the high season. Dave was ready to wind up this tour and get back home to deposit the lockerful of cash he'd collected in a safe place. Not a fan of the banking system, Dave kept his life savings stashed in a dozen different cubby holes around the half-acre plot of land he owned in the bayside town of Crown Point.

The Swamp Thing carried a capacity crowd, more than twenty passengers in all. Some were locals on a Sunday excursion. Most fell into the category of out-of-town guests who were so vital to keeping the economic health of Louisiana on life support.

Captain Dave had been talking steadily into his hand-held mic for the last hour, pointing out various highlights of the natural beauty found within Barataria Bay. Now he was content to shut up and steer for a while. Just listening to the dull rumble of *The Swamp Thing*'s motor, accentuated by a rhythmic slapping of waves against the hull, comprised an indelible part of the tour experience he offered.

In addition to a lecture on some of the more recognizable types of flora indigenous to the bay—lush mangroves, waving clusters of Spanish moss, robust live oaks—the Captain had also given his passengers an eyeful of the local fauna. Smartphones pointed every which way; the group had photographed a veritable menagerie of foraging armadillos, frolicking otters, sunbathing turtles, frogs with impossibly bright green skin, and four different species of ducks.

All good fun, but Dave's patrons had forked over $18-per-head to see Barataria's most iconic resident: the American alligator. After finding some usually reliable spots empty, Dave steered *The Swamp Thing* into less traveled waters. His gambit paid off. Pulling close to the shallows near the bay's southwestern lip, he switched off the motor and treated his guests to an intimate look at no less than fourteen adults of the species.

Customary gasps arose as he leaned over the boat's stern rail, reaching an arm out to tempt the nearest gator with some marshmallows. Dave knew precisely how long to keep the bait in his grip, watching the massive reptile advance across the water's cloudy surface with elegant sweeps of its tail. At the last possible moment, his fingers splayed and the marshmallow fell. The creature's toothy maw snapped shut, loud as a firecracker. Oohs and ahhs filled the boat, right on cue.

The passengers loved seeing the big gators, but Dave had one more surprise in store for them. Before docking back at Crown Point, they'd have the chance to hold a baby in their bare hands. Eight weeks old and twice as many inches long, it was now squirming in a wooden box at Captain Dave's feet.

"This here on the starboard's worth looking at," he mumbled into his mic, speaking in a Cajun dialect that sounded like a linguistic collision between the South of France and Flatbush.

The passengers all scrambled to the boat's rail, necks craning and phones held aloft to capture whatever marvelous sight the Captain had just alerted them to. There wasn't much see—just another small island covered with bushy mangroves.

"That's where I saw the strangest sight ever to greet my eyes in forty-odd years on this bay. I come out early of a morning with my oyster pots, and right there on that muddy spit, I seen a full-grown male gator squaring off against three snapping turtles. Them turtles put up a hell of a fight, too."

Turning off the mic, Dave chortled into his beard. The story was true, but he had no way of knowing whether it had taken place on the small island they'd just passed or one of a thousand other virtually identical outcroppings in these waters.

"What's that?" a woman shouted from the stern. "Oh my God!"

A quick shuffle of hurried feet followed her startled cry. Many passengers were rushing aftward to see what had caused the stir.

"Slow down, folks," Captain Dave growled with irritation at the carelessness of these landlubbing fools. "Ain't no running on *The Swamp Thing*."

He was half-way to the stern when he heard a stout male voice shout, "Man overboard!"

Dave's blood went cold. In all his days with the Barataria Tour Company, he'd never had a passenger fall out of the boat. All safety measures were up to code, but that didn't prevent some bullshit liability suit from landing on his head.

He grabbed a life preserver and pushed aside two stoned-looking teenagers who'd spent most of the tour buried in their iPhones.

"Captain, we have a man overboard," repeated a silver-haired passenger from New England decked out in preppy nautical garb.

"Where?" Dave asked furiously, his head turning on a swivel.

"Two o'clock off the port side," the man replied, pointing off toward a cluster of sawgrass marshes in the distance.

Sweet Jesus and Mary, Dave thought. *How'd we get so far away? How long ago did the jackass tumble out?*

"Not one of ours," the New Englander commented. "I suppose we ought to haul him in just the same, don't you?"

"Give me room," Dave said, pushing the man aside to peer over the rail. Off to his right, some thirty yards away, a figure was thrashing wildly in the shallows.

Seeing a tangle of long black hair, Captain Dave initially thought it was a woman. A second glance told him it was a man struggling to pull himself out of the muck and onto a patch of sawgrass.

With a profound swell of relief, Dave confirmed the New Englander's claim that it wasn't one of his passengers.

"Everyone take a seat," he ordered, and there was no need to repeat it. The whole group assumed a rapt seriousness of manner. They were clearly excited about this unscripted addition to the tour, but weren't sure how to behave.

"Y'all are getting a bonus today, and it ain't even gonna cost you extra."

Dave strode back to the wheelhouse and fired up the motor. He swung the boat around in a wide arc and hit the emergency horn. Throttle held at full tilt, *The Swamp Thing* turned into the westward sun and held a straight line toward the clump of sawgrass onto which the distant figure still fought to climb.

Sounding the horn again, Captain Dave had to shake his shaggy head in wonder. Life on Barataria Bay was something a man simply could not take for granted, even if he knew these vast depths as well as his own backyard. Just when he thought he'd done all there was to do as a tour guide, he was about to make his very first rescue.

18.

Dr. Philip Roque impatiently swiped his card key through the digital reader. The magnetic strip didn't register on his first attempt, or the second. Roque swore under his breath, cursing the reader's faulty design. He tried again at a more measured pace and heard a motorized lock slide open.

Roque admonished himself not to be too impatient—or at least not to let it show—and stepped into the medical office plaza's foyer.

Heeding that inner advice was a challenge. He had been on edge for the past several hours. Ever since his iPhone started ringing a few minutes before seven o'clock, waking him from the first decent dream he'd enjoyed in weeks.

He'd ignored it at first, figuring no one of any importance would bother him so early on a Sunday morning. The call went to voicemail. But no digital chirp followed to indicate a new message. Ten seconds later, it started ringing again.

Sprawled across a king-sized mattress in the master bedroom of his expansive Uptown home (soon to be his sole residence once the divorce papers went through) Roque felt no inclination to answer the phone. It kept ringing, but he lay there stubbornly, fleshy limbs entangled in satin sheets.

His mistress Yvonne was snoring next to him, with considerable volume. Some women snored in a gentle way that was more endearing than annoying, Roque had found over the course of a busy philandering career. Yvonne was of a different breed, sawing logs with the intensity of a lumberjack on meth. This had just recently come to his attention, despite the fact that they'd been sleeping together for well over a year.

It struck him as ominous that her apnea-induced barrage revealed itself only now that she was within weeks of becoming the next Mrs. Philip Roque. As he let the phone ring unanswered for a third time, Roque pondered the matter uneasily.

They hadn't made love last night, nor the past three nights. She'd claimed a persistent case of cramps, also an unprecedented phenomenon. Taken together, the snoring and sudden lack of carnal interest raised troubling questions. What other traits was she waiting to unveil once that marquis diamond was safely on her finger?

An unsettling proposition, but the goddamned ringing didn't allow Roque to stew over it for long. He climbed out of bed with an annoyed grumble and retrieved the iPhone. His grumble turned into a groan when he saw Claude Sherman's number on the screen. Christ, of all the people to bother him now!

Roque couldn't fathom why Abellard had given Sherman his cell number, after being explicitly told not to do so. It was a moot point, and he'd never quite found the nerve to complain about it. Carrying the phone out of the bedroom, he answered with as much pique as he could muster. It didn't hold up for long.

Sherman was flat-out raving on the other end of the line, insisting the doctor meet him at the clinic within an hour. When Roque pointed out it was a Sunday, most of which he planned to spend on the greens of Riverside, Sherman exploded with such fury it seemed wise not to provoke the man further. For all he knew, Abellard had given him this address along with the cell number.

Philip Roque wasn't willing to risk the possibility of Claude Sherman showing up here in such an unhinged state. Even meeting at the clinic provided not nearly as much distance as he wished to keep from the man.

So he consented to drive over to Magazine by nine o'clock. No sooner. After a few more minutes of arguing, Claude agreed to meet him at that time.

Now, riding the elevator to the medical plaza's third floor, Roque considered a mystery he'd ignored until this moment.

Why was it so urgent to meet right away? What business refused to wait until tomorrow afternoon, when Claude could make an appearance under his flimsy but useful veneer as the overnight custodian?

Roque stepped off the elevator and flinched at the sight of a dark shape lurking by the clinic's front door. It could only be Claude Sherman. The uncombed mane and strangely tilted posture was impossible to mistake.

For a surreal moment it appeared he'd grown a hunch. Claude clutched a shiny black garbage bag in his hands, slung over one shoulder. The image of a dozen drowned cats crept into Roque's head. He brushed it away and approached with measured steps.

"I certainly hope this is important."

"You're late. We said nine."

Roque entered the office without reply. He flicked on the overhead lamp, bringing a dull white glow to the reception room. He'd never been here on a Sunday before, and something about the emptiness of this familiar space unnerved him.

"Let's make this brief, Claude. What's so pressing it couldn't wait a day?"

"You got work to do."

"You're right. On my short game at Riverside, which is where I should be right now."

"No, real work. We're staying here till it's done."

"This office is closed, in case you hadn't noticed. Not to mention, there's no one here whose presence might allow for the kind of work that you're interested in to proceed."

"Don't need no one else. Just need the...finalizing part done."

Roque glanced at the garbage bag and back at the bearded face of the man carrying it. A chill ran through him.

"I'm not following you, Claude."

"So shut up and listen."

"You might as well save your breath. The last time we spoke, I was perfectly clear about where we stand with this arrangement."

"You mean the money? That's not important now."

"Not to you, maybe. But you'll recall I said there would be no more deliveries until my terms were met. Did you pass that along to our mutual acquaintance?"

"I said forget the money!" Claude shouted. "We'll work that out later."

A silent caution lit up inside Roque, telling him to lower the tone.

"Calm down, please. This isn't personal. We're just two guys negotiating, nothing more."

"I'll split my cut with you, OK? Fifty-fifty, whatever. Right now we got *work* to do."

Suddenly the room felt smaller, as if all four walls had constricted in the blink of an eye. Roque decided he didn't want to find out what kind of work he'd been summoned here to perform.

"That's a generous offer," he said slowly. "But I wouldn't take money out of your pocket. Wouldn't be right. Abellard can afford to meet my price, and until he agrees to—"

"No more talking," Claude said, cutting off Roque's access to the door with two quick steps. "Operation room, now."

"I don't let anyone boss me around, Claude. Least of all in my own goddamn office."

A moment passed that might have appeared ludicrous to a detached observer. Two grown men playing a sandlot game of who will blink first. It was a short contest.

"Alright," Roque said quietly. "Let's make it quick."

He turned and strode past Margaret's desk, toward his office and the adjacent operating room beyond. Feeling his unwanted companion less than two steps behind all the way.

The lights in the operating room fluttered on with the touch of a switch. Roque stepped around the operating table, positioning himself at the far end of the room. Furthest point from the only exit available, but he wanted to keep some tangible obstacle between himself and Sherman right now.

Claude lowered his load onto the clean white table, producing a small flinch from Roque. Even though it would be fully sanitized before his next patient lay there, seeing a garbage bag on the table made him feel slightly sick.

"We need a batch. We need it right away. I told you, and you didn't listen."

"I listened, Claude. I honestly did."

"And you told me it was impossible."

"Nothing more than the truth. This isn't a mill, you understand? There's no guarantee of regularity, which I made clear from the beginning."

"You said you'd deliver what we needed. Talked like a big man, how it wouldn't be a problem."

"I never promised—"

"Bullshit. You said five batches a month wasn't out of the question. I was there, I heard it."

"That's true, depending on the month. I delivered that many in March, didn't I?"

"Doesn't do shit for us now, doc."

"And when it became clear I couldn't maintain that schedule," Roque pressed on, "what did I do? I put my professional reputation on the line to get you a job at Bon Coeur. What a fiasco that turned out to be! Don't think I didn't get an angry call from the administrator, demanding to know what the hell I was thinking when I gave you that referral."

"That's history," Claude interrupted, in no mood to revisit the topic of his brief employment at the maternity ward. If Roque had continued to deliver as promised, Claude would never have had to make such a desperate move.

It was a fiasco, Roque was right about that. And when the Lavalle girl threatened to spill to the cops, things only got more complicated.

"Forget all that," Claude snapped. "All that matters is this new batch."

"I realize it's been slow," Roque said in a conciliatory tone. "Springtime always sees a reduction at the clinic, don't ask me why."

In fact, Roque had a theory of why the influx of new patients had slowed to a trickle in recent weeks. It was a seasonal phenomenon he'd long noticed in his practice. More people in Louisiana seemed inclined to procreate, intentionally or other otherwise, during the spring, which made for a dependably busy fall and winter. Now, in the early weeks of May, the clinic was experiencing a predictable lull.

Roque hadn't mentioned the slowdown when he'd entered into this deal with Joseph Abellard three months ago. With the aid of hindsight, his recklessness now staggered him. If it wasn't for the goddamned divorce, and the avalanche of bills threatening to bury him…

Loss of his medical license was a certainty if this went public. Jail time wasn't out of the question either. But that seemed like a risk worth taking. At least it did for a while. Now he just wanted out.

"Claude," he said, "I haven't had any new patients in almost two weeks. Don't you understand that? I can't deliver a new batch because I've got no material to work with."

"You do now."

Sherman's fingers went to work on the yellow ties sealing the garbage bag's opening.

Roque involuntarily backed away, an inner caution telling him not to look at what lay hidden in those folds of plastic. He bumped up against the wall and realized he could retreat no further. No more room to run.

Claude yanked at the bag's opening, pulling down with both hands and revealing a bundle of dark blue towels. At least Roque thought they were blue. It was hard to say for sure, given the many rust-colored splashes dotting them that he knew in a horrified instant was blood.

"Jesus God," he uttered, barely a whisper. "What did you do?"

"What you *made* me do, fucker. You and Abellard both!"

Claude undraped the top towel covering the bundle. It fell onto the gleaming tabletop, revealing the butchered mass within.

Philip Roque groaned like a man who'd just taken a lance in the soft part of his midsection. Not a fatal wound, but one that caused indescribable anguish.

"Cover it up. Please."

"Oh, no. I told you, doc. We got work to do."

"Cover it! I don't want to see it!"

A deranged grin spread across Claude's face. He knew this was good. This was even better than he'd imagined. Seeing the doctor squirm and shudder felt incredibly satisfying. For just a moment, it was almost enough to take away Claude's own lingering horror over what he'd done to fill this wad of towels.

"You're gonna do a whole lot more than look at it. Whatever needs doing to get this ready…harvested, whatever the word is…you're doing it right now, and I'm gonna stand here and watch till you're done."

"Where did…" the question faltered somewhere behind Roque's tongue. A new light of understanding filled his eyes. "That woman in the Quarter."

"She didn't suffer much. Whole thing couldn't have taken more than three or four minutes."

"Christ almighty."

"It might've gone quicker, if I'd chosen a better knife. Probably should have asked you first. You could've given me some good advice, being a doctor and all."

Roque raised his head. It took him a moment to recognize the four-inch blade gripped in Claude's right hand. Recoiling, he turned to the glass case behind him. He looked inside and saw the empty slot where the blade belonged with its sterling silver companions.

"You sick bastard!" he screamed, his terror giving way to a rush of fury. "I'll call the police!"

The smile on Sherman's face vanished.

"Like hell you will. And tell 'em about our little operation here?"

"I don't care. I never hurt anyone. All the material I gave you…it was going to be disposed of anyway."

"Don't make it legal, doc. Just calm down and think about what you're saying. Nobody's calling the damn cops."

"You're a murderer. A fucking murderer!"

Roque spun away from the table. Claude lunged. He kept

the knife high, only looking to stop his progress toward the door. Roque slammed against the opposite wall and rebounded, driving himself into the other man.

The ankle Claude injured from jumping off Marceline Lavalle's front porch sent out flares of pain. He lost his balance. Roque pushed forward and ran through the doorway connecting the operating room to his office.

Three paces got him into the hallway. Five more brought him into the reception area. One hand pulled his phone from his pocket. He madly tried to dial 911 while his other hand reached for the door.

Claude came charging out of the hallway and into the reception area.

Roque caught a flash of fluorescent light on the knife. Claude lunged again. The blade caught Roque on the forearm. It tore through his shirt and opened up a gash.

Screaming, Roque swung his other arm. The phone's glass screen smashed into Claude's mouth, drawing blood, staggering him back a step.

Philip Roque released the door handle. He flung himself into Claude Sherman. He clenched the wrist of the hand holding the knife, digging in with his fingernails. The blade fell to the floor.

Everything froze for a heartbeat, the furious struggle giving way to suspended animation. Both men looking down at the knife.

They dove at the same moment. Two bodies collided hard. Roque took a knee to the groin. He barely felt it.

His hands lunged but only knocked the blade further away. It disappeared into a darkened spot beneath Margaret's desk.

Claude scrambled across the carpet for it. Roque clutched a fistful of greasy hair and yanked. He liberated a clump at the roots and produced a shriek from Claude, whose right foot knocked over a lamp next to the desk. Its glass shade slammed into the water cooler, knocking the five-gallon jug onto the floor and creating a miniature flood.

Roque clambered to reach the surgical knife. His right hand

shot under the desk.

Claude wrapped him in a chokehold. Roque threw a wild elbow backward, thudding against Sherman's temple.

The two men thrashed and rolled on the floor. They fought with lunatic intensity to take hold of the fallen blade.

Roque's hand grabbed it first. He clutched the handle tightly, but didn't know if he could hold on long enough to finish the job.

19.

The Barataria Tour Company's office building was a ramshackle affair, built of unvarnished timbers supporting a corrugated tin roof that looked in need of serious hurricane proofing. It occupied a small plot of land in Crown Point on the eastern side of the bay, about thirty miles outside the New Orleans city line.

A smattering of woodframe houses stood clustered along the shore, almost all with watercraft of some sort anchored in front. Crown Point was populated almost exclusively by people who made their living afloat. Shrimpers, crabbers, crawfish catchers, and the odd gator wrangler.

And then there were men like Dave Thibodeaux, who did all of the above and also supplemented his income by guiding tour boats deep into the waters that had served as his backyard since birth.

Captain Dave docked *The Swamp Thing* ten minutes ago. Most of the passengers had already gotten in their cars and driven away. A handful remained, lingering around the gift shop and pondering the wisdom of taking home some gator jerky for supper.

Rusty sat in a shady spot next to a vending machine dating back to the seventies. Its smudged plastic front advertised Tab in faded pink and white hues. He'd occupied this spot since being deposited here by Captain Dave, who'd waddled away with a promise to return shortly.

Rusty was making a concerted effort to do nothing except monitor his breath until some sense of calm returned. It was an uphill battle. Every time he closed his eyes, the same vision materialized: Abellard launching himself over the desk, meaty hands closing around his throat.

Gonna get that motherfucker, Rusty thought over and over, the words swirling like a silent mantra. *Even if he's not responsible for whatever happened to Marcie, I'm going to get that motherfucker.*

Captain Dave pocketed the last of the money owed him from the tour and walked over. He took a knee, one hand lifting Rusty's chin.

"Color's just about returned. I believe you've made it through the thickest part of the woods."

"Thanks again, Captain. I don't have the first clue how I might be able to repay you. Name it and I'll do my best."

"No repayment required. You gave me a whopper of a yarn to lay on the guests. Hell, I ought to cut you a percentage up front."

Rusty managed a grim smirk.

"Feel ready to go on in?" Dave asked. "You'll need to make an account of what happened, which is bound to tax a bit more of your time."

"No need," Rusty said. "Only account I plan to make is to the rental car company at Armstrong, seeing as my ride's a lost cause. That bayou rum is some powerful swill. Think I'll stick to beer next time I go fishing."

The captain shook his head, a look that split the difference between bewilderment and contempt spreading across his face.

"You mean to say you don't know where you left your vehicle?"

Rusty shrugged.

"I was half in the bag before I lit out from New Orleans. Big breakfast at Pat O's, they serve those bottomless Hurricanes. I know it was sheer stupidity to get behind the wheel and drive out here with that kind of front-load on. But sometimes a man's got to fish."

"Hmm," the Captain grumbled, looking at him with a more jaundiced eye. "Lucky you didn't finish your bender as gator bait."

"That I am," Rusty nodded, pushing his back against the

plank wall behind him to stand upright. "What I need now's a ride. I'll make it more than worthwhile for whoever gets me back to NOLA the fastest."

"I'll give you a ride, straight to Vacherie Medical. Gotta get you checked out, make sure you're OK to go."

"Don't trouble yourself. I'm fine. Just a little embarrassed is all."

"Ain't that simple, hoss. I got an obligation to report this, one way or another. The bay's a protected wetland, meaning us swamp folk operate under the eye of the feds. Anytime something strange happens on one of my tours—like, say, fishing a fella out of the mangroves—I'm bound to let the authorities know about it. Could lose my license if I don't."

Those words were spoken calmly, without the slightest hesitation. Rusty looked into the captain's leathered face, meeting his determined gaze.

"What if we both agree you never saw me? I swam back here on my own, chalk it up to dumb luck or whatever."

Dave glanced over his shoulder, where a few tour guests were still milling about.

"Too many eyeball witnesses to shoot that story down. Me personally, I'd be happy to pretend nothing out of the ordinary floated to the surface on this tour. Afraid I can't take that chance."

"Hell, there's nothing to report. I got a little loaded and lost my footing in the shallows trying to reel one in. Must happen all the time around here."

"Actually, it don't. Oh, I've pulled plenty of odd things out of the swamp in my day. Nice leather ottoman. Baby manatee. One time I almost went overboard trying to reel in the fender of a '57 Dodge. But you're the first two-legged critter to flop onto my boat, and I can't pass you off as catch of the day."

"I don't want to argue with you," Rusty said, starting to turn away. The captain laid a heavy hand on his shoulder.

"I'm guessing you don't want to talk to the sheriff neither. We can avoid that, but at the very least I got to turn you over to Vacherie Medical. After that it's not my problem anymore.

Sounds like a wise choice to me, but it's your call."

Rusty tried to swallow, realizing how parched he was after disgorging all that swamp water.

"Don't give a guy much leeway. Do you, Captain?"

"Only when I got some to spare. Sheriff or hospital, hoss. Say the word."

Further conversation was clearly pointless. Rusty nodded. "Hospital."

• • •

Monday Reed spread out a blanket on a patch of grass in Audobon Park, a favorite spot that almost no one seemed to know about but her. Just a stone's throw from the placid lagoon, she could hear the quacking of ducks as they splashed about in the sun-dappled water. Farther away, a streetcar faintly rumbled and clattered down St. Charles.

This was her day off, from both of her jobs. Monday worked three shifts a week at Bon Coeur, on a rotating basis determined by the other nurses' schedules. She served drinks at Temptations five nights a week on average, but it was a causal arrangement and left to her discretion.

The club's owner, a squat Greek gentleman named Angelo, made it clear upon hiring her last year that she'd have to put out sooner or later. All the girls did. Monday had never allowed him so much as a quick feel, and her unwavering rejection of his crude overtures had the opposite effect of what she'd anticipated. Rather than fire her, Angelo treated her with a kind of quiet reverence, allowing her to work as much or as little as she felt like in a given week.

She enjoyed her free Sundays. As often as the weather allowed, she ended up here in the park. She was more than content to keep to her secluded little section near the lagoon, away from screaming babies and leering drunks, the two categories of humans she encountered most often while working.

Monday removed her button-down shirt, kicked off her sandals and stretched out on the blanket in a bikini top and a pair of denim cutoffs. Fishing a used Harold Robbins paperback from her bag, she scanned the back cover for some motivation to keep reading. She liked raunchy fiction, but preferred a more imaginative touch than Robbins brought to the material.

Tossing the book aside, Monday realized she'd forgotten to bring sunblock. Her fair complexion, the natural result of her parents' Irish-Swedish union, was not made to endure high exposure to UV rays. She went straight from freckled alabaster to boiled lobster in no time flat, a painful tendency she had no intention of allowing today.

But the sun felt so good pouring over her skin. She didn't want to abandon it for the safety of the shade just yet.

Five minutes, she told herself. Then she'd place the blanket under the protection of a gnarled oak and see if Mr. Robbins had what it took to hold her attention for another ten pages.

She lay back, head resting on the soft ground. Unprompted, Rusty Diamond appeared in her mind. Was it the thought of sexy reading material that conjured his image? Monday pondered that question with a smile. He hadn't entirely dissipated from her thoughts since they'd parted ways at Temptations. Monday had taken a mild dislike to Rusty upon first sight at the hospital, based on what Marceline had said about him.

She hadn't felt any immediate thawing last night, but by the end of their conversation he'd convinced her of two things. One, he was in no way involved with Marceline's disappearance, and, two, he sincerely wanted to ensure her well-being. How much of his concern was personal and how much expressed on behalf of Prosper Lavalle, Monday couldn't say. But she sensed something genuine and resolved in him, and she liked it.

All that aside, the guy was hot. Just her type, she realized with an inward groan. The last thing she needed right now was another ill-considered entanglement, having just broken one off last month. She was enjoying sleeping alone for the time being, or had at least partially convinced herself of that. Anyway, given Rusty's history with Marceline, it wouldn't feel right.

She felt her phone vibrating in the hip pocket of her cutoffs. The number wasn't familiar.

"Hello?"

"Monday. It's Rusty Diamond."

"Damn, dude," she said, irritated to feel a thrill at his voice. "You must have ESP."

"I gotta ask you a favor. It's not a small one."

"What is it?"

"Need a ride back to NOLA. I'm at the Vacherie Medical Clinic. They're ready to release me but I got no wheels."

Monday sat upright on the blanket.

"Jesus, what happened? Did you see Abellard?"

"Yeah. He's every bit the gentleman you'd led me to expect."

"Are you alright?"

"I'm fine. Just need to knock some swamp water out of my ears."

"What are you doing in the hospital? And what happened to your car?"

"I'll explain all that on the ride, if you can come get me. I know it's a lot to ask, but I'd rather not wait for a damn bus, which I've been told won't leave till after sundown. Otherwise, I'll have to try and pay someone for a lift. Don't see any likely candidates at the moment."

"I'm coming."

A pause elapsed, and she heard him expel a relieved sigh.

"Thanks, Monday. Hope I'm not breaking up your day too badly."

"Sit tight," she told him. "I should be there by five o'clock, give or take."

Before he could hang up, Monday asked if there was any good news about Marceline, unable to keep the question to herself.

"I don't know if it's good or not," he answered. "But we may be closer to knowing something than we were yesterday. Get out here soon as you can and I'll fill you in."

20.

Monday's 2012 Chevy Volt, its Crystal Red Tintcoat exterior not a bad match for the lipstick she'd applied with a rushed glance in the mirror, sped eastward on the I-10, back to NOLA. Rusty slumped in the passenger's seat. He was both wired and exhausted, a feeling not entirely alien to him. Felt like he could easily close his eyes and sleep for ten hours or stay on his feet for the next three days, depending on what kind of curves appeared in the road ahead.

He'd already apologized for the dank, swampy smell filling the car and no doubt seeping into the upholstery. Monday told him not to worry about it. Her beloved Volt was due for a detailing and she'd send him the bill.

It took her barely ninety minutes to reach Vacherie after they got off the phone. Rusty was surprised to see her walk into the clinic's lobby a few minutes past five, expecting to wait at least another hour. As soon as they got on the road, his surprise faded. Monday kept her foot heavily planted on the pedal, rarely decelerating below eighty.

He gave a detailed account of everything that had happened since they last spoke. Monday listened intently, never letting up on the gas. When Rusty mentioned his viewing of the dead woman at the forensics center, she took one hand off the wheel to give his shoulder a squeeze.

"Jesus. That must have been awful."

"Yeah. I was relieved, of course. But I won't forget her face any time soon."

He went on to describe his encounter with Abellard.

Monday's eyes grew wider as he outlined the chain of violence that started in the Carnival's back office and ended with his immersion into the bay.

"That's fucking unbelievable!" she cried, pounding a fist on the wheel. "I told you Abellard was scum."

"You did at that."

"So he's obviously got Marcie. Holding her against her will somewhere till she has the baby. Or...with his temper, I guess..."

She didn't finish the sentence.

"I'm not so sure," Rusty said. "He was cryptic, didn't give away much. But I got the feeling he's as worried as we are, in his own way."

"Right, real worried," Monday replied acerbically. "That's why he tries to off a total stranger who comes asking about her. Exactly what an innocent man would do."

"I was studying him, Monday. The whole time he was talking. Laugh if you want, but I'm pretty good at reading people. I think he was being straight, to a point."

"Mentalism, huh?" she asked, glancing at him with an arched brow.

"It's actually not bullshit, even though most people who claim to practice it are frauds."

"You've got to be kidding, Rusty."

"I won't try to convince you now. I'm more interested in the phone call I overheard. This Professor Guillory. Abellard became a totally different person talking to him. He sounded...I don't know, cowed. Desperate. He said something like, 'Is she OK? I want to hear her voice.' What does that sound like to you?"

Monday didn't answer, still fuming at the suggestion that Joseph Abellard might not be every inch the criminal she thought him to be.

"Did you call this Hubbard guy back?" she asked, changing the subject.

"Uh huh, after I saw the body. He said he was glad for my sake, then offered the number of a private detective. Says he's a good man."

"Are you thinking about going that way?"

"Last night, I wasn't too sold on the idea. Private dicks get paid by the hour, which seems like a pretty strong disincentive to deliver fast results."

Monday didn't respond, just accelerated past a tour bus hauling a sunburned church group from Salt Lake City.

"What do you think?" Rusty asked.

"About hiring a private eye? I'm not a big fan of them, to be honest. My ex-boyfriend sicced one on me after I kicked him curbside. Seemed to think I was balling his best friend, which is total bullshit and wouldn't have been any of his business anyway. This private eye, I cornered him once. Digging through my garbage with his bare hands. Absolute slime."

She paused, frowning in disgust at the memory. "You've got to call Hubbard though," she continued, "after what happened today."

"I've been thinking about that."

"What's there to think about? The man tried to kill you, Rusty. Mind-reading, whatever…no offense, but save that crap for Vegas. Even if Abellard doesn't know where Marceline is, he should be in jail."

"It's my word against his. Everything that happened today, I got no proof. He'll just deny ever seeing me."

Monday chewed her lip, pondering the options.

"You said there was a security camera at the casino. That would show you walking in and never walking out, right?"

"Abellard could've erased the footage by now, if the camera was even running. And if there is proof of me walking in, all he has to do is say I got drunk, made a scene, and they hustled me out the back. The clinic drew blood when they checked me out, they'll confirm the booze in my gullet. Not to mention the Vacherie Sheriff may be in Abellard's pocket for all we know."

Monday's face revealed intense frustration as she pressed a little harder on the gas.

"Anyway," Rusty said, "I think this all may have been worth it. I've got something to follow. Something *we* can follow, if you want to help."

"This Professor…what's the name, Guillory?"

"It's not much. But maybe it'll give us some leverage with Abellard. Or put us on the scent without even having to deal with him."

Rusty got no reply to that suggestion. The next five minutes passed in silence. He couldn't tell if Monday was annoyed with him or just wrapped up in some private concern. A sign on the road told him New Orleans was only twenty miles away.

"Before you go dismissing Abellard as the prime suspect, there's something you should know."

She let that hang for a moment, seeing how he'd respond. Rusty just waited to hear more.

"That incident at the hospital…when Abellard showed up and they got into an argument?"

"Yeah. You said a couple of security guys had to drag him out."

"That was the last thing you mentioned to him, right? When he attacked you?"

"I was just trying to push buttons, get a reaction before he showed me the door. What are you not telling me?"

"The argument with Marceline. I said I didn't know what it was about. That wasn't completely true."

"Well shit, don't hold out now."

"Just listen. After the guards hauled him away, I asked Marcie what happened. She was upset, as you might imagine, but angry more than afraid. She didn't want to talk about it, wouldn't say anything except it was over. But something else happened, a few days before. I really didn't think there was any connection. Now, I don't know."

Monday veered into the left lane to pass a sluggish Winnebago, then cut in front with a cozy foot or two to spare.

"There was an incident involving one of the night janitors. It happened in the lab unit, where postpartum tissue is stored."

"Postpartum tissue?"

"Some parents choose to bank the umbilical cord blood after delivery. Others don't. The cord blood has all kinds of medical applications, but a lot of people prefer to just dispose of it. In that case, we keep the tissue in a refrigerated storage facility before it goes to a crematorium."

Rusty felt a sense of alarm in his gut. He didn't know where this story was going but he knew it was nowhere good.

"This janitor, he was new. Only worked the overnight shift for a week or so. He got caught trying to steal something. A security guard saw it on one of the cameras and stopped him. The administrators fired him the next day, it all went down very quickly. They called in the nurses and the rest of the ward staff for a meeting. Said we weren't to mention what happened, at the risk of being terminated. It was a private matter that had been dealt with appropriately. Nothing but negative attention would come to Bon Coeur if it went public."

"What was the janitor trying to steal?"

"We were never told, officially. Like I said, the brass wanted to keep it quiet. Most of us figured he'd raided the dispensary for drugs."

She hesitated.

"Keep talking, Monday."

"Word got around, a few days later. The security guard's got a thing going with one of the nurses. He told her and it spread. The guy was stealing a discarded umbilical cord."

"Jesus," Rusty said, repulsed. "Why would anyone do that?"

"Way I see it, there are two possibilities. One, the guy's some total sicko who planned to use the cord for purposes I'd rather not imagine."

"Agreed, let's leave that page blank. What's the other possibility?"

"Umbilical cords are loaded with fetal stem cells. Pluripotent cells, to be specific, the kind that can regenerate damaged tissue in any part of the body. That's what makes them so fruitful for treating serious illness."

"Right. Supposed to offer miracle cures, I've heard."

"The research is promising, there's just one problem. Louisiana has a ban on any medical procedures involving stem cells. We're one of the strictest states in the U.S. when it comes to that."

"Pro-lifer deal, huh?"

"Correct. That sentiment runs pretty strong down here."

"So what value does an umbilical cord have, if it's illegal to use for treatment?"

Monday glanced at him with a raised brow.

"Think about it. If you had ALS or lung cancer or some other terminal disease, would you be shy about breaking the law to find a cure? Assuming you could afford it?"

"Black market," Rusty nodded. "I thought that kind of thing happened mostly in Eastern Europe, places like that."

"I can't see why it wouldn't happen here. Plenty of rich sick people in this state."

"And plenty of doctors willing to perform off-the-books treatment, if the money's right."

"Exactly. When the hospital brass learned the full story was out, they called us in for another meeting. This time the threat was explicit. Say a word and we'd not only be fired but sued for breaching the confidentiality clause in our employment contracts."

"Did that surprise you?"

"Not really. Bon Coeur is an elite hospital. Can you imagine what this would do to their reputation? All those Uptown parents-to-be hear about some freak stealing biological tissue from the maternity ward? Fucking nightmare on the PR side. God knows how much lost revenue."

"So they never reported it to the police?"

Monday shook her head.

"Not as far as I know. The administrators decided canning the guy was enough. They just wanted it to go away."

"The janitor. Do you know his name?"

"Never met him. Just saw him once, when I was clocking out from my afternoon shift."

The knot in Rusty's stomach coiled tighter, a deepening sense that what he was hearing boded ill in ways he couldn't fathom.

"And this happened how long before Abellard showed up at the ward?"

"Couple days. A week, maybe. I honestly never connected the two things in my mind. There may *be* no connection. It's just…hearing about what happened today got me thinking."

"Goddamn, Monday. I wish you'd mentioned it last night."

"Would it have stopped you from seeing Abellard?"

"No. But I might have thought twice before I mentioned him getting dragged out of the ward. I'm not sure what he thinks I know, but I'm starting to get a better idea why he was so hot to sink me in the bay."

Monday reached over and gave his hand a squeeze.

"I'm sorry. I should have said something about it."

"Hell. No permanent damage done."

"So what's next?"

"Research on Professor Guillory. If it's a dead end, probably won't take long to find out. Then I guess it'll be time to call that private eye."

"And just forget about what Abellard did to you?"

"I didn't say that. But I don't want any payback on my behalf getting in the way of finding her."

Rusty pulled his cell phone from his pocket and made a few futile jabs at the screen.

"Shit. My phone drowned."

"We can try the rice method at my place. That's worked for me a few times. We'll use my iPad to do some digging on Guillory."

The invitation surprised Rusty. He'd expected she would drop him off at his hotel and they'd regroup later tonight or in the morning. But there was no denying that her offer pleased him, if for no other reason than sparing him the embarrassment of entering the Cornstalk's elegant lobby in his waterlogged state.

"Sounds good," he nodded, and for the next few miles they made a game of avoiding eye contact so as not to acknowledge any other possibilities implied in the offer.

"Might have to hose you off first," she eventually added.

"Wouldn't be the first time, I'm afraid."

Monday took the Esplanade exit and turned right on Rampart, heading into the Quarter just as twilight took hold.

They got stalled behind an Abita delivery truck and sat there listening to Etta James waft from the Volt's speakers. Rusty smiled at the thought that New Orleans was probably the only city in America where the beer trucks delivered on Sunday.

Feeling the weight of Monday's glance, he rotated his head to face her.

"What?" he asked.

"Nothing. Just thinking, you're a pretty brave son of a bitch. Pretty resourceful too, getting out of that swamp in one piece."

"Lucked out," Rusty said with a shrug. "Didn't see any gators and nary a leech on me when they pulled me into the boat. I'd have drowned for sure if Captain Dave hadn't picked me up."

"Sure, play it down. I mean, *anyone* could free themselves from being tied up and tossed overboard. Piece of cake."

"Well, a lifetime devoted to learning strange skills can come in handy sometimes."

"Makes me wish I'd seen you on the big stage."

"I was pretty badass. Can't lie."

"Ah," Monday grinned. "Nice to see that false modesty go out the window."

21.

Rusty stood in the shower for fifteen minutes, letting jets of hot water scald away the swamp muck that felt like it had seeped into his bloodstream through every pore. He gave his hair two vigorous washings, the strawberry scent of Monday's shampoo not exactly his style but a vast improvement nonetheless.

She'd insisted he leave the door open a few inches. Her tiny bathroom wasn't sufficiently ventilated to prevent the buildup of mold with the shower running. As Rusty turned the ivory handle to kill the stream, he heard her say something from the adjoining room.

"What's that?" he asked, stepping onto a fluffy bath mat.

"I said there's a fresh towel on top of the medicine cabinet."

He dried himself, detecting a faint alpine scent in the detergent. It blended unexpectedly well with the shampoo. Examining himself in the mirror, he saw an ugly bruise on the small of his back where the chair in Abellard's office had jabbed him, though the pain had dissipated to a dull throb. The kick to the head didn't even seem worth remembering.

"So'd you find anything on Guillory?" he asked.

"Actually, yeah. Didn't take much Googling, and it's pretty juicy."

Rusty wrapped the towel around his waist and stepped out of the bathroom.

Monday's home was a snug studio on Rampart, on the second floor of an aged Mediterranean-style building that overlooked Congo Square. Vintage black and white prints of jazz greats like Jelly Roll Morton and Professor Longhair hung from the walls. A pair of brass lamps in opposite corners stood draped with silk sashes, filling the room with a mellow amber glow. Some early Delta blues played from unseen speakers.

"I like your place," he said, sitting in a chair next to a corner window. Through the fogged glass, he could see the arched gateway of Congo Square across the street. Its yellow lights burned in soft contrast to the purple bruise of the sky. Full dark was imminent, inviting all manner of criminal activity into the Square, a well-trafficked tourist site by day that Rusty had long ago learned to avoid after sundown.

"Kind of a rough neighborhood, isn't it?"

Monday glanced up at him. She was seated in a black leather beanbag, an iPad held by her crossed legs. Rusty caught himself looking at her bare feet, which were perfectly shaped and tipped with glossy, blood-red nails.

"I can take care of myself. Never leave home without pepper spray, and I know which streets to avoid." She nodded toward the queen bed, neatly made up with thick lavender covers. A visibly nicked Louisville Slugger leaned against the night stand.

"Hope you haven't had to use that on any intruders."

"Not yet."

She hit him hard with those green eyes. A slight curl of her lips let him in on the joke.

"Your clothes are still in the washer," she said, returning to the iPad. "There's probably a pair of jeans somewhere in the closet that'll fit. My asshole ex left a bunch of stuff, and I've been too lazy to clear it out."

Rusty stood and opened the closet door, barely dodging a small avalanche of clothes, well-thumbed paperbacks, and other sundry items that came tumbling out.

"Heads up," Monday cautioned with an amused glance.

"Just when I thought the day's danger was over," he replied, going down on a knee to dig through the pile for some jeans. "So what do we know about this mysterious professor? Guy's got to have some heavy stones to make Abellard beg like a dog."

"First off, it's not a guy. Anne Guillory is the author of at least a dozen articles in various academic publications."

"No shit."

"The Journal of Ecology and Natural Environment, March 2005. The Ecological Society of America's Quarterly Newsletter. Biological Conservation, Winter Issue 2007. The list goes on. A rather eminent figure, this lady."

"Can't be the same Guillory," Rusty said with a dismissive scowl. "No chance a thug like Abellard is in the orbit of someone with that kind of pedigree."

"And yet the byline from one of her articles would suggest just that," Monday said, clicking a link. "Professor Anne M. Guillory, head of the Entomology department at Tulane. That's awfully close for a coincidence, don't you think?"

"Hmmm. You said he's had some dealings with Tulane?"

"Not exactly. I said that's where he met Marceline, at some charity fundraiser. I doubt he has any official ties to the school."

"All the same," Rusty said, pulling a pair of men's acid-wash jeans from the pile and quickly discarding them, "kind of a stretch to think there's another professor with that name in the area."

"I agree. Just to make sure, I searched the faculty directory at Tulane's website. No Guillory's."

"Other than this Anne, you mean."

"Nope, not even her. Seems she no longer holds her position there. These articles, they're all kind of old. Most recent I can find is from 2008."

"So she's not even a professor anymore," Rusty said, annoyed. "Which gives us diddly-shit to go on."

"Slow down," Monday said, raising a palm. "I see you're not a fan of acid-wash. Me neither. There should be some wearable chinos in there if you keep digging."

Rusty resumed his seat by the window, no longer concerned with locating a pair of pants.

"OK," Monday said, opening a new window in her browser, "how's this for a headline: 'The Case of the Vanishing Entomologist.' First paragraph: 'Why did an esteemed professor at Tulane, head of her department and the youngest woman ever to earn tenure at Louisiana's most prestigious university, suddenly abandon her post in the middle of the 2011 spring semester? Can the whiff of academic misconduct—or worse—be far from such an unprecedented departure?"'

"Where's that from?" Rusty asked.

"The *Gambit*," Monday replied, assuming he would recognize the name of NOLA's venerable free weekly. "Dated February 10th, 2012. Cover story, in fact. Seems the professor's disappearing act was kind of a big deal. Par for the course, I guess, when someone famous goes off the grid."

This oblique reference to Rusty's well-publicized flight from Vegas lingered in the air like a provocation. He ignored it.

"What's the upshot of the article?"

"Hush and listen. 'Anne Guillory was a standout among the elite faculty at Tulane. Even before earning tenure at the scarily impressive age of twenty-nine, her works on insect and animal-borne pathogens had garnered national notice. An invitation to speak before Congress in 2002, during which she gave impassioned testimony on the vanishing wetlands of Louisiana's Gulf Coast, received coverage not only on C-SPAN but also more mainstream news outlets. It cemented her reputation as one of the leading voices on the inevitable ecological disaster to the region due to unregulated human encroachment. That she was a woman, under thirty and attractive to boot, only served to boost her burgeoning notoriety.'"

Monday took a sip of tea from a mug on the floor and continued.

"'Flash forward eighteen months. The Board of Regents at Tulane, in a ceremony orchestrated for maximum public exposure, named Anne M. Guillory head of the Entomology Department. She was by far the youngest person to achieve that distinction, regardless of gender.'"

"This is all really fascinating," Rusty interrupted from his perch by the window, "but I'm waiting for the juicy part."

Monday shot him an icy glance, the likes of which he hadn't seen since their first meeting in the maternity ward.

"Sorry," he said. "Ignore me."

"I'll skip ahead a few paragraphs," she muttered, a fingernail flicking the iPad's screen. "'And then, seven years after her deservedly touted promotion, Anne Guillory stepped down. Just like that, with little fanfare and less explanation, she abdicated her post as head of the department. By that point, the novelty of her position had worn off, and thus her departure from the university was met with notably less interest than her rapid rise though its hierarchy.

"'But now, one sizable question remains. Why? Why would a tenured professor, nationally published and regarded as a leader in a rarified field of study with broad implications on human and animal life in the most perilous regions of the state, suddenly abandon her post?

"'For answers, at least of the official variety, we must rely on two separate press releases, disseminated within days of each other and equally terse in wording. On April 3rd, 2011, Professor Guillory announced her retirement in an open letter to the Student Body. In it, she sounded the obligatory notes of gratitude for the opportunity to work at such a distinguished institution, expressed high hopes for the students she'd been privileged to instruct, and made passing reference to personal matters that required more of her attention than she was able to give as head of the department. A statement from the University released two days later proved equally murky, doing little more than rephrasing Guillory's goodbye message and offering best wishes for future success in other arenas.

"'But the story hardly ends there. Based on a lengthy investigation including off-the-record interviews with both faculty and students, this paper has pieced together a disturbing narrative that puts Guillory's departure in a notably different light. A follow-up article in next week's *Gambit* will make the case that she did not step down for 'personal reasons' but was forced to resign lest she bring scandal and possible criminal prosecution to the University.'"

Monday rubbed her eyes, weary of reading aloud.

"Talk about a tease," she said. "There's a link to the follow-up article if you want to hear it."

She got no response. Glancing up from the iPad, she saw

Rusty had given up on finding a pair of pants and lay sprawled on her bed clad only in the towel around his waist.

Monday almost told him not to get any ideas, but stopped when she heard a muted snore.

She walked over and sat on the bed next to him. His chest rose slowly as it filled with oxygen, seeming to animate the complex sprawl of tattoos on his pectorals.

Monday just looked for a few minutes, allowing herself a casual and thorough review of his physique. She'd long had a weakness for stylish body art. Though she'd limited herself to only the one bleeding rose, knowing all too well how badly ink treats female flesh over the course of time, she couldn't help feeling a familiar tingle at seeing such artistic designs spread across such a well-crafted body.

Reaching out, she placed the tip of her index finger just above his left nipple and tracked a feathery line along the twisting serpent tattoo that reached down toward his ribcage. Strewn along both arms from wrist to shoulder were matching vines of symbols and incantations. Monday retained little memory of the rudimentary Latin she'd memorized as a schoolgirl at the Academy of Our Lady in Shreveport, but she recognized a three-word phrase spelled out on Rusty's right bicep.

Actum ne gas.

"Do not redo that which has been done," she whispered with a grin. "Probably good advice for a magician."

She let her hand fall to his stomach, dipping a finger in his damp navel before traveling lower. Rusty's eyes opened as Monday reached under the towel to apply a friendly but purposeful grip where it counted the most.

"I know," she smiled down at him. "Bad idea, right?"

"That wasn't the first thing to pop into my mind, actually."

"Wish I wasn't such a sucker for ink on muscles, but we are what we are."

"Indeed we are. Nothing we can do about it."

A long, mutually pleasurable moment of silence passed. Monday could see how much Rusty was enjoying her touch, but she saw something else in his gaze.

"You really care about her a lot, don't you?"

"Oh, yeah. She meant the world to me, for a long time. If anything's happened to her…anything bad…"

He trailed off, not wanting to finish that thought. Monday's hand was moving with soft, practiced strokes.

"Are you still in love with her?"

"No. That's long over. I just want to see her safe and sound."

"Me too."

Monday leaned down to place her lips on his. They kissed deeply, both surprised by the intensity of it, then she rose from the bed. With two quick motions that flowed so smoothly from one to the next that Rusty barely saw them, she pulled off her tank top and slid free of her shorts. She stood naked before him for a moment, liking the way his eyes canvassed her figure.

Rusty tossed the towel to the floor and she slid on top of him, their bodies finding an easy fit on first contact.

"You know," he said as his fingertips roved down her back, "it's been sort of an asskicker of a day."

"I'd say it's improving, wouldn't you?"

"By leaps and bounds," Rusty whispered, allowing a hand to slide between her thighs and finding her wet. "Just saying I might not bring my A-game at the moment."

"Oh, I see. You're saying I have to do all the work here."

"Let's call it a 60/40 split."

"That's not a very enticing offer, my friend."

"Yeah, but my forty is like a solid eighty for the average guy."

"Is that right?" she asked with a laugh, biting his lip just shy of the point of pain. "Talk is cheap, magic man."

22.

"Odd place for a theft," the clerk at the Hertz office grumbled, glancing up from a claim report he was filling out on his computer. "Usually this kind of thing happens in the city." He quickly added, "Not that it's common, mind you."

"Yeah," Rusty said with a commiserating nod. "Surprised the hell out of me too. Just when you think it's safe to do a little fishing out in the sticks."

The clerk didn't offer any reply to that, turning back to the computer screen.

Morning lit up the French Quarter in a blaze of brilliant sunshine. It was a few minutes past eight o'clock, and the rental car office had just opened. Rusty walked here from Monday's apartment, enjoying a meandering course through empty streets filled with silent echoes of the Quarter's colorful, violent past.

He'd waited outside the Hertz office for twenty minutes, entering as soon as the clerk unlocked the front door. There was much to be done today, none of which he could do without wheels.

Rusty had already decided on going with something a little roomier than the Mustang. Being tied up in the back of Abellard's Escalade made him think a conveyance that size might come in handy.

"And you're sure," the clerk droned on, still typing, "you locked the vehicle before you went fishing?"

Rusty flashed a polite smile, probably his fifth since this conversation began. He decided it would be the last.

"Definitely. I'm very consistent about that, even in my

garage at home. Force of habit."

Not that it really matters, you little prick. That's what comprehensive coverage is for.

"Just glad I went full-boat with the insurance," he continued, verbalizing his thoughts in a more agreeable fashion. "I'm real consistent about that too."

"We always recommend the maximum coverage," the clerk said with an approving nod. "Some credit card companies tell you they provide full protection, but it gets a lot more complicated in the case of a total loss. We don't process too many of these, fortunately."

He might as well have added, *Because we don't often rent to irresponsible lowlifes such as you, Mr. Diamond.* Somehow that message got through even without being spoken.

Rusty leaned hard against the counter and cleared his throat.

"We about done here? I'd like to get my replacement and not waste the whole day doing it. Let's make it an SUV, something in the deluxe class."

The clerk stopped typing and looked up with a worried frown.

"You're sure you want another deluxe vehicle? Perhaps one of our excellent economy options might be more sensible."

A laminated placard showed all the vehicles for rent. Rusty laid a finger on the Lincoln Navigator.

"This one. Full coverage. Never know if I'll be victimized by another thief in this lawless town."

The clerk winced as if personally insulted, then made some final keyboard clicks and started printing out a new rental agreement.

Rusty's phone vibrated in his pocket. Monday's remedy of letting it sit in a bowl of dry rice had revived it from yesterday's dousing in Barataria Bay.

"Hey there," he said, turning away from the counter. "You're an early riser. I was surprised to wake up alone."

"Disappointed too, I'm guessing."

"That's true."

"My shift at the ward started at six. Did you help yourself to coffee?"

"Sure did. And I unplugged the machine before I left, just like your note instructed."

"Yeah," Monday said in a kind of languid half-sigh that stirred Rusty's loins, memories of last night flooding his mind in Technicolor. "I'm borderline OCD about not leaving any appliances plugged in when I'm not home."

"We all got our quirks."

"It's not totally irrational. My building's over a hundred years old. I doubt it's up to code. Visions of a three-story tinderbox keep me up at night."

"Not last night, I hope."

"No, sir," she said, and he could hear her smile over the fiber optic line. "I was plum tuckered out by the time I closed my eyes."

"Told you my forty's not bad."

"Don't get cocky. You still owe me sixty."

Rusty caught the clerk's expectant gaze. He grabbed a pen from the counter and scribbled his signature on the rental agreement.

"I hit paydirt on our mystery janitor," Monday said. "Name's Claude Sherman. He was hired on March 25th, dismissed without severance on April 3rd."

"Good work. How'd you track all that down?"

"Waited for Nurse Ballbuster to use the ladies' and snuck on her computer. It hadn't gone to sleep so I didn't have to log in. Which is good, since I don't know the password. Anyway, I looked through the personnel records for recent hires and found him."

"I'm impressed. Is there a home address?"

"Negative. A notation says Mr. Sherman preferred to pick up his paycheck at the hospital. No mailing address, no direct deposit."

Rusty shook his head, hearing a false note in what she'd just said.

"Strike you as kind of odd the hospital would hire someone without any contact info? Even a night janitor?"

"He came with a strong referral. I guess that was enough."

"Who referred him?"

"Dr. Philip Roque, of the Uptown Family Planning Clinic."

"You familiar with the place?"

"Can't say I am, but I'm guessing it's where the well-to-do fix their bedroom mistakes. Swanky address on Magazine Street. Apparently Sherman worked there as a custodian."

"And if we're lucky, he still does."

"Plucked the words from my mouth, sir."

Rusty grabbed the Lincoln's keys from the clerk, whose final words were, "Please try to be careful!"

Walking to the rear lot where the rentals awaited pickup, he resumed his conversation with Monday.

"You did an awesome job. Really."

"That sounds like you think I'm done," she said, sounding let down.

"I think you are, for now. I'm going to the clinic. Worst case scenario, maybe I can snag a home address for Sherman. If he's there, I'll figure out a way to get him alone."

"And he'll just spill whatever you want to know, right?"

"Yes," Rusty said coldly. "He will."

"Slow down there, cowboy. I've got a better plan. Let's go to the clinic together."

"I don't know—"

"Think about it," she cut him off. "Works a whole lot better if you show up with a woman, right? I'll ask for a private consultation with Roque and you…do whatever it is you're gonna do."

Rusty couldn't argue with her logic. He slid behind the wheel of a 2015 silver Navigator, liking the vehicle's heft.

"When do you get off?"

"Two o'clock. Meet me in front of Bon Coeur. We'll head straight over."

"Maybe we should call for an appointment."

"They take walk-ins. I checked."

"You're impressing the hell out of me, Monday. Might have missed your calling as a private snoop."

"Gotta run."

A brief pause, then she added:

"One more thing. There's a photo of Sherman on his employment profile. I snapped it on my phone, texting it to you now."

"Great," Rusty said, then a thought hit him. "That detective, Hubbard. He should get this photo, see if it matches anyone they've got on file."

"Good point."

"You should really tell him what you know about Sherman getting canned. I know that could cost you your job—"

"Fuck the hospital brass," Monday said without hesitation. "If they fire me, fine. That lawsuit threat was bullshit, it would just mean more bad press. They should've reported this when it happened."

Rusty fired the ignition as she continued, "Guess we'll have to swing by the Sixth Precinct so I can give a statement in person."

"After we check out this Dr. Roque," Rusty said. "Hubbard would only tell us not to do it, so why give him the chance?"

"I like the way you think. Two o'clock, sharp."

With that, Monday ended the call. Three seconds later, Rusty saw a text message icon pop up on his screen. He opened Monday's message, then clicked on the attachment.

The face staring up at him through the cracked screen made him recoil in his seat.

Thick mat of poorly combed brown hair. A week-old beard growing in uneven patches across jagged facial contours. Beady eyes looking not directly into the camera's lens but off to the left as if momentarily distracted. All in all, a collection of features tailor-made for criminal phrenologists of days past.

Damn it, Rusty thought, peering at the photo with a shiver of distaste. *I've seen this face before.*

He was sure of it, but he didn't know where. Putting the Lincoln in gear, he edged out of the Hertz lot onto St. Peter. He decided to roll over to the French Market and see if it was more economical to place a bulk order for chicory coffee in person than to do it online. For the past year, he'd had regular shipments sent to his rented home in coastal Maryland.

Thinking of his house in Ocean Pines made him wistful. Rusty missed the quiet seclusion of the place that had been so critical for sustaining any peace of mind in the long months since abandoning Las Vegas. He felt nostalgic for the blissful ignorance of just three days ago, when he'd locked the door and driven to the Baltimore airport with no knowledge of what awaited him on the Louisiana soil.

Figured the worst I'd have to deal with is an awkward moment or two. Amazing, what we don't know we don't know.

Rusty slammed on the brakes, almost getting rear-ended by a sports car that had been following too closely. He ignored the angry honks behind him, reached for his phone, and opened up Monday's message again. A second look at Claude Sherman's crude face sent a jolt through him like he'd stepped on a live wire.

The son of a bitch who jumped me at Marcie's apartment.

Rusty hit the gas and tore through a red light, all thoughts of chicory coffee and the quiet refuge of coastal Maryland erased from his mind.

23.

The live oaks of Uptown stretched along both sides of St. Charles, creating a green canopy through which rays of sun danced on the windshields of passing cards. Colorful strands of plastic beads hung from tall branches, remnants of this year's Mardi Gras parades. Soft gusts blew in from the river, sweetened with honeysuckle and goldenrod.

Rusty piloted the Lincoln Navigator along the avenue, keeping his speed low. He was in no particular rush to arrive at the Uptown Family Planning Clinic. They needed time to talk.

"You're sure it was him?" Monday asked when Rusty told her he'd identified Claude Sherman as the intruder at Marceline's apartment.

"I'd say, hell, ninety-eight percent sure."

In the five hours since making that connection, Rusty had peered at the photo a dozen times. His certainty rose and fell with each glance.

"Let's say it was him," Monday said. "Two questions: what was he doing there, and does it still make sense for you to confront him at the clinic?"

"Yes, to the second question. It was pitch black in the apartment, no way he could have gotten a good look at me. I only glimpsed him when he ran out onto the stoop. As for the first question, I really don't know. But if we go on the theory that the argument at the hospital was related to Sherman getting fired—"

"That's a pretty big assumption, but OK."

"If we assume that, it creates another link to Abellard being involved with her disappearance."

Monday wrinkled her nose, not following.

"Maybe to scare her," Rusty said, "or just keep her quiet." He stopped there, not wanting to verbalize any more extreme possibilities.

"We'd need to establish a connection between Abellard and Sherman before that holds water."

"Correct. And that's what I intend to do while you're talking to Dr. Roque."

Rusty could see the skepticism on her face but he didn't challenge it.

"I've been thinking," he said. "Roque does family planning, right? Wouldn't that give him access to stem cells every time he—"

"Aborts a fetus? Indeed, it would. I was thinking the same thing myself."

"Glad we're in step. Want to go over our cover again?"

Monday shrugged, a mischievous smile on her face.

"Shouldn't be too complicated. Just another white trash couple who got a nasty surprise last month. What with both of us unemployed and you a two-time loser fresh out of the joint—"

"With a bad huffing habit," Rusty added.

"Right. I've managed to wean myself off paint thinner, but you're still struggling with that demon."

"Man's got to have a hobby."

"Anyway, we're just not sure this is the right time to bring a new life into the world."

"And we're hoping the doc can give us some sound advice."

"But I'd feel more comfortable talking with him alone," Monday said, enjoying the cover story. "See, I'm not a hundred percent sure it's yours, and I'd rather not say that in front of you. What with your temper and all."

"Right. So I'll cool my heels in the lobby—"

"And see what you can learn about Claude Sherman. Even if it means seducing Roque's secretary."

Rusty smiled and steered right onto Magazine. Two blocks later, the red brick facade of the medical plaza came into view.

He started to hit the turn signal but stopped, foot landing on the brake.

Two NOPD patrol cars were parked by the curb. Three more filled the driveway. Bright yellow banners of crime scene tape sealed off the entrance.

Rusty and Monday turned to face each other.

"Oh shit," she whispered. "Are you getting a bad feeling too?"

"Let's see what we can find out."

Rusty nosed the Navigator in as close as he could get to the yellow tape.

A young cop leaning against one of the prowlers flicked away a cigarette. He loped over with a chest-out posture probably picked up from too many bad action movies.

"Back it up. This building's off-limits."

"What's going on?" Rusty asked, trying to sound oblivious.

"Can't come in here, sir. That's what the tape there's telling you."

"Well, shoot. We got an appointment with Dr. Roque."

"It's canceled. He won't be seeing anyone today."

"What happened?" Monday asked, leaning across the center console to gift the cop with a bountiful eyeful of cleavage.

"Not at liberty to say, miss."

"Damnit," Rusty uttered, "we made the appointment three weeks ago."

"Sorry for the inconvenience. Back this thing up, please."

"We *really* need to see Dr. Roque," Monday pressed, raising her voice to a little girl whine. "We got a, well…an embarrassing problem to deal with."

"I'm sorry, miss. You'll have to find yourself a new doctor. There's been a homicide here. Dr. Roque was killed."

"Oh my God," Monday said, covering her mouth with a hand. Rusty wasn't sure how much of her reaction was feigned. He himself felt a greater sense of shock than seemed logical at learning of a total stranger's demise.

"What in the world happened?" he asked the cop.

"We haven't released that information yet. I can tell you

this much. Receptionist came in this morning, found him on the lobby floor."

"How'd he die?" Monday asked.

"Stabbed. Hard to say how many times, but my guess would be north of twenty."

Rusty felt Monday's hand grip his arm, and he knew this reaction wasn't faked.

"That's horrible."

"Yep, pretty messy," the cop added, warming to his role. His chest swelled slightly.

"Strangest bit," he added, unable to help himself, "looks like Roque got done with one of his own surgical knives."

"How do you know that?" Monday asked quickly, before the cop thought better of revealing more information.

"There's one missing from a case in the operating room."

"No shit," Rusty said.

"Spotted it myself," the cop lied. "The case was open just a bit, empty slot where the knife should've been. Of course we'll need the coroner to confirm things."

"Do you know who did it?" Monday asked.

The young officer started to reply but his mouth clamped shut like he'd suddenly awakened to his gross indiscretion.

"Back it up now," he said brusquely. "This is an active crime scene. I don't wanna have to book you for tampering."

"Thanks," Rusty said.

"We'll be watching for you on the news," Monday added.

Rusty put the gearshift in reverse and inched out of the driveway. He drove a few blocks up Magazine and parked in an open space behind the Balcony Bar, letting the engine idle.

"So much for bracing Claude Sherman," he said through clenched teeth.

"What odds do you give he's the one who iced Roque?"

"Fuck, who knows? All I wanted from the guy was some info that connected him to Abellard. I was hoping he'd put up a fight so I could get it out of him the hard way."

"So what now?" Monday asked. "Talk to your detective friend at the Sixth Precinct?"

Rusty didn't answer. Monday noticed how his eyes were focused on something high above the Navigator's hood. She followed his gaze upward to an inflatable skeleton hung from the rafters of the Balcony Bar, looking like it had been there since last Halloween.

Marceline waved a hand in front of his eyes, bringing him back to the moment.

"Are we going to the cops, or what?"

"Yeah. Depending on how that goes, I've got another idea."

24.

Claude Sherman drove in a state of controlled panic. Pedal pushed to a quarter inch off the floorboard, needle holding tight at 75 MPH. The flatlands of rural Louisiana flew past him in the Pontiac's flyspecked windshield, and he barely noticed any of it. Hands gripping the wheel, his eyes never left the road.

It was an odd kind of panic. Not entirely unpleasant. He felt almost liberated by taking the life of Philip Roque. The abortionist's overfed body deserved every one of those stab wounds. Claude just wished he'd made a cleaner job of it. Roque had shown more fight than Claude gave him credit for, eliminating the possibility of a quick kill.

Well, spilled milk. It wasn't like he'd walked into the Uptown Family Planning yesterday with homicide in mind. Roque brought that on himself. Claude just wanted the man to perform the function for which he'd been contracted. He balked, then struggled, then threatened to call the police. What other outcome did he expect for such reckless behavior?

Claude's eyes flicked up to read a road sign indicating that State Highway 22 was five miles away. In the thirty-odd hours since leaving the clinic, he hadn't been plagued by too much unease, other than worrying over the smartest next move if he wanted to stay alive and out of jail.

But no guilt. That was paramount, and totally different to how he felt after dumping that unknown woman's body in a dumpster behind Decatur.

Claude knew the only reason he wasn't in handcuffs was that he'd convinced the abortionist to meet him at the clinic on Sunday morning. He saw no one on his frantic exit from Roque's office, down the elevator and out to where he'd parked the Pontiac on Magazine. His image may have been recorded by a dozen cameras as he left the empty medical plaza, but that hardly mattered. Unlike the murder in the alley, Claude had no illusions about escaping detection for Roque's death. His prints were all over the scene. The police were surely looking for him by now.

He reached the exit for State Highway 22 and turned north into rural Livingston Parish. Large parcels of land passed with no signs of habitation, until he reached Maurepas. He took care to observe the speed limit inside the tiny town, which had no red lights but was notorious for radar-armed prowlers hidden in roadside alcoves.

Getting pulled over by a Maurepas cop was no picnic in the best of circumstances. But when you're the prime suspect in the murder of a prominent New Orleans physician, it was something to be avoided at all costs. Claude giggled madly at the thought, then brushed away a sudden impulse to head back to NOLA and turn himself in.

Why not? The worst fate prosecutors could throw his way was the needle, and even that could probably be avoided. With Claude's history of institutionalization, a sharp lawyer could most likely wheedle him into an insanity rap.

Besides, the consequences awaiting him through legal prosecution were mild compared to what Joseph Abellard would do if he ever got his hands on Claude. Killing Dr. Roque was a necessity, but Abellard wouldn't see it that way. Not only had he terminated their sole source for acquiring stem cells, but the murder would invite scrutiny onto their whole operation.

Despite those concerns, Claude wasn't turning himself in. Nor would he allow Abellard the opportunity to erase him as a liability on the balance sheet.

A third option lay available.

Professor Guillory. Claude would be at her doorstep in minutes, and he'd make her listen. A woman with her smarts couldn't fail to recognize the value of his proposition. Hell, she owed him. He'd done everything she had asked. Even snatched the Lavalle girl, a move that would've bought him a ticket to the bottom of Barataria Bay if Mr. Abellard ever learned of his role in it.

Professor Guillory would see that it was in her best interest for the one man still alive who could connect her to everything—not just the sale of banned material, but kidnapping and murder—to safely disappear.

She had the resources to bring that about. Claude knew with enough cash and the kind of phony documentation she surely could provide, he'd be able to vanish. Never have to look Abellard in the face, never sweat under the hot lamps of a police interrogation. And best of all, never have to think about the blood on his hands.

Fifteen miles north of Maurepas, the landscape grew more desolate. Claude reduced his speed and started scanning the roadside for a mail box topped with a large brass fleur-de-lis.

Just as he felt certain he'd passed it or had made a wrong turn, he spotted it up on the left.

Claude eased into the driveway, advancing slowly around a bend bordered by lush crepe myrtles. The drive straightened out and narrowed. After some thirty yards, a weathervane in the shape of a schooner appeared over a cluster of treetops.

The driveway turned again, bringing the house fully into view. It was a two-story brick structure, with a shingled roof surmounted by a cupola supporting the weathervane. A columned portico filled out the front, with gallery porches extending around all sides and embellished with elaborate cast-iron grillwork. A sallyport crouched beside the house, its twin doors lowered to conceal any vehicles inside.

Claude braked in front of twin stone walls connected by an iron gate that blocked the driveway. He reached out to press a button on a metal callbox built into the left wall.

It rang four times before he got an answer. A buzz of static was followed by an echoey male voice.

"State your business, please."

"It's Claude Sherman. I need to talk to Professor Guillory."

A pause, then:

"She's not expecting you, Mr. Sherman."

"Gotta talk to her, Pierre. Tell her it's what she's been waiting for. The package. She'll see me right now, I think."

* * *

The grandness of the house always had the same effect on him. He felt woefully out of place, despite having been invited here a handful of times. Before meeting Anne Guillory on his inaugural visit with Abellard, Claude had never been within a hundred yards of such an opulent residence.

The voice from the intercom met him at the front door, housed in a large muscular body. Claude knew the man only as Pierre. He acted like a butler but didn't dress like one. Pierre appeared to be an ex-bodybuilder trying to pass himself off as a moneyed man of the world: tailored Burberry suit, carefully groomed five o'clock shadow, mirror-shined shoes. Claude had heard Guillory use the term majordomo in reference to the man but had no concept of its meaning. If pressed, he'd wager it meant a combination of handyman, bodyguard, and house stud.

Pierre wordlessly led Claude down an oak-paneled hallway lined with oil portraits. They turned left into another passage that opened up into a large hexagonal conservatory. As he followed the majordomo inside, Claude felt the same surreal swoon he did the first time he entered this unlikely space, feeling as if one step had transported him from a refined southern estate to the Amazonian wilds.

The conservatory seethed with the hothouse pulse of an oversized terrarium. Bamboo furniture spread out across a floor of varnished pine planks. Traditional southern plantings abounded but were overwhelmed by an assortment of lush tropical varieties: palmettos, moth orchids, succulents, and dozens more filled every available nook.

Claude started sweating, as he did every time he found himself here. The thermostat had to be set well above eighty, with a humidifier adding an invisible mist to the air.

"Sit, please," Pierre said. "You'll be attended to shortly."

Claude took the closest bamboo chair as Pierre turned and exited the room. Bereft of any human companionship, he was far from alone. Rows of translucent cases held bustling colonies of insects and lizards, while tall latticed cages housed an aviary of squawking birds. Feathers brighter than neon, beaks capable of chipping plaster, they merged into a kaleidoscopic whirl in Claude's overheated brain.

The sound of crisp footsteps came from behind him. Turning in the chair, Claude saw her and everything became real again.

"I'm sorry..." he stammered, rising. "Sorry to show up like this. I know the rules."

"It's a bit of a surprise," Anne Guillory said, moving across the planks with a kind of precise fluidity he'd noted before. "But let's not put too much emphasis on so-called rules, Mr. Sherman. You obviously have something important to discuss."

"Yes, very important. I wouldn't bother you otherwise."

"Of course," she replied, smoothing her skirt before lowering herself onto a sofa.

She gestured for him to sit and then remained motionless, studying him. Not for the first time, Claude felt like a kind of bug trapped under glass for her inspection. Nothing more than mild curiosity betrayed itself in her gaze as she waited for him to speak.

"First of all," he began. "There's a problem..."

Pierre stepped into the room carrying a silver tray. Claude's mouth snapped shut mid-sentence. He wasn't about to say what needed saying for an audience of two.

"I thought some sweet tea and king cake might be refreshing," Guillory said. "Hardly seasonal for the cake, I admit. But it seems almost shameful to limit such a delicacy to Mardi Gras, don't you agree?"

Pierre offered Claude some iced tea in a crystal glass and set down a plate holding a slice of three-colored cake on the circular table next to his chair. The muscled servant then repeated the procedure for Guillory.

"I said *thin* slices, Pierre," she murmured, accepting the plate. She offered a slightly toothy grin for Claude's benefit.

Pierre gave a small nod and with five steps had once again vanished from sight.

"I'm not hungry," Claude muttered, wondering how he was going to state his case if he didn't even feel comfortable maintaining eye contact with his host.

Claude pegged her at mid-forties. He wouldn't call her beautiful, but she was certainly striking. Her dark hair was pulled back into a tight ponytail. A pair of horn-rimmed glasses sat high on her aquiline nose. A low-wattage erotic current emanated from within, neatly contained by the well-manicured exterior.

"I don't have what you want," he ventured. "There's not gonna be any delivery today."

"I won't say I'm not disappointed, but I will admit to not being surprised. If this was a pro forma visit, you certainly wouldn't be here unaccompanied."

Claude eased the dryness in his mouth with a sip of tea. It smelled of jasmine and tasted like a summer day in Audobon Park. He wasn't much of a tea drinker, but he'd never tasted better.

"Things have gotten kind of mixed up. More than you might already know about."

"This room makes you uncomfortable, doesn't it?"

Claude gave a noncommittal shake of the head. He hated the conservatory, but giving an honest answer to her question seemed rude.

"It's really no more than a fancy indoor garden," she said warmly. "Or a miniature zoo."

"Look here," she continued, rising and walking to an oblong glass terrarium. Inside lay a mini ecosystem of grass, dirt, and a few thick branches. Scuttling about were at least fifty insects, all similar in appearance: roughly an inch in length, brown and black bodies, with large forceps extending from their abdomens.

"These little darlings belong to the order Dermaptera. But you might know their more common name. The earwig."

"Don't those crawl into your ear while you're asleep and lay eggs?" Claude asked uneasily.

Guillory's brows raised with delight.

"Bravo. That's indeed the legend. Entirely unfounded, of course. The female of the species wouldn't find an ear canal very accommodating to her needs."

Guillory retrieved a thin wooden straw from below the terrarium. She gently nudged it under one of the larger insects. Legs and antennae twitching, it climbed up onto the tip.

"Could you hand me that bottle, please?"

She pointed to a small bottle of brown glass resting on a nearby table. Claude placed it in her free hand.

"Watch now," Anne Guillory said, lowering the straw so that the tip descended toward the rim. The earwig crawled up the straw, away from the bottle.

"You see? She has no interest in entering such a tight darkened space. The human head is the last place this insect would willingly choose to burrow. But, with a little encouragement…"

She titled the straw higher. Unable to fight gravity, the earwig scrambled down and disappeared into the bottle.

Setting aside the straw, Guillory left the bottle's rim open, uncovered by her fingers.

"Here's the interesting part. Our little friend is limited by an evolutionary fluke. Inside a constricted space, the earwig can't turn around or move in reverse. There's plenty of room for her to escape, but she doesn't. She's trapped, by her own genetic deficiency. All she can do is keep trying to move forward. Imagine finding this creature *inside your head*, unable to free itself, only digging deeper and deeper. Twitching and scraping inside you, nothing you could do to dislodge it. How long would it take before madness took hold, for death to seem preferable? A day? Less? It's easy to see where that old wives tale derives its power, don't you think?"

"Uh, yeah," Claude said, bewildered by the sight of the bug feverishly clawing against the brown glass. "That's interesting. But we got some serious problems—"

"He doesn't know you're here," Guillory interrupted, setting down the bottle. "Does he?"

"You mean Mr. Abellard?"

"Who else could I possibly mean?"

"I haven't talked to him. Thought it was best to see you myself. There's a problem. More than a problem. I need your help."

Guillory opened her arms slightly as if to communicate any help she could muster was his for the taking.

"It's the best thing, for everyone. I'm not just thinking about myself. I…"

He couldn't find the words to continue. Dark circles of sweat were widening beneath his armpits, a trickle descending the back of his neck. He took another sip of tea.

"The delay has been disappointing," Guillory said, rescuing him from his verbal paralysis. "To put it mildly."

"Wasn't our fault. The main supplier, he cut out on us. You know that already. The backup plan had problems. You know that too."

"I don't think we need to dwell on your termination from Bon Coeur. As I said at the time, I admired your resourcefulness for devising an alternate delivery source when Dr. Roque's output proved disappointing. You should have been more careful, but what happened happened."

Claude almost flinched at the mention of the abortionist's name, as well as his own embarrassing termination from the ward. But Guillory had a soothing, almost narcotic way of speaking. He couldn't help but feel lulled into a sense that maybe the situation wasn't as catastrophically fucked as he'd feared.

"We had to take the girl," he said, nodding so vigorously that he felt slightly dizzy. "You were right about that. She knows my face from the casino, put two and two together…we had to do it."

Claude saw Guillory grin slightly, and he felt that he'd been working too hard to convince himself of something. He had somehow lost track of what he'd come here to discuss, every thought that surfaced in his head faded before assuming clarity.

"I can guarantee you," Guillory said, "he suspects no participation on your part in that enterprise."

"No shit," Claude replied, clumsily lifting the glass for another sip. "I'd be fertilizer right now if he did."

"I spoke to him about it just yesterday."

"What?"

"Seemed pointless to keep it from him any longer. Frankly, I'm surprised he hadn't put the pieces together by now. Your employer is not quite the mastermind he fancies himself, I'm afraid."

Claude still hadn't recovered from what he just heard. It made absolutely no sense, and the room felt like it was tilting to one side.

"Hold it. You told him we kidnapped her?"

"Calm yourself, Mr. Sherman. As I said, he has no knowledge of your involvement. I left out that little detail."

"So…but…*why'd* you tell him?"

"Because the girl's value as a motivating force has been greatly diminished. And we have your handiwork to thank for that, don't we?"

The sharpness of those words snapped Claude out of his thickening haze. He remembered his purpose for being here and made one last stab at steering the conversation.

"We've got more than a delay to deal with now," he said, the words tumbling thickly from his tongue. "Our source…no more batches coming from him."

"Mr. Sherman, you don't need to be so coy. Roque is dead. That's what you're trying to say, isn't it?"

Claude's eyes seemed to shift out of focus. The conservatory's seething jungle atmosphere swam before him. The shriek of a cockatiel a few feet from his head produced an interior flinch, but his muscles were too numbed to move.

"It's been on the TV virtually nonstop since this morning," Guillory continued. "What can you expect from those Uptown snobs anyway? The Lower Ninth averages four homicides a week and it hardly merits a headline. Huge tracts of wetlands are raped routinely, nobody seems to notice. But a prominent physician, knifed in his own clinic less than ten blocks from Tulane…well, that's bound to ruffle a few feathers."

Feeling a fiery dryness in his throat, Claude reached again for the tea. His fingers brushed against the glass, knocking it to the floor.

Something was wrong. His appendages had hardened like sunbaked blocks of clay, dumb insensate slabs disconnected from his body. Guillory kept speaking to him as if she didn't notice the total collapse his nervous system was experiencing.

"You did the right thing by coming here," she said softly. "There was really no other choice, was there?"

Claude tried to nod, but he couldn't tell if he was moving his head or his entire torso. Not that it mattered. Whatever the tea had been laced with was taking hold of him completely, and he sensed Professor Guillory didn't really expect an answer to her question.

He knew the tea was drugged or poisoned without fully grasping the ramifications of that fact. From some faraway place, a voice whispered: *You knew it was bad before you took the first sip, but you drank it anyway. Why? Because you deserve this.*

It occurred to Claude, the thought forming slowly in his mind as if traveling a great distance to get there, that he'd quite possibly been dosed with the same toxin he'd used to subdue the Lavalle woman before carrying her from her home in the middle of the night.

Curare. That's what had Guillory had called it. The extract from some woody vines that grew in South America. A skeletal-muscle relaxant, Amazonian tribes had used *curare* to make poison-tipped arrows for centuries, or so she had said when instructing Claude how to soak a rag in the fluid and place it over the sleeping woman's face.

Guillory had stressed the importance of removing the rag the instant she stopped resisting, as overexposure to *curare* could produce death by respiratory paralysis. Claude did as instructed. He always did as instructed, and this was his reward?

"I can see you're struggling to follow me, so I'll wrap it up with thanks. You proved yourself a useful contractor, until you weren't."

Claude couldn't understand what was being said anymore.

The words buzzed in his ear like an electrical fan with a faulty motor. No meaning, no comprehension. A kind of weightless euphoria washed over him. One knee dropped to the red planks below. His unshaven cheek seemed to kiss the floor rather than collide with it.

"Don't lose heart," Guillory said, standing a mile above him. Claude was vaguely aware of another gargantuan presence. The burly manservant called Pierre had returned.

The last thought to fully form in Claude's mind was not comforting. If this was the same toxin used on Lavalle, then it might not kill him. But why slip him a non-lethal dose? If the professor had decided he was no longer needed for making deliveries, what did she think he was needed for?

As if reading his clouded mind, Guillory answered, "There's still a useful task to which you can be put."

Claude didn't like the sound of that. Even as he was sucked deeper toward oblivion, those two words thundered ominously in his head.

Useful task?

Then the last fiber of lucidity dissipated like smoke from an extinguished match, and he knew no more.

25.

Monday and Rusty lay on her bed as afternoon street noises wafted in through the open window. They both directed their attention to the screen of her iPad, propped up against a pillow. The web browser displayed a page on YouTube.

"Ready for this?" she asked.

"Let's see it."

The video was paused on an arresting image shot in grainy low resolution. A shirtless, hooded man faced the camera. His muscular frame stood poised in front of a large red flag with an insignia depicting a snake coiled around the letter V.

A caption underneath the video screen read: VECTOR Manifesto—Public Access Broadcast, 10/3/2010.

Monday clicked the mouse. The hooded man pointed to the camera and started speaking in the bombastic cadence of a tinpot dictator.

"Citizens of Louisiana, hear the VECTOR Manifesto! We are no longer willing to sit by and watch the Gulf's most vulnerable ecosystems suffer wanton despoilment at the hands of money-grubbing politicians and their corporate masters. The time for entrusting these natural treasures to the so-called protection of toothless legal threats at state and federal levels is over. The time for war is now!"

The hooded man shook a knuckled fist to drive home his words.

"See where this is going?" Monday murmured.

"Tree huggers gone wild?"

The hooded man paused, switching his gaze to another cue

card outside the frame.

"We vow swift, merciless retaliation against the governor and members of the legislature who voted for state measure 2197-A, as well as two private firms whose ready cash pushed the deal through. The wetlands south of Beaux Bridge will *not* be ripped asunder to make room for another mixed-use eyesore intended to reap maximum profit by forcing grotesque levels of human encroachment onto precious land. VECTOR will not allow this to happen! Our proactive assault will not be delivered with guns or explosives, but by targeted deployment of natural lifeforms serving as transmitters of deadly pathogens."

"Otherwise known as vectors," Monday said, pausing the video. "Bugs, rats, anything that carries disease."

In response to Rusty's raised brow she added, "I looked it up."

She started the video again.

"Serving on the front lines of Mother Nature's army," the hooded man continued after another cue card switch, "are mosquitos genetically engineered to spread West Nile Virus. We will unleash these and other vectors across an array of strategic locales to wreak widespread havoc on the agents of venality. Nature is indeed red in tooth and claw. The people of this state, and the world, will soon learn that to their horror. VECTOR has spoken!"

The hooded man brought both his elbows together by his navel, forming a V with his forearms. On the back of his right hand was a tattoo of the flag's insignia: green snake wrapped around the same capital letter.

The screen cut to black.

"That's all?" Rusty said after a pause. "I was just getting into it."

"It's the only video I could find. Apparently there were more back in 2010. All broadcast on a public access station out of Shreveport."

"I did a little Googling," she continued, sitting up. "Seems these nuts earned a low-priority slot on the FBI's watch list for domestic terrorist cells."

"FBI?" Rusty replied. "Surprised they got taken so seriously. That wasn't exactly a high-end production. Looks like it was shot in someone's basement."

"Indeed," Monday replied, giving his back a playful scratch. "But not just any basement. And that's where our Professor fits in."

She clicked on a bookmarked page from the *Gambit's* website.

"The follow-up article, remember? This is where it gets juicy."

Rusty rose from the bed and sat in the chair by the window to listen as she read aloud.

"'More than one source in Tulane's administrative department has confirmed that Anne Guillory did not step down by choice. Rather, she was forced to leave so that the University might be spared the scandal sure to boil over when her ties to a radical eco-terrorist group came to light.'"

"Ah," Rusty said. "It all becomes clear."

"'By early 2011,' Monday continued, "'rumors were spreading in the Entomology department that Guillory had moved beyond advocating extreme conservationist tactics in the classroom, and was actively funding criminal activity. Whispers of a small but devoted cell operating under her largesse became the stuff of widespread speculation. The end came in April 2011, when Tulane's Board of Regents learned she'd made university facilities available to members of VECTOR, including the Level 3 Biosafety Lab. She was gone within forty-eight hours of that news hitting the Dean's desk.'"

Monday looked up from the screen.

"OK," Rusty said, "let's start with the fact Professor Guillory's some kind of nut with violent friends. That makes it more plausible she might have ties with a guy like Abellard, agreed?"

Monday nodded.

"I'll admit," he added, "I can't see exactly where the connection goes from there."

"Let's not assume his connection to her has anything to do with these VECTOR freaks. The fact that Guillory is tight with that element might explain why he sounded so obsequious on the phone with her."

Rusty raised another brow. "Obsequious?"

"It means kissing her ass. One of my favorite words."

"Got it, and I agree. No way Abellard's scared of Guillory herself, but if she's backed by a bunch of psycho tree huggers—"

"Who probably aren't afraid to use any methods to get what they want," Monday broke in. "Including the abduction and ransom of certain people we might know."

Rusty rose from the chair and started pacing the hardwood floor. Monday watched him, noticing the tautness that seeped into his entire body. She could sense something building within, a steel spring coiling tighter.

"What's going on in there?" she asked. "You look a little scary all of a sudden."

Rusty stopped pacing and stared out the window for so long that Monday started to wonder if he'd heard. He reached for his jacket and grabbed the keys to the Navigator.

"Let's go. He should be getting home soon."

• • •

Prosper Lavalle dozed in a tufted wingback chair, his favorite piece of furniture in the shotgun house on Felicity Street. He found himself occupying the chair more and more often in recent days. Its position in a sunny corner of the front room made for an ideal napping spot.

Prosper had never been much of a napper in his seventy-plus years. He preferred to wake at dawn and spend a few hours listening to his collection of vintage jazz records before leaving to catch the streetcar so he could open the Mystic Arts Emporium promptly at nine o'clock. He rarely got home before sundown—much later on weekend nights—spending the entire day on his feet and seldom feeling fatigued.

That long-held pattern had started to change recently. He'd close the shop early so he could come home and drowse in his chair for a spell before rising to make dinner for one.

Prior to last week, Prosper had chalked up this variance of his schedule to the limitations of advanced age. But ever since Marceline had disappeared, each day without her return growing more intolerable than the last, he'd found a new reason to nap through the afternoons. Sleep was his only refuge from the constant worry that gnawed at him like a cancer in his bones.

He didn't trust anyone to mind the shop other than himself. His part-time sales clerk was competent, but didn't possess the slightest interest in magic. Prosper had no one to share his storehouse of knowledge with in the waning years of his life. He didn't even *want* someone like that. He'd already had the most accomplished student any mentor could hope to find, years ago.

He was dreaming about Rusty Diamond this afternoon when a soft tapping brought him awake. Lifting his head, he made out a tall shape through the lace curtains by the front door.

The tapping grew louder. A cold stab of panic hit him.

It was a policeman. He knew it. Probably that detective, come to tell him they'd found Marceline. Or what was left of her. No chance it was Marcie herself standing out on the stoop. She had her own key and would let herself in rather than knock.

Prosper rose with an unbalancing sense of dread. He shuffled over to the door.

"Who's there?"

"It's Rusty. Let me in, we need to talk."

"Did you find her, Rusty? Tell me right now before I open this door!"

"No. I haven't found her yet. But I've got an idea where she is."

The old man unlatched the door and opened it an inch, leaving on the chain.

"I would've called," Rusty said, "but this is a conversation we need to have in person."

Prosper gave a cool glance at the woman standing next to him. He saw only a mass of dark red hair and a neck tattoo, and formed the uncharitable assumption she was some Bourbon Street pickup Rusty had inexplicably chosen to bring here.

Then a sense of recognition set in.

"I know you."

"This is Monday Reed. She works with Marceline at Bon Coeur."

"Yes," Prosper nodded slowly. "You and Marcie take lunch together."

"That's right, sir. I saw you last week, when you brought over those flyers."

"Did they do any good?"

"I honestly don't know," Monday answered. "I handed them out to the other nurses, tacked up a bunch around my neighborhood. Has anyone called you?"

The old man shook his head.

"You haven't learned anything?" he asked, looking hard at Rusty.

"Actually we have. We just haven't found her yet."

"Shouldn't have expected no better," Prosper whispered. "I didn't expect no better."

"We need your help," Rusty said, risking his nose by pressing it up close to the door's gap. "Can we come in, please?"

Prosper glanced down at his napping chair, knowing it would offer no further sanctuary this day.

He unlatched the chain and opened the door.

Twenty minutes later, the three of them were seated in the shotgun's front room. Rusty and Monday occupied a two-seater brocade couch while Prosper sat in his chair.

Hands on his chest, fingers steepled, he listened as Rusty gave an overview of what happened in Vacherie and everything he and Monday had learned since. His large brown eyes flared every time Abellard's name was mentioned, small utterances of contempt forming on his lips.

When Rusty described his escape from Barataria Bay, making brief reference to the stage breathing techniques he'd used to survive, the older magician leaned forward. Hands on his knees, his interest was clearly piqued. Rusty noticed the change in posture, and felt a small thrill despite himself. For the student to see his mentor enraptured by an account of how hard-earned skills were brought to bear in a life-or-death situation…it felt like a miniscule victory of sorts.

"I knew it," Proper muttered. "That sonofabitch wasn't gonna let her go. Why wouldn't she listen to me?"

"I tried to warn her too," Monday said. "She didn't want to hear it. She said there was something good about him I just couldn't see."

Prosper gave a weary sigh, not finding Monday's comment particularly useful.

"You told all this to that detective Hubbard?" he asked.

Rusty nodded.

"We went straight to the Sixth Precinct from Roque's office. He knows everything you do."

"So they gonna arrest the sonofabitch, yes? Go at him with a phone book till he confesses what he's done with her, is that right?"

"Things don't work that way anymore," Monday said. "Unfortunately."

She and Rusty traded a glance. On the drive over here from her place they'd debated how to describe Hubbard's reaction to their story. It was considerably less impactful than they'd hoped for when walking into the precinct two hours before.

"Hubbard's more interested in this guy Sherman," Rusty said. "He's the prime suspect for killing the doctor. Hubbard thinks he might've also pulled another homicide, some woman down in the Quarter. Similar weapon and m.o."

"I heard about that," Prosper said. "What's it got to do with my daughter?"

Rusty almost described his visit to the Forensics Center but stopped himself, instead saying:

"As far as the NOPD is concerned, nothing. Sherman's the suspect in two murders that are getting a lot of press. He's the priority. Hubbard's still not convinced anything bad has happened to Marceline. He thinks any connection between her disappearing and Sherman being fired from the ward is circumstantial at best."

"And what about Abellard being dragged away from there?" Prosper cried. "You told him that part too, right?"

"Hubbard says that could've been a personal dispute. Since the hospital didn't see fit to report either event to the cops, he's not impressed."

In response to the look on Prosper's face, Monday added, "I know, it's infuriating."

Rusty leaned forward and risked placing a hand on the elderly man's knee.

"I'm not willing to wait around for the cops to take this seriously. I told you I wouldn't leave New Orleans till she's home safe, and I meant it."

Prosper receded back into his chair, grumbling unhappily. His eyelids sank to a near-closed position.

"Is he still awake?" Monday whispered after a protracted silence.

"I'm awake, girl."

His eyes opened, and Rusty felt the full power of his gaze as he hadn't in many years.

"Tell me something. If I ask you a question, can I believe the answer you give me?"

"Of course," Rusty replied, feeling a wary tautness in his chest. "Whatever you want to know."

"Last time I saw you in Vegas, you were riding high. Twelve shows a week, selling 'em out. But you'd changed. Success, if you can call it that, brought out the very worst in you."

"Fair enough. So you and Marcie ditched me. I woke up one morning and you were gone. Not even a note."

"Made no sense for us to stay. We felt like we'd already lost you. You weren't Rusty Diamond anymore. You'd become the Raven. Just a silly stage name, but you started thinking it was real. We didn't want no part of that."

Rusty noticed Monday had withdrawn slightly from his side.

"What do you want to ask me?"

"After we came back home, we put you out of our minds. At least I did. Every so often I'd hear your name, from a street performer or someone in the Emporium. Then…"

Prosper pressed his hands together and pulled them apart with the theatrical flourish Rusty had seen many times before.

"You disappear, like smoke. Nobody knows where. Hottest magician to hit Vegas in years up and vanishes. It was a big story, for a while. Over time, people forgot about you. I think we all assumed the story had some sad, sordid end. Some figured you for dead, including me. But here you are, alive and well."

Prosper leaned forward, hands planted on his thighs.

"Tell me, son. What happened out in that desert?"

The tension inside Rusty had tightened to a balled fist, constricting his breath. He felt on the verge of something he'd avoided for the past two and a half years.

"I killed someone."

Silence greeted those words. It filled the room.

"Or maybe not. I really don't know. I *do* know I hurt someone, badly. There was no time to stick around and see just how badly. It was either run or die. I ran."

Prosper and Monday remained mute. Rusty stood, facing them.

"Paul Ponti," he said to Prosper. "Name mean anything to you?"

"Some gangster, right?"

"There aren't any gangsters in Vegas anymore, not like the old days. But close enough. Ponti's what they call an operator. Parking garages, escort services, disposable cell phones, and probably some flat-out illegal shit. Not someone to cross."

"Sounds like he'd get along great with Abellard," Monday whispered.

"It started out simple. An invitation to a party. Ponti's daughter was having her sweet sixteen. Big bash at his house in the hills north of town.

"Remember Rocco?" Rusty asked Prosper, not waiting for an answer. "Door guy at the Etruscan Room? He delivered the invitation. Mr. Ponti would be honored if I'd agree to a private performance. No fee mentioned, but I was made to understand it would be generous. I was also made to understand saying no wasn't an option. When a guy like that extends an invitation, you accept gracefully.

"So I drive out there. Jesus, you wouldn't believe this place.

On a bluff outside the city limits. Best view of the Strip I ever saw. The party's underway, a good hundred people or more. Big tent out back by an Olympic-sized pool. Two bands. Bubblegum pop for the kids, jazz for the grownups. I was nervous as fuck. I always got nervous before performing. That's something not even you knew, did you, Prosper?"

The old man tapped his foot on the rug, impatient to hear the story.

"I managed my nerves with frequent trips to the bathroom to snort some excellent cocaine. Place had a gold fucking toilet. After about eight bumps and as many glasses of champagne, I'm way too loaded. But the crowd scares me so I just keep doing more. Felt like I was trapped in a scene from *Goodfellas* except everyone had better manners."

"What about the host?" Monday asked. "What was he like?"

"Barely shook his hand. I got a very clear feeling it wasn't his idea to hire me. There he is in his Armani, shaking hands with some dude all inked up in Goth regalia. If it wasn't his daughter's birthday, he probably would've had me hauled off in a dumpster.

"All of a sudden, it's time to perform. I'm standing by the tent. There's a spotlight rigged on the roof, blinding me. Whole party is crowded around to see the show. I can't see them, just outlines in the glare. I'm sweating hard, and not just from the coke.

"I start out with some small stuff. Throwing cards. A minor pyro stunt with a handkerchief and some flash paper. Very safe, very stale. I can tell the audience is unimpressed. Getting bored in a way that feels hostile. Somebody shouts at me, why don't I do a trick with the guest of honor? Christ, the most obvious thing in the world, but somehow it hadn't occurred to me. So I call her out into the spotlight. Pauline, named after her daddy. Pretty girl, a little on the heavy side. She's shy, doesn't want to come, but everyone starts chanting her name and she finally gives in."

Rusty stopped talking, keeping his silence for so long he wasn't sure he knew how to start again.

"I…can't say why I chose the trick. Maybe it was that hostility I was feeling. Maybe I wanted to show Ponti exactly who I was, what I was capable of. Shit, maybe I was just stoned. I take the girl by the hand and ask her if she could help me with a brand-new trick I'd just devised. Never done it on stage before, I said, which was true. I'd only practiced it a few times and damn sure didn't have it down cold."

"What was the trick?" Prosper asked, his mien darkening.

"Something I came up with after you and Marcie skipped town. I was in a pretty unhinged frame of mind at the time. A variation of Kronstein's Deathtrap, only this one involved neodymium magnets and gunpowder."

"For God's sake," the older magician uttered, barely more than a whisper. Rusty saw the recrimination in his eyes, and the profound disappointment.

"It went wrong," he said, speaking faster to get it all out. "My fingers were numb from the coke, too much sweat on my palms. I lost control as I was handing her a magnet for the big reveal. The powder ignited. Not a big bang, just a tailpipe backfiring. Smoke everywhere. I never heard the scream, not the first one. The smoke cleared fast, there was an empty space in front of me where she'd been standing. I look down, she's on the concrete near the lip of the pool. Hands covering her face. I could see blood seeping through her fingers."

"Jesus Christ," Monday said quietly.

"Things went completely crazy. People charging in, grabbing me. There were screams, someone hit me and cracked a rib. I can't say how I got out of that house alive. I have no memory of driving back to Vegas. Soon as I got to my suite, I really started bingeing on the coke. Just to make it go away. I didn't sober up till late the next night. I knew it was over. Everything I had in Vegas, gone. I was a dead man if I stayed. Prison was the least scary option, and the least likely. Ponti would get to me first. So I grabbed a few things, emptied out the safe. Got in my car and started driving east. No destination in mind.

"While I was living on the road, I tried to find out what happened. There was nothing in the news. Ponti probably decided the public didn't need to know about it. I saw my own name in a few headlines. 'What happened to Rusty Diamond? Vegas performer disappears halfway through 18-month engagement at Caesars. Casino managers scrambling to find a replacement.' Et cetera. After three months of living in motels, I ended up back in Ocean Pines. I've been there ever since."

He stopped talking, spent and revolted by the tale. Monday and Prosper remained silent. Rusty glanced from one to the other, failing to meet their eyes. He had a feeling neither would ever look at him in quite the same way again.

Without glancing up, Prosper asked, "Did the girl recover?"

"I don't know."

"How can you not know?!" Prosper almost shouted.

Stepping over to the chair where he sat, Rusty kneeled.

"Judge me all you want, old man. I deserve your scorn, and worse. Write me off, never speak to me again. But right now we have to think of Marceline. I think I know where she is. How to find her, and get her back. And I need your help."

26.

Anne Guillory's leggy frame reclined along a blue velvet sofa in the conservatory. Feet on a pillow, she faced north, gazing out at the rear grounds as a curtain of peach-orange sunlight streamed in over her left shoulder.

The conservatory was quiet, except for a soft purr from the humidifier. Kept at precisely 82.5 degrees, an ideal temperature for the many plant and animal lifeforms amassed within, the humidifier puffed out tiny clouds of vapor that dissipated before they left any trace of condensation on the panes.

All fifteen birdcages were covered with sheets, which explained the silence. If undraped, the cages would rattle and shriek with conjoined bedlam. Guillory often enjoyed sitting in here alone, listening to the crazed orchestra of birdcalls. If she closed her eyes, she could envision herself someplace far from central Louisiana and all its disappointments. She might be in Peru, or Ecuador, or some uncharted tropical region where one's missteps vanished into the overgrowth and were never thought of again.

This afternoon, however, she didn't want the birds to carry her off to any imaginary refuge. She needed to be alert, focused on her immediate problems and their most economical solutions.

"Lower," Anne Guillory said, closing her eyes as she issued the command.

Pierre Montord did as he was told. He dropped his fingertips an inch, finding exactly the spot below her third cervical vertebra that most needed his attention. He'd been massaging her neck and shoulders for the past hour. The task didn't bore him. Each small murmur of satisfaction stoked his desire by incremental degrees. He'd stand here, responding to her directions and honing in on tender areas, until she was ready to move things to the master bedroom upstairs. At least that's how their arrangement normally progressed. But nothing about today was normal, and Pierre couldn't quite envision how it might end.

"It's final?" he asked quietly. "You're absolutely sure this is how to proceed?"

Guillory didn't answer him. She had no desire to speak at the moment, or to be spoken to. Pierre's most valuable qualities seldom intersected with the needs of her mind, and right now her mind needed only to process data uninterrupted. She required his hands, not his mouth.

They were impressive hands, if oddly delicate on such a solidly built man. His nails were manicured to glossy perfection, at Guillory's insistence. The hairless skin stretching from his knuckles to the wrist of his right hand contained a splotchy reddened patch indicative of ink removal. The tattoo once there had depicted a snake coiled around the letter V.

The tattoo was more to Pierre's liking than the nail gloss, but he gladly made some allowances for the privilege of serving Anne Guillory in a range of vital functions. Left to his own devices, Pierre would gnaw his nails down to the cuticle, unconsciously mimicking the self-grooming habits of the Louisiana muskrat, one of his favorite members of the Cricetidae family of rodents indigenous to the state.

If only things had gone differently. If VECTOR had been granted adequate time to flourish with proper funding and personnel, they most certainly would have employed the muskrat as one of many warriors in a righteous campaign against the despoilers of the Gulf's most vulnerable wetlands.

It wasn't to be. Hell, they never even got close to launching an opening salvo. But that was all ancient history by now. With a little luck, and smart application of the money accumulated from their arrangement with Abellard, VECTOR might one day rise again.

"I asked you a question. Are you quite sure—"

"Please shut up and go back to that spot you were working on before. No, to the left. That's it."

A vintage Bakelite phone on the bamboo coffee table rang. Guillory rotated on the sofa to glance up at Pierre.

"Why don't I check caller ID in the great room?" he asked.

"Just pick it up."

Pierre did as he was told.

"Hello? Yes, Mr. Abellard. I believe she's available. Hold the line."

Covering the mouthpiece, he whispered, "What exactly are you going to tell him?"

Guillory grabbed the receiver and nodded for Pierre to resume his handiwork on her tendons.

"Hello, Joseph."

"We're on," Abellard answered gruffly, not bothering with any preliminaries.

"I'll be frank. You've caught me off guard. That's not what I was expecting to hear."

"Told you I make good on my deals."

"I'm not sure I want to know just how this delivery was obtained, Joseph. In light of some recent newsworthy events."

"If you're worried that incompetent piece of shit Sherman's involved, you can scratch that. Motherfucker hasn't shown his face for two days. No answer on his phone neither. He's on the run."

"My. Such an unexpected breach of protocol must prove worrisome."

"No, I ain't worried. I'll find him, and he'll have plenty to answer for when I do."

Anne Guillory held the phone in place for a moment, savoring the crack of two fused vertebrae as Pierre pressed on just the right spot with his thumbs. A real talent of his, finding the right sensitive spot. On top of which, he was a fairly accomplished chef who was willing to do all manner of housework. He earned his keep. That was why she'd kept him around all this time, despite the tremendous deficit to her professional reputation their liaison had cost her.

"I'll spare you some pointless legwork, Joseph. You won't need to look for Mr. Sherman. I can tell you exactly where he is at this moment. More to the point, I can promise you he's beyond the reach of incarceration. So if you've been sprouting gray hairs over what he might divulge under the pressure of a police inquiry, you can relax."

She waited as Abellard let a moment pass before replying. Guillory had the impression the time was spent attempting to erase any note of surprise from his voice.

"I'm sure you'll be more specific," he said, "so I know what the fuck you're talking about."

"He's safely out of the way, and fulfilling a purpose beyond any I imagine he ever dreamed himself worthy."

Guillory's breath caught as Pierre bore down fiendishly on a sensitive nerve. She shot him an admonishing glance saying: *That's too hard and you know it.* He responded with a winsome grin saying: *No it isn't, and you know it.*

"Sherman's not a problem," she said sharply into the phone, cutting off a string of full-throated protestations from Abellard. "You can take my word for that, or see for yourself. But if you can regain a measure of calm, there's something more important I have to tell you."

Pierre's hands slowly stopped moving as he listened to one side of the brief, tense conversation that followed. He heard Anne Guillory tell Joseph Abellard that the Lavalle woman was safely interred right here on the property, as she had been for almost a week. This wasn't new information. The professor had divulged as much in a similar conversation less than twenty-four hours ago. Now she added a new bit of intel, casually informing Joseph Abellard that the man who executed the abduction was none other than his own wayward employee Claude Sherman.

Immediately after this revelation was aired, Guillory had to yank the receiver away to spare her ear the volcanic barrage of obscenities that followed. From his position behind her, Pierre could hear each word as if it was being shouted inches from his face.

"Joseph," Guillory tried to interject. "Joseph! Calm down. I told you she's been treated perfectly well. If anything, she may end up missing the level of comfort she's been afforded here."

A silence followed. Pierre could no longer hear any emanations of wrath coming through the phone.

"Let's pare things down to their most vital components. You deliver what's owed to me and I release her into your care. We sever our arrangement and don't cross paths from that point onward. Agreed?"

Abellard grumbled some more in reply. Guillory covered the receiver and glanced up at Pierre with an amused glint in her eye.

"Can you hear him panting? Like a Bull Mastiff in heat."

Pierre didn't share her mirth, shaking his head with disapproval.

"I told you this wasn't a good approach," he said. "If you could occasionally listen to—"

Guillory raised a silencing hand.

"Could you repeat that, Joseph?"

"Tonight, goddamnit!" Abellard roared, loud enough for Pierre to hear plainly. "Have her ready for me. And tell that fuckin' pretty boy not to try anything that makes this go another way."

The line went dead. Guillory handed the phone back and briskly stood, no longer interested in a neck massage.

"Appraise me of the girl's condition."

"Looks fine," Pierre said with a shrug. "She's given up on her little hunger strike."

"That wasn't destined to last long, was it? Go out and make sure she's presentable. I don't have to tell you to employ the usual precautions."

"Why'd you tell him Sherman was the one who grabbed her?"

"Two reasons. He's clearly distracted by wondering where Mr. Sherman is at the moment, and I want him focused on more pertinent matters."

"What's the other reason?"

Guillory looked at Pierre with a kind of disappointment

he'd seen in her face before. It reminded him of his days as her student at Tulane, when she'd had to explain an academic point he should have figured out on his own.

"Think, darling. When I told Joseph the truth about Miss Lavalle's predicament yesterday, who do you think he assumed performed the abduction?"

"I don't care if he thinks I did it."

"I care, given the chances of him looking to settle that score. I thought it best to remove you from the line of fire, but don't thank me now. I'm sure you'll find some creative way of doing so later, when this tiresome episode is behind us."

With that, she turned and walked out of the conservatory, her stockinged feet padding silently across the planks.

"Does he really think we're letting her go?" Pierre asked as she stepped into the main house.

He got no answer from Anne Guillory.

27.

Joseph Abellard tried to calm himself after getting off the phone. The walls of his cramped office at the Carnival felt tighter than ever before. Either that or the suppressed wrath boiling within him had stretched his corporeal frame to new dimensions. He was working very hard not to physically wreck the office.

Viewed in sum, the call went about as intended. He'd expressed the primary message clearly enough. An exchange was going down tonight, one which would erase all outstanding debts and conclude his business dealings with Guillory. Abellard would deliver a new batch of viable embryonic stem cells, one he'd personally procured in Shreveport this very morning.

Locating an alternate source of the material had been a challenge. He'd resorted to pouring through copious bookmaking ledgers to find a client in the family planning profession. There was only one candidate, a degenerate gambler with his own clinic who'd lost over twenty grand last year on ill-advised college basketball wagering. Abellard called the man, said he'd wipe the slate in return for a favor. He didn't mention specifics over the phone, just made the drive to Shreveport at sunrise.

Dr. Sidney Golden responded with shocked outrage to the proposed favor, but some physical intimidation proved sufficient to induce his cooperation. Several hours later, the quaking abortionist met Abellard in the clinic's parking lot, handed him a cooler the size of a shoe box, and swore to never place another bet as long as he lived.

That cooler now sat in the back of Abellard's Escalade, which Antoine should be bringing around any minute. Abellard would most definitely check to make sure everything was in order before leaving. He'd also be checking to confirm a snub-nosed .38 was hidden in the rear console, where he'd instructed Antoine to stash it with six rounds in the chamber.

Thus armed, he'd be prepared for whatever happened at Guillory's house. And no matter what did happen, he'd be bringing his woman back home.

All good enough. But Abellard was still reeling from the one revelation he almost couldn't believe had escaped him until a few moments ago, which Professor Bitch had disclosed with a smile he could almost see over the phone.

Fucking Claude Sherman. Abellard's dirty job specialist. A traitor in his own house.

Ever since Guillory dropped the bomb twenty-four hours ago, revealing that Marceline had been under her watch all this time, Abellard figured it was that manicured freak Pierre who'd pulled the snatch. Made sense. He was a big, rangy bastard who seemed plenty capable of handling his business, despite the glossed veneer that made him look half a fruit. And Pierre's connections to that weird eco-terrorist shit, about which Abellard knew little and didn't care to learn more, probably gave him all kinds of deviant inclinations.

But no. Today Guillory nonchalantly said Pierre wasn't the abductor. It was Sherman, a man on Abellard's own goddamn payroll. The same motherfucker who'd continued to work in his employ the past week like nothing happened.

Sick, deceitful back-stabber. Stealing a pregnant woman from her bed as she slept. *His* woman—and yes, that's what Marceline Lavalle was and would remain, regardless of any temporary falling out—held captive in conditions Abellard couldn't even begin to conceive, despite Guillory's velvety assurances of safety and comfort. Quite possibly rendered docile by drugs, all the while carrying his child in her belly.

Abellard could no longer claim he knew what he was getting into by agreeing to broker illicit human tissue for Anne Guillory. When presented with the scheme after making her acquaintance at some stuck-up charity bash at Tulane, he'd seen it as just another chance to wet his beak. No different in principle from the escorts he ran in the Quarter, the heavily stepped-on coke his boys slung all over the Lower Ninth, or the rigged games he used to soak compulsive gamblers right here in the Carnival.

A knock at the door pulled him from his incensed reverie.

"Come in!"

The door opened and Antoine's bulbous head appeared through the gap.

"All gassed up, boss."

"What about the console? Am I gonna find what I'm looking for in there? Don't make me come back once I'm out the door."

"It's cool. Everything like you said."

Abellard mulled the reliability of Antoine's pledge, then nodded.

"Alright. I'll be leaving before the hour's up. Till then, no interruptions. Any little kind of mess, deal with it yourself."

"You know we'll handle business." Antoine paused before asking, "Sure you don't want backup, or at least a driver?"

"What did I say, motherfucker? Get your fat ass on that floor!"

Antoine grunted in affirmation and closed the door, leaving Joseph Abellard with his rage and his plans for putting things right.

• • •

As he stepped out of the casino's back office, still smarting from the rebuke about his weight, Antoine could only shake his head. Abellard had never been a particularly easy man to work for. Rarely more than two or three days passed without someone getting royally chewed out. It was part and parcel of working at the Carnival.

But things were different now. Something was eating the boss up inside, and it was making everyone's life miserable.

Antoine crossed the casino floor to resume his post by the metal detector. As he passed the blackjack area, he gave a nod to

Charles, the wispy-moustached dealer. Charles was scooping up the deck after winning a hand off the three players at his table.

The CAT Diesel man filled out his usual spot on third base. On his right was a skeletal woman who studied her cards as if they contained some hieroglyphic message for her rheumy eyes alone. At first base sat an elderly gent whose salt & pepper beard looked to be comprised of cracker crumbs as much as hair, nattering soft curses every time he lost a hand.

Charles had already cheated this trio out of a c-note collectively, but failed to savor any sense of accomplishment. How difficult was it to steal from wasted losers like these? He yearned for a chance to test his skills on a more seasoned crop of gamblers, but that type seldom frequented the Carnival.

Charles heard an angry grumble as he dealt from a freshly doctored deck. The bearded oldster on first base pointed a gnarled finger his way.

"I saw that, boy."

Charles kept dealing, finishing with an upcard to himself. It was an Ace.

"Anyone want insurance?" he asked, ignoring the old man's quaking finger.

"I said I saw what you did."

"No insurance?" Charles pressed on, scanning the table. The woman and Mr. CAT Diesel both shook their heads.

"Damnit!" the old main shouted, throwing his cards away. "I don't expect much from a shithole like this, but I ain't gonna sit here and be cheated!"

"Take it easy, pops," CAT Diesel mumbled.

"Like hell I will," the old man railed. "You think I never seen bottom-dealing before?"

Charles felt his cheeks flush and lifted a casual hand to get Antoine's attention. Best to extinguish this situation as quickly as possible.

"Don't tell me *you* didn't see it?" the oldster demanded of the woman on his left. She gave a noncommittal half-shrug and developed a serious interest in her gin and tonic.

"Why don't you take a break, sir?" Charles said nervously.

"Come back another time, have better luck."

"I ain't leaving till I get a refund!" the gambler yelled, slamming a liver-spotted fist on the table.

A group of slots players had pivoted around on their stools, drawn by the noise. Sensing he had an audience, the old man raised his voice even louder so that it cut through a Buddy Bolden track on the juke.

"Place is nothing but a goddamn clip joint," he shouted, waving to the slots players. "Watered down drinks, tight slots, hell, that's par for the course. But a cheating dealer is too goddamn much!"

Charles was starting to panic, but relaxed when he saw Antoine rise from his stool. About time the fatass started doing his job. With any luck, this ancient cracker would be hustled out the back before Mr. Abellard got wind of the disturbance.

"We got a problem here?" Antoine said.

"Damn right we do," the gambler replied.

"Gentleman's had too much to drink," Charles offered. "Cards haven't being going his way."

"That's because you're dealing 'em crooked, you little bastard!"

Antoine had heard enough. He felt certain a racial epithet was begging to spring from the old man's spittle-flecked lips, an eventuality sure to cause more trouble than anyone wanted.

"Come on," he said, laying a persuasive hand on the man's shoulder. "Let's step out the back way, nice and easy. Nobody's making a fuss here."

The oldster cast a last pleading look at his two fellow gamblers, searching for some sign of solidarity. Both were ignoring him, which appeared to deflate his ire. The moment had passed. Nodding like he'd expected no better, he pushed himself away from the table and allowed Antoine to steer him toward the rear exit.

"Don't seem right," he muttered quietly.

"Everybody gets their ass handed to 'em sometimes," the security guard mumbled in commiseration as they stepped off the casino floor and turned into the rear hallway. "Shake it off and win it back another day."

Antoine never saw the kick launched at his left kneecap. It struck dead-center, hard enough to open a hairline fracture in the bone. A much harder blow than he would have imagined possible from such a feeble attacker. He didn't even feel the pain immediately. What he felt was gravity yanking him down hard as his leg buckled from the kick's precisely aimed impact. He landed flat on his face, tasting carpet.

A knee dug into his back with enough force to rob him of his breath. Then the tip of something very sharp nudged up against his jugular vein.

"Feel that, big man?" Rusty said through the tangled fibers of the false beard. "I'll split you like a can opener if you don't do exactly what I say. Got it?"

"Fuck you," Antoine growled. He still didn't know what was going on. The voice sounded somehow familiar, but more confounding was how the old bastard had felled him with one crippling kick. The numbness in his knee was rapidly oozing into a febrile throb.

"Think twice, Antoine. You'll bleed out before the boss even gets a whiff there's something wrong."

A jab of the razor-like tip verified that threat. Antoine nodded in assent.

Rusty gripped the Marrow Seeker's handle tightly, careful not to press too hard. He knew perfectly well what kind of damage the deceptively sharp wooden blade could do. He wanted to incapacitate Antoine, but not lethally.

"Listen real close," he said, spitting away some hairs from the beard. The damn thing had irritated his skin since Prosper applied it along with the prosthetics hours earlier, using an excess of spirit gum in Rusty's opinion.

"You're taking me to Abellard's office," he continued. "Knock three times like I saw you do before."

"He ain't here."

"Better hope that's bullshit," Rusty said, making a downward slash with the blade that ripped open the collar of Antoine's shirt and took away some skin in the process. The security guard yelped like a kicked puppy.

"He's here, he's here!"

"Good news for you. Now what are we doing?"

"Knocking on the door three times."

"When he asks what you want, tell him there's a situation on the casino floor that demands his attention."

"He said not to be bothered for nothing."

"Then you'll have to convince him. Trust me, it's in your interest for him to open that door."

"Then what?"

"Step aside. Get in my way, you bleed. Are we clear?"

Another terse nod. Rusty retracted the blade but kept it within striking range.

"On your feet. Let's do this."

Antoine lumbered into an upright position and stepped forward. Rusty followed closely behind. He sensed a compression of energy as the security guard pondered making a quick move.

"Don't do anything stupid, Antoine. Your boss ain't worth opening a vein for. You know damn well he wouldn't do it for you."

The guard raised a fist and rapped on the door three times.

"Goddamnit!" Abellard's muffled voice came through the two-inch oak. "What the fuck did I say!"

"Tell him the Sheriff's here," Rusty nudged. "Investigating a complaint about that crooked blackjack dealer."

"This is important, boss. Man out here from the Sheriff's Office. Wants to talk to you, shoving around a piece of paper supposed to be a warrant."

Rusty nodded in approval.

No reply came. Five seconds passed, then ten.

"Prod him some more," Rusty hissed in Antoine's ear.

"What else am I supposed—"

The door opened, stopping his unfinished question. Joseph Abellard filled the frame, backlit by the office's bright lamps.

Rusty collapsed Antoine's left leg with a hammering kick to the back of the knee, the same one he'd targeted before. The security guard staggered forward, all his weight falling into Abellard. The half-second it took for the two men to right themselves gave Rusty time to press the Marrow Seeker against Abellard's neck. Pulling him to the floor in a wrestler's takedown, Rusty shouted at Antoine.

"Shut that door!"

Antoine's eyes flicked from his boss to Rusty and back. Abellard bucked against the weight pushing down on top of him, but the knife's advancing pressure persuaded him to stop.

"Shut the door or he dies!"

"Do it," Abellard said, nodding furiously. Antoine pushed the door closed.

"Good. Now back off into the corner. Sit on that safe. Hands on top of your head."

"You're dead, old man," Abellard mumbled. "Whoever the fuck you are, you're dead."

"Shut up," Rusty said, watching the guard do as he'd been told.

The moment Antoine lowered himself onto the metal safe, Rusty used his free hand to drive a fist into Abellard's mouth. A pair of prominent upper teeth tore through the shriveled, liver-spotted latex on Rusty's knuckles, digging into the skin beneath. It felt good.

"Come here to rob me, old man?" Abellard demanded, blood running from his split lip. He jerked his head toward the safe. "Think I'm opening that for your ass?"

"I'm not here for money, Joseph. You and I got some unfinished business."

Abellard froze, recognizing the voice without being able to place it. Rusty slammed another fist into his face, breaking the nose.

"Remember me now, asshole? You fucked up on the bay. Should've stuck around to make sure I never found the surface."

Abellard's breath came in ragged gulps as he pieced together what was happening. His eyes rotated around in their sockets, scanning the office for some sign of how to reverse this situation.

"Never walking out of here, motherfucker," he muttered without much conviction, still dazed.

"Shut up and listen. I told you yesterday why I'm here. Nothing's changed, except now you're gonna take me to her."

Rusty sensed movement in the corner of one eye. He whipped his head to the left in time to see Antoine clumsily lifting himself from the safe.

"You wanna see him die? I wouldn't blame you, but that's gonna leave you with a whole lot of questions to answer. Sit down, Antoine."

The security guard stood in place until Abellard yelled for him to be seated.

"Alright," Rusty said. "You and me are going for a drive, Joseph. We're taking that nice Escalade of yours."

He saw Abellard shake his head, regaining some composure. The casino boss appeared to recover quickly from the shock of being attacked by a man he thought was dead. Now he was obviously focusing on how to regain the advantage.

"I ain't going nowhere. Go ahead, shiv me. See how far you make it out of here."

"I got no interest in cutting you just yet. I need you alive, so you can take me to Guillory's place. Guillory has her, isn't that right?"

Those words brought a moment of silence, the only sound heard in the office a muted bassline from the jukebox thumping through one wall.

"There's no point lying now, Joseph."

"Man, I told you it's none of your damn—"

"Shut up. You're taking me to see Guillory, and I'll take it from there. You just better pray she hasn't been hurt. Where are the keys?"

"Go fuck yourself."

Rusty pressed harder on the Marrow Seeker's handle. The tip dug into the skin below Abellard's chin, drawing a pinprick of blood.

"The keys!"

"On the desk," Abellard said through gritted teeth.

"Toss them to me," Rusty ordered to Antoine. "Slowly."

Antoine stepped over to the desk. He picked up a heavy

key ring and gave it a heave. Rusty caught it with his free hand, slipping the keys into his jacket pocket.

"Is it parked out back?" Rusty asked him. Antoine nodded. "Back on the safe, big man."

The security guard again seated himself.

"OK, me and Joseph are stepping into the hall and walking to the right. Same way you fuckers carried me out yesterday. Sound the alarm or try to stop our progress in any way, he dies. Understand?"

"I hear you," Antoine replied.

"We good, Joseph?"

Abellard didn't move, then gave one terse nod of the head.

"Alright, up nice and easy."

Both men slowly rose from the floor. Rusty placed a hand on the back of Abellard's neck and turned him around toward the door.

"Step out and make for the exit. I'm right behind you."

Abellard opened the door and the casino's juke filled the room. Rusty nudged him and Abellard stepped into the hall, looking left to see if there was anyone whose assistance he could flag down.

"Other way," Rusty said, giving a jab to encourage forward movement. "Let's go."

He shot a final glance at Antoine, still perched on the safe. The security guard didn't move as Rusty and his hostage disappeared out of the office. The look on Antoine's face was one of ambivalent consternation, as if trying to calculate how long he should wait before sounding the alarm. And wondering if it was even worth trying to save his miserable boss at this point.

28.

The black Escalade rolled out of the Carnival's badly paved lot, sending up a small hailstorm of dust and gravel. Abellard fumed in the driver's seat, safety belt securely tightened at Rusty's insistence. Rusty occupied the passenger seat, leaving the belt off so his left hand could hold the knife within an inch of Abellard's neck.

Neither man said much as they passed over the Mississippi and turned eastbound on the I-10. Abellard merged into the fast lane and floored it. Rusty cautioned him to watch his speed, getting stoney silence in response.

"I hope you're not planning to do something stupid," Rusty said, "like driving in such a way that gets us pulled over. Maybe Antoine's already put the call out to some cop on your payroll and there's a patrol car looking for us right now. Word to the wise: anyone tries to flag us down, it's not gonna go well for you."

Abellard did not reply, just goosed the accelerator.

"Or maybe you're thinking about getting us in a wreck," Rusty continued. "You can forget that too. Even if the airbag keeps you safe, nothing will stop this blade from doing its work."

"You gonna talk the whole fuckin' way? You're getting what you want, so why not shut up?"

"Just making sure our position is clear. You're worth something to me as long as I think you'll take me to where she is. The minute I stop believing that, your life loses any value."

Rusty used his free hand to peel off his salt & pepper wig, then the beard. He hadn't disguised himself since performing in

Vegas, and he hadn't missed it much. The beard's rough, ticklish fibers had been driving him nuts since Prosper applied it in his kitchen at the house on Camp Street, pulling out a closet's worth of professional makeup and stagecraft devices. Monday had watched with rapt fascination, offering some helpful comments.

Itchy as the beard was, the liver-spotted latex nose bugged Rusty a hell of a lot more. He detached it from his face with a moist pop, enjoying his first unrestricted inhalation in hours. Then the latex applications covering his hands came off, one finger at a time like form-fitting gloves.

"Jesus Christ," Abellard sighed with a disgusted shake of the head. "Nothing but a dime store Halloween mask."

"Not even close, but nice try."

"Fatass lets you walk right in the door…"

"Don't be so hard on him. These are expert prosthetics, applied by a master. You wouldn't have made me either."

Abellard didn't reply. He flipped on the headlights as the sky descended into something deeper than twilight.

They'd driven another twenty miles on the interstate, retracing the route Rusty had taken from New Orleans, when the Escalade turned left onto State Highway 22.

"We're heading north?" Rusty asked.

"Livingston Parish, outside Maurepas."

"Are you sure you're taking me to Guillory?"

Abellard nodded.

"Her house or somewhere else?"

"House. I know the place."

"And that's where Marceline is?"

"If she ain't, she's somewhere close by. I'm getting her back tonight," the big man continued, voice steadily rising. "Already laid the groundwork to make that happen, it's all set."

"Guess I'm ruining your plans, huh?"

"Smirk all you want, motherfucker. I was doing this my way, and you're fucking it up!"

"You've had plenty of time to do it your way, Joseph. I'd say you've done a shit job so far. We'll do it my way from now on."

Rusty could practically see the gears of Abellard's mind at

work, seeking a way to alter the circumstances.

When he spoke again, his voice was quiet and devoid of the usual thuggish edge.

"I'm telling you, man. I care about that girl more than your dumb ass will ever understand. She don't want to be with me, that's her call. I'll still provide for her and the child, and she's free to do as she wants."

Rusty watched the play of approaching headlights across his face. Abellard's expression had softened with the same elasticity he'd noticed before. In place of rage and frustration was a hint of something like real remorse.

"She's not free now, is she? And that's your fault, Joseph."

Abellard opened his mouth to refute that statement, but the words didn't make it.

"At first I thought you'd snatched her, or worse. Jealous man, can't stand the idea of her walking out, especially with a kid on the way. But when I met you, I got a different impression. Didn't really want to believe it. I wanted to think you knew where she was. But that's not what my eyes told me. You were genuinely worried about her."

"Shit," Abellard muttered. "I told you as much."

"Thing is," Rusty continued, "I saw more than worry in your face. I saw guilt, and I knew you had something to do with it."

"You don't know jackshit."

"I can take a stab at it, since we've got some time on our hands. Claude Sherman tried to steal a goddamn umbilical cord from Bon Coeur. You got him that job, or pressured Dr. Roque to provide a reference. The same Dr. Roque who got diced up with one of his own surgical knives. My guess is you and this wacko professor are running some kind of medical scam. Selling biological material that's too scarce to come by or flat-out illegal. Roque was in on the scam but someone decided to ice him."

Abellard mumbled under his breath, but didn't say anything to contradict what he was hearing.

"I don't give a shit about that part," Rusty continued. "When Sherman got caught, Marcie connected him to you and threatened to talk, since the hospital brass was too chickenshit to report it. So you show up at the ward like the fucking hothead you are, and it gets ugly. The damage is done, and the risk is there as long as she's free to talk. Three days later, she vanishes. Only it wasn't you that grabbed her."

Abellard's hands tightened on the wheel like it was his passenger's trachea.

"I'm guessing it was Sherman who pulled the abduction. I walked in on him at her place a few nights ago. Maybe he was there to collect some evidence he'd left behind, I don't know. Anyway, I don't think he was acting on your orders. Guillory sent him there."

"Pieced that together yourself, huh?"

"I'm not saying I have it all right. All I know is Marceline got caught in the crosshairs of whatever's going down between you and Guillory. I'm bringing her home, and then I'm getting an assurance you'll never bother her again."

"Is that right?" Abellard said. Despite speaking calmly, Rusty could see the casino boss was inwardly going nuclear. "Just how you plan on getting an assurance like that?"

"Think about it, Joseph. I got to you once, I can do it again. And next time I'll have more than a goddamned wooden knife in my hand."

• • •

Night had fallen by the time the Escalade approached the end of Guillory's driveway. Rusty kept track of their course as far as Route 17 outside Maurepas but couldn't identify the two-lane road they'd been on for the past several minutes. As Abellard slowed to turn left, Rusty noted an elaborate mailbox with a mounted brass fleur-de-lis.

"We here?"

"Home of Professor Bitch," Abellard grunted. "Let me do the talking or we won't get so far as the door."

They traveled down the winding, wooded driveway and pulled to a stop in front of the iron gate. Abellard reached out to press the button on the callbox.

A crackle of static was followed by Pierre's voice.

"Is that you, Mr. Abellard? We've been expecting you for some time."

"It's me. Open the damn gate."

The gate swung inward with a clang. Abellard gassed through until the house's dark peaks came into view against a starry nightscape. The Escalade pulled all the way around the circular drive and came to a stop.

"I'll follow your lead until I don't," Rusty said quietly. "When I make my move, don't try to stop me."

Abellard looked Rusty in the eye for the first time since they'd left the casino.

"Put that fucking blade down and listen to how this is gonna go."

Rusty retracted the knife a few inches, still close enough for a quick slash.

"You got the drop on me, fine. You wanted to come out to where they been keeping her, you're here. But pay attention to what I say now. If you want this to go the right way, sit here and let me deal with it."

"Can't do that."

"Goddamnit, what do you think's gonna happen when I walk in there with some dude they never seen before?"

"Tell me. You know these people, I don't."

"It's a delicate situation, motherfucker. Not the kind of play where you want to throw a curve ball at the last minute. Understand what I'm saying?"

Rusty nudged the blade closer to Abellard's neck, drawing his eyes down for a fraction of a second. He used that tiny misdirection to pull a pair of plastic "Cobra" handcuffs from his jacket and snap one end on Abellard's right wrist. Less than another second was required to close the other cuff around the Escalade's steering wheel.

In the blink of an eye, the big man had been shackled to his vehicle.

"What the fuck?! Did you listen to a goddamn thing I said?"

Abellard bucked in the driver's seat and wrenched his arm

back, trying to free himself.

"Don't waste your energy. Cobra Cuffs aren't metal—I couldn't get them into the casino if they were—but that plastic's got a tensile strength of three hundred pounds. They used to stop a huge cinderblock from crushing me onstage, so I figure they'll keep you snug. Just calm yourself."

Abellard thrashed wildly in the seat, jerking his arm like a piston. If he couldn't snap the cuff he'd settle for ripping the wheel from its housing.

"Can't leave you like this, Joseph. Too much of an unknown variable."

Rusty took aim and jammed the Marrow Seeker's flat teak handle into the base of Abellard's neck. The big man bellowed and his body shook with a surprised spasm, but the blow appeared to have little effect. Rusty swung again, digging the handle's hard edge directly into the patch of skin covering the medulla oblongata.

Pretty much a guaranteed knockout spot, if properly struck. Rusty knew as much from painful personal experience. It took a third and fourth blow to yield the reaction he was looking for. Abellard's eyelids fluttered and his head drooped forward. Rusty gave him another for good measure. Then he pulled the keys from the ignition and got out.

He approached the house, passing a row of columns on the front portico. Monday answered his call on the first ring.

"Where are you? I've been going crazy."

"Inside the property line, at Guillory's. Got a handle on my coordinates?"

"Yup. This GPS app is the shit. Says you're about twenty miles northeast of a town called Maurepas, in Livingston Parish."

"Sounds right. We passed through Maurepas a while ago."

"Doesn't look like you're on a marked road," Monday said. Rusty pictured her biting her lower lip the way she did when intently focused. "Closest I can see is Route 17, a bit to the south."

"Yeah, we turned left off 17 onto an unmarked road. About five miles after the turn there's a private driveway leading to Guillory's place."

"That's where I'll be."

"You can't miss the entrance, there's a mailbox with a fancy brass flower on top. Pull around and park a little past it. The driveway's gated, you won't be able to get through. Which is fine. The property might be surveilled so let's lean toward caution."

"Got it."

"I'll text you as soon as I know she's here. Keep the engine warm, we may be coming out in a hurry."

"Copy that," Monday said, ending the call.

Rusty pocketed his phone and took a last buttressing breath. The front door opened just as he was about to raise the knocker.

"Where's Mr. Abellard?" Pierre said, his wide frame filling the doorway.

"Sleeping it off. I'll take it from here."

Pierre's eyes darted toward the Escalade. The door started to close. Rusty stopped it with his right foot, confident in the manufacture of his steel-toed boots.

"I'm the one you want to talk to. The deal's changed."

The pressure on his foot increased as Pierre pushed harder on the door.

Rusty held up his phone. A 504 area code number was visible on the dial pad, his thumb hovering over the Send button.

"See that? Direct dial to Detective Dan Hubbard with the New Orleans Police Department, Sixth District. He's waiting to hear from me. He'll reach the Livingston Parish cops with one call, if I tell him to. They take a fairly serious view on kidnapping, I'm told."

"What do you want?" Pierre demanded.

"I want to meet the vanishing entomologist."

29.

Pierre told him to wait in the great room, a wide rectangular space separated from the entrance by a dimly lit foyer. The great room was lushly furnished, with a baby grand piano framed by a set of French doors at the far end. It had seen many festive gatherings since the house's construction in 1849.

Rusty was the sole occupant now. He stood in a corner nearest to the foyer, trying not to bounce on the balls of his feet with pent-up adrenaline. Pierre had offered him a seat but he declined.

He heard floorboards creaking above his head and a brief murmur of conversation, the number of voices impossible to decipher. Waiting to see what happened next, Rusty sent Monday a text.

IN HOUSE. BE READY.

He saw a reply pop on the screen just as footsteps echoed down the main staircase.

ENGINE RUNNING. BE CAREFUL.

Rusty pocketed his phone as Pierre reentered the great room, followed by a woman of striking features and regal bearing.

"The last time this house had an uninvited guest," she said with a smile, "I was just a child. A vacationing couple from Maine broke down on Highway 22 outside Maurepas. My parents were hosting a crawfish broil and asked them to join us while they waited for a mechanic. I think it may have been the highlight of their trip, actually."

"Was Marceline Lavalle invited? I got the impression she was brought here kind of suddenly."

Guillory let the remark pass, taking a curious look at him.

"I suppose it's unnecessary to say you're not who I was expecting."

"Abellard's been detained. I'm here to close the deal."

"You have his proxy?"

"Hardly. I gave him two options, take me to where she's being held or bleed to death on the floor of his office. He made the sensible choice."

"Joseph, sensible? First time for everything, I suppose."

Guillory seated herself on a sofa near the French doors, passing by Rusty as if his presence in her home was of no greater concern than a fluttering moth. He took a few steps toward her but remained standing.

Pierre positioned himself off to one side, halfway between them. It felt to Rusty like a Mexican standoff performed with an absurd level of decorum by three participants who didn't all know what they were playing for.

"If you won't sit," Guillory said, "I won't bother Pierre with bringing in refreshments."

"I'm not gonna be here long."

"Maybe you'll stay long enough for me to correct a few erroneous impressions you seem to have formed."

Rusty didn't have a quick response to that. Whatever he'd been expecting, this wasn't it. He'd seen Anne Guillory's photo in the *Gambit*, taken on the day of her promotion to head of Tulane's Entomology department. The photo showed an attractive if somewhat stern woman with thick-framed glasses and dark hair pulled back tightly over her high forehead. Rusty had envisioned a kind of mousy asexuality totally unlike the study in elegant angularity and poise seated before him.

"Should I call you Professor? I've heard Abellard use that term, but I thought he was just needling you with it."

The irritation produced by that remark wrote itself across Guillory's face and quickly passed.

"Why don't you call me Anne. And if you give me your name, we'll be able to have a cordial discussion."

"You don't need my name. I'm the guy who might not turn

you in for felony kidnapping and false imprisonment, if you play your cards right."

"That sounds ominous. Or it might, assuming I had any idea what you're talking about."

"Just to be clear, I don't have whatever you're expecting to get in exchange for releasing her. You can work that out with Abellard when we're gone."

Guillory and Pierre traded a glance Rusty couldn't decipher.

"At first," he ventured, "I thought it had something to do with VECTOR."

"Ah. I haven't heard that name in a while. VECTOR made for some lurid fiction disguised as journalism, but don't believe everything you read. In truth, our little group was no more than a bit of wide-eyed idealism gone astray. It bore scant resemblance to the boogeyman created in the pages of the *Gambit*."

"It was serious enough to ruin your career."

Rusty saw her posture stiffen. He'd made contact with a patch of sensitive tissue beneath the buffed exterior.

"My involvement was…well, perhaps it's a bit much to call it a folly of youth. Let's say a product of misguided naiveté. In any case, VECTOR has been defunct for years. It was only my limited patronage that kept it afloat for its short, fruitless existence."

"Getting mixed up with terrorists on the FBI watch list is your idea of naive?"

"Terrorists," Guillory parroted with a dismissive wave of her hand. "VECTOR's goals had nothing to do with terror, and if we garnered federal interest it was only from those ludicrous articles. Our sole purpose was restoring some shred of natural order to the Gulf region."

"How about getting mixed up with a hood like Joseph Abellard?" Rusty asked, tiring of the conversation. "Chalk that up to youthful naiveté?"

"Just the opposite," she answered with a smile. "Mature necessity."

When Rusty didn't respond, she said, "I found a market for a product I can't acquire on my own. I needed someone with the kind of resources to handle supply while I oversaw demand. Simple as that."

"You know what? I don't give a shit. I'm just here to bring home someone I care about."

"My. This young lady certainly doesn't lack for guardians. Has it occurred to you that Miss Lavalle might be staying here as my guest, by her own choice?"

"Sure. She disappears, doesn't tell anyone at her job, leaves her father in a state of total panic. Just so she can enjoy your hospitality. Makes a lot of sense."

"Can you consider the possibility I'm offering her the one thing she can't find in New Orleans?"

"And that would be?"

"Protection, from the crude thug whose child she's carrying."

Rusty absorbed that. It was pretty much the last thing he'd expected to hear. Even though it ran contrary to a long list of logical reasons, he couldn't dismiss it immediately. If Marceline wanted to escape Abellard, was it impossible to believe she might have sought refuge here?

He shook the idea from his head, angry to have been lulled by this woman's commanding presence.

Pierre inched forward across the carpet.

"Keep your distance," Rusty said without turning his head.

"Do you know what I'm doing right now?" Guillory asked. "I'm trying to piece together the tortured logic that brought you here. You seem to think Miss Lavalle is being held against her will. If that were true, why would I release her to you?"

"Because it's the only way you avoid jail. Like I said, I don't care what you've got cooking with Abellard. Marcie's a pawn in it, maybe by her own doing. If you've kept her safely away from him for the past week, I might even thank you for it. But she's leaving with me."

Anne Guillory rose briskly from the couch.

"Why don't we let Miss Lavalle decide that?"

She gave Pierre a nod and then walked toward the French doors, again brushing past Rusty as if his presence barely registered.

The two men stood facing each other, both wondering if the suppressed violence that permeated the room was about to break loose. Rusty had moved the Marrow Seeker into his right boot in case he'd had to submit to a frisk before entering the house. Unarmed, he'd have his work cut out for him with this musclebound individual.

Take him low, he's top heavy. Upset the balance and slam a palm into his throat.

Both men tensed.

Guillory's voice halted their next movements.

"Are you coming or not?"

Rusty rotated his gaze away from Pierre to see her standing by the French doors with an impatient frown.

"Where?"

"To see the lady in question. Isn't that why you're here?"

30.

A cobbled path stretched out behind the main house, tracing a curve around an ancient stone well. Anne Guillory led the way, Rusty and Pierre following and keeping a guarded distance from each other. Copper electric lanterns in the style of antique gas lamps stood at intervals, lighting their progress across the grounds. The grass grew thick, not looking to have been mown in some time.

At the end of the path stood a two-story, red brick building. It looked to Rusty like a barn or stable, but as they drew closer he saw a matching set of doors and windows clearly designed for human habitation.

"The carriage house," Guillory said. "Oldest structure on the property."

Rusty glanced back over his shoulder. His mind captured an image for future reference. He assessed the distance separating the carriage house from the main building. Roughly a hundred feet, with the stone well at a midway point.

He turned back to find Pierre glaring at him.

"I had it refurbished for guest quarters when I took ownership of the estate," Guillory said, speaking as if Rusty was an interested buyer. "Partially refurbished, anyway. There's still quite a bit of work to be done."

"Let me guess. Used to be the slave quarters."

"My family gave considerable thought to demolishing it over the years," Guillory replied. "I gather the idea was to wipe away ugly memories. My father came quite close to tearing it down in the sixties but fortunately had a change of heart. You can't erase the past by destroying its material vestiges."

"So you've kept it standing as a place to hold someone against their will. Sounds like real progress."

"What an asinine remark. Why don't you come in and see just how wrong you are."

Pulling open the unlocked door, she stepped into the carriage house. She flicked on a light switch by the door, illuminating a narrow antechamber.

Pierre waited for Rusty to follow.

"You first," Rusty said, having no intention of turning his back on the man.

Pierre shrugged like it wasn't worth debating and stepped into the carriage house. Rusty took a last look behind and followed. The antechamber led to a bannistered stairway. Guillory had already walked up to the second floor landing, where she turned on another overhead light.

Rusty paused before going any further. None of it made sense, but he couldn't exactly describe this building as a prison. It did look like a tastefully appointed guest house—shiny fixtures, unblemished wallpaper, the scent of clean wood in the air. The stairs gleamed under the light of an overhead lamp wrapped in a frosted glass sconce.

"Are you coming or not?" Guillory asked. Rusty could no longer see her from where she stood on the second floor.

He ascended the stairs rapidly, pushing past Pierre. Any shred of patience he'd been maintaining was gone. He needed to see, now.

Reaching the landing, he turned left at a gesture from Guillory. At the far end stood a wooden door, secured to the adjacent wall by a bulky padlock on a brass hasp. Carved into the door at eye level was a square Judas window with bars crisscrossing over the embedded glass.

Rusty walked over and yanked open the Judas window.

He found himself peering into a simple, well-furnished room. With its antique canopy bed, three-mirrored vanity, and hooked rugs spread across the floor, it looked remarkably similar to his suite at the Cornstalk Hotel. Neat, well-maintained, and comfortable.

Rusty flinched at the sight of a body lying on the bed under a pile of plush comforters. Turned away from him, legs tucked into a fetal ball, long, black hair spread across the pillow. He thought he heard a faint sigh, like someone emerging from sleep.

Was that Marceline Lavalle?

It could be her. It had to be her.

Rusty's hand fell to the padlock dangling from the door's hasp.

"Locked on the outside, huh?"

He said it without turning around, feeling every muscle in his body tense. Seeing her—*it has to be her!*—so close and apparently in one piece, electrified him. He had to contain it, to channel it, or lose control of the situation.

"For her safety only," Guillory calmly intoned. "We have no way of knowing when Mr. Abellard might show up and try to take her against her will."

"If I have to listen to one more lie—"

"Pierre, open it."

The manservant stepped past Rusty and removed a key from his pocket. He opened the padlock and lifted it from the hasp.

"Want me to warm her up for you?" he said with a leer, placing his hand on the door. It took everything Rusty had not to strike him.

"No? OK, she's all yours."

He stepped aside, pocketing the lock.

Rusty reached for the door. His hand froze. It was simple, too simple.

"If either one of you tries to stop us from leaving," he said, "I'm going to cut both your throats."

Those words rang slightly false. The Marrow Seeker was still secured in his boot. He'd have to subdue or at least stun the man next to him before gaining control of the weapon, and he felt less than total certainty of accomplishing that.

"Are we clear?"

Neither Pierre nor Guillory answered.

Rusty's left hand reached for the door handle even as he detected movement in the peripheral vision of his right eye. Pierre was pivoting toward him, arms held low.

He felt a fist slam into his kidneys. It was a glancing blow, diminished by his split-second reaction of turning away. He registered little pain. Everything slowed in his mind. He seemed to observe rather than participate in what happened next.

Can't reach the blade.

Next best thing…

Rusty's right hand flew up in a knifehand strike aimed at Pierre's throat. Direct hit. He felt the man's Adam's apple recede half an inch as the flat edge of his palm made contact.

A strangled gasp escaped the servant's mouth. Rusty watched him stagger back before realizing he'd been struck a second time in the midsection. This one did more damage. It felt capable of fracturing a rib and caused him to double over.

He saw Pierre's left hand emerging from his coat pocket. It held something silver.

Gun!

No.

A cylindrical aerosol can. Four inches long with a red nozzle at the top.

Close your eyes!

Rusty didn't know where that intuition came from, but he followed it—an instant too late. Pierre's thumb pressed the nozzle. A cloud of white mist sprayed forth with a discordant hiss. Rusty's screams drowned out the noise even as the vaporous assault continued.

He fell to a crouch, both hands clasping his face. Several seconds passed before the pain fully kicked in. Both eyes filled with fire, like they'd been sprayed with battery acid. He screamed louder and his legs buckled, the thud of the stone floor against his kneecap overwhelmed by the agony filling both eye sockets.

He rubbed furiously at his face, feeling a sticky wetness coating his skin that had to be blood. The fire spread deeper into his head until he felt sure both eyeballs had been burned or gouged out. The wetness streaming down his face grew more viscous.

Blood. It's got to be blood.

But it wasn't blood, because he couldn't wipe it away. His eyes were open, but sightless. He used his fingers to spread the lids as far as they would go to prove to himself they were open. Nothing, except a red curtain that darkened to black.

He was blind.

Stumbling to his feet, his upward progress was halted by Pierre's arm wrapping him in a chokehold. Rusty kicked and swung but only made contact with air. He was suspended two inches from the ground, oxygen supply rapidly being cut off. Pierre tightened the vice until Rusty stopped fighting.

"You're doubtless wondering what's eating away at your ocular membranes," he heard Guillory say from somewhere very close. "It's called Excoecaria, a plant genus of the family Euphorbiaceae. That's a mouthful, isn't it? In the tropics, you'll find it more commonly called blind-your-eye tree. I don't need to tell you why. Consider it an honor to be the test subject for a project that never enjoyed the opportunity it deserved. If VECTOR came to full fruition, Excoecaria would have been deployed on the front lines."

Pierre's hands released Rusty's neck. Before he could react, a hard shove launched him through the doorway and into the chamber. His balance gave out completely, the misery in his eyes overpowering every other sensation.

"You wanted her," he barely heard Pierre say. "She's yours."

The door shut noisily, followed by the sound of the lock snapping into place on the hasp.

Rusty leaned unsteadily against the door. Giving it a hard push, he felt it open an inch only to be stopped by the padlock.

He could just barely make out the sound of descending footsteps over his own ragged breathing. The footsteps faded to silence. After a few more seconds, he heard the lower door being closed.

Then he heard her voice.

31.

Monday sat at the wheel of the rented Lincoln Navigator, clutching her cell phone tightly like the application of manual pressure might force it to ring. She was parked on the roadside about ten yards east of Anne Guillory's driveway. Rusty had been right, the elaborate mailbox was hard to miss. Headlights turned off, the engine had been idling for almost twenty minutes.

He'd said to give him a half hour. Monday had accepted that timeframe, but now she wondered why? If Marceline was being held somewhere on the property and Rusty was going to bring her out by persuasion or force, why assume thirty minutes was sufficient? Why not ten minutes, or five hours? So much of what he'd presented as a viable plan back in New Orleans now struck her as woefully half-baked.

She'd sent a series of texts:

WHATS HAPPENING?

IS SHE THERE?

SHOULD I COME GET U?

IM COMING IN 5.

None received a reply. She could fathom no explanation of why Rusty wouldn't get back to her unless something had gone wrong.

Monday took a last fruitless look at her phone and decided she wasn't waiting any longer.

She backed up to the driveway's entrance and eased onto the property with her headlamps still dark. The trees thinned as the Navigator rounded a bend. A pair of stone walls appeared, connected by a metal gate obstructing further progress. Just as

Rusty had described.

Monday got out for a closer look. A hard tug on the gate proved it immovable. She peered through the metal bars and saw the lights of the house at the end of the driveway. Abellard's black SUV was parked by the front porch. About fifteen feet inside the gate a wire ran across the driveway, connected to a flat metal sensor.

Monday found a toehold in the stone wall and hoisted herself up. Thankful to be wearing tennis shoes instead of high heels, she climbed over and dropped to the other side. She walked over to the ground sensor and stepped on it.

Nothing. She jumped in the air and landed with both feet. The gate swung inward.

Monday ran to the Navigator and dove behind the wheel, barely managing to pull into the driveway before the gate crashed shut against her rear bumper.

So far, so good. Even if she was going off-script, Monday felt better just to be taking some kind of action rather than twiddling her thumbs out on the road. If nothing else, she'd be able to provide a faster getaway.

Monday slowed as she passed the Escalade. Nothing was visible through the tinted windows. She pulled to a stop two cars' lengths in front and just sat there for a minute, unsure of how to proceed.

She didn't relish the idea of waiting here in plain view of anyone inside the house. Reaching for her phone with the hope of seeing a new message that would tell her this was all over, she found none.

Monday turned off the engine. She had no idea whether to approach the house or put the Lincoln in gear and drive back out to her lonely roadside sentinel. The one option that seemed least intelligent was to stay here in the driveway like a sitting duck.

Deciding she could cough up some bogus story about running out of gas if necessary, she got out of the Navigator and approached the house. She'd just passed one of the front columns when the driver's door of the Escalade swung open.

Before she could react, she heard the shot. Just one

brisk pop, sounding very much like the report of a medium caliber handgun.

She whipped her head around and saw the rough outline of Joseph Abellard reeling from the vehicle. A nickel-plated revolver flashed in his hand. Hanging from his wrist was one severed half of the Cobra cuff.

Abellard swayed on his feet, looking slightly dazed.

Monday slid behind the nearest column, breathing hard. He hadn't seen her yet but she couldn't stay hidden for long.

The front door of the house was barely five feet away, the Navigator three times that distance. She'd never make it to the vehicle without attracting his notice. The house door was closer, but what reason did she have to think it was unlocked?

No choice. She lunged for the door, her right hand gripping the brass knob and pulling hard.

It didn't budge.

She tried pushing, knowing it was pointless. The door was firmly bolted.

Then she heard heavy footsteps behind her. Monday turned around just in time for Abellard to smash the gun butt into her face.

32.

"Rusty. Oh my God, say something."

It was her voice. There was no mistaking it. No matter how much time had passed since he'd last heard it, that voice would always resonate in his ear with total recognition. It cut through the torment that dripped like molten lava into his cranium, burning red pathways across the back of his skull. He anchored himself to her voice.

"Talk to me, Rusty. Please."

He tried to speak but it came out as a hoarse croak. He clenched against the pain and tried again, articulating her name one syllable at a time. A third attempt came more easily.

"God," Marceline uttered, her lips close to his ear. "I just can't believe—"

"It's me, Marcie. Christ, I can't believe it's *you*."

He felt her fingers touching his face. Their touch was familiar. Strong fingers wiping away the sticky residue covering his eyes.

"Can you see?"

He shook his head. "Blind as a bat."

"What did they do to you?"

"I'm not sure. Some kind of...venom, or poison. I let that fucker get the drop on me."

Marceline's fingertips traveled from his face to his neck, making exploratory gestures as if testing his reality. The sense of tactile recognition hit him even harder than before. Then her hands clasped his and she helped him to stand.

"Come on. Let's get you over to the bed."

Rusty rose awkwardly and allowed her to guide him across the room. He heard the groan of floorboards under his feet, followed by the squeak of aged springs as Marceline lowered him onto the bed.

"How'd you get here, Rusty? God, I don't even know where *here* is."

"Are we alone?" he asked. He tried opening his streaming eyes but quickly shut them. If all he could see was black, he'd just as soon do it with his lids closed.

"I've been alone the whole time," she said. "Ever since I woke up, five nights ago. I've been keeping track."

He felt her fingertips tentatively touch his face again. The discomfort in each eye was slowly receding from a stabbing needle to a pounding hammer, but he was still completely sightless.

"What is this stuff?"

"I don't know. She said it was some kind of toxic plant residue."

"Who?"

"Guillory. I think it's just her and the other one. Didn't see anyone else."

"I don't know who you're talking about."

"Is that door the only way out?" he asked, craning his head in different directions, futilely attempting to conjure some spatial sense of the room imprisoning them.

"Uh huh. I've been trying to pick the lock since I got here. There's a transom up by the ceiling, but it's too high to reach. Bolted too."

"Is there something we can climb up on?"

"There's a dresser. It's just barely tall enough for me to reach the transom when I'm on top. No luck. That window's got to be three-inch glass. Steel frame built right into the ceiling. No way out, but at least it lets in some sunlight."

"Well, then. Guess we'll have to take another look at that door."

"Come here first."

She took his hand and led him across the chamber, flicking on a light inside the adjacent bathroom. Then she filled a drinking glass with water and placed a folded towel on the rim on the sink.

"Lay your head down here," she said. "Open your eyes."

Rusty was reluctant to follow that command, sensing it would usher in more discomfort. He was right. Both lids immediately shut of their own will after barely a second. The pain didn't upset him nearly as much as the yawning expanse of darkness it revealed.

"Open them, Rusty."

He did as he was told, bracing himself. Marceline titled the glass and flushed his eyes with a steady stream of cool water. Rusty winced, fingers gripping the sink, but the water's sting lasted only a moment before it offered some cooling relief.

"Nursing 101," Marceline said, and he could almost hear the trace of a smile in her voice. "SOP whenever the eye gets exposed to an irritant."

"Should've known I was in good hands."

Marceline repeated the flush three more times. She grabbed some dry towels and guided him back toward the bed. Rusty lay his head in her lap and she started cleaning the affected area.

"What's the last thing you remember before you woke up here?"

Marceline paused before answering.

"I was home, after a shift at the ward. Went to bed early. Someone was on top of me, in my bed. I didn't have time to resist, he shoved a rag over my face. I smelled something…like a chemical only not exactly like that. I was out. Next thing I remember, I woke up in here."

"Do you have any idea where we are?"

"None. I can't see anything but some treetops through the transom. It's quiet out here, so we can't be near the city."

"We're at the house of someone named Anne Guillory, about twenty miles north of Maurepas. Any of that mean anything to you?"

"No. I don't…none of this makes any sense."

Rusty could hear the rudderless despair in her voice, but the foundation beneath it was weighted far more heavily toward anger than fear.

"So you've never seen anyone, all this time?"

"A man comes to the door twice a day, wearing a hood. Slides in a fresh tray, grabs the old one and leaves. Won't say a word, no matter how much I scream at him. When I tell him I need toilet paper and some other things, he brings 'em. Fresh towels, linens. Couple of aspirin, whatever. It's like being a prisoner in some plush hotel."

The flow of watery discharge from Rusty's eyes had slowed, drying to a thin crust on his cheeks. She brushed it away with a kind of thoughtless intimacy.

"And the food," Marceline continued, her voice betraying amazement. "I swear, it's like eating at Commanders' Palace every day."

A pause, then Rusty felt a jab to his ribs from her finger. "I'm eating for two, so no judgment."

"The guy who brings it, you never saw his face? Or anyone else?"

"Nope," she said. "Thought about trying to pull his damn hood off, but what good would that do? Figure I'm safer not knowing. Kidnappers can't let you go if you know who they are, can they?"

"I think that's how it usually works."

"How in the world did you find me?" she asked, wiping away more flakes from his face.

"Your ex-boyfriend."

Rusty heard a startled inhalation at those words, which he'd spoken with open hatred. He understood too late the casual reference to Abellard must have come as a shock.

"Sorry. I shouldn't have put it like that."

"Joseph knows I'm here?" she asked in a slightly strangled voice. "He's known all this time?"

Rusty lifted his head from her lap. He figured the mix of emotions she was feeling had to be dizzying—fear of the man whose violent temper had caused her to break off the relationship even as his child grew within her, combined with hurt astonishment that he might have gone so far as to make her a prisoner.

"When I found out you'd gone missing, I figured he was probably behind it. Turns out it's this Guillory, she's been using you as a kind of…I don't know, bargaining chip. So Abellard will come through on whatever scheme they're in on."

"This is about Claude Sherman," Marceline said after a long pause.

"Yeah. He's the one who broke into your place and… grabbed you. But Abellard didn't put him up to it, if that makes any difference."

Marceline didn't say anything for some time. Rusty knew she was still right next to him, could hear her breathing. He didn't know how much of what he'd just told her she'd already pieced together on her own, but her stony silence suggested a boatload of her worst suspicions had just been confirmed.

"Dad," Marceline said quietly. "He must be going of his mind."

"He's the one who told me you've been missing."

"God. Is he OK?"

"He will be, soon as he sees you're OK."

"What about Joseph? Where is he now?"

"Secured, for the moment. Look, I know this is a hell of a lot to deal with, but let's get out of here and have a nervous breakdown later. Agreed?"

Another silence. When she spoke again her voice was firm.

"Agreed."

Rusty heard her stand and walk across the room. He sat up from the bed and did what he'd been dreading for the past few minutes. He opened his eyes and blinked hard a few times, then looked around in a series of directions. Left to right, up and down.

"Any better?" Marceline asked quietly.

"No."

He stood.

"But we're still getting out of here."

33.

Monday saw stars, but the impact of the gun's metal butt didn't knock her out. The pain ballooning across her cheekbone was sharp enough to keep her upright. She wobbled slightly, then a hand roughly grabbed her arm before she could fall.

Abellard twisted her around and yanked the arm up behind her back in a crushing grip. It hurt more than the gun. Monday cried out and tried to claw at his face with her other hand.

Abellard wrenched the arm higher and she stopped fighting.

"OK, OK. Jesus, that hurts!"

"I know you," he uttered in her ear, barely a whisper. "I seen you before."

"Let go. I'll tell you—"

"You work with her, at the ward. Ain't that right? Answer me, bitch!"

"Yes, OK. I'm a nurse at Bon Coeur. I'm a friend of Marceline's. I'm trying to help her."

"You're in this with Diamond. Driving the fuckin' getaway car, that it?"

"I'm just trying to help. I'm worried about her."

"Bullshit."

"Fuck you if you don't believe me. You're the reason she's—"

Abellard yanked the arm high enough to tear ligaments. Another half inch and he'd dislocate it entirely from her shoulder. He silenced Monday's screams by pressing the .38's muzzle up against her eye. She clamped her mouth shut and stopped resisting.

"We call this the chickenwing. Hurts like a mother, don't it?"

Monday's chin fell to her chest, as much from disgusted resignation as physical stress. She'd let him get her and now Rusty and Marceline faced an added threat on top of whatever was going on inside the house.

"Where's Diamond?"

"I don't know," she said through gritted teeth. "I thought you'd done something to him."

"This is how it's gonna go. You and me, we're going inside. Open your mouth or make one fuckin' move, you're the first one to die. We're gonna find them, both of 'em. Then I'm cleanin' all this shit up for good."

Even in the midst of despair, Monday wanted to talk reason into this brute. To explain that they shared a common concern. She wanted Abellard to understand she was truly Marceline's friend. That she'd only come out here in hopes of restoring her to safety.

Monday wanted to communicate all this, but it was impossible. Abellard was already forcing her toward the front door. Her only option was to confuse him.

If she could redirect his fury onto herself, even momentarily, it might buy Rusty some critical time to finish doing whatever he was doing in there. It might make all the difference.

With that resolve, she spat into his face. Hoping to anger him enough to create even a brief distraction, disrupt his momentum for just an instant.

Abellard didn't take the bait. He backhanded her hard enough to split her lip, then pushed her hard against the brick wall next to the front door.

"Stop fucking around," he said, using his gun hand to slam the brass knocker.

They stood there for a moment, hearing nothing but their own breaths and the surrounding hum of a million nocturnal insects.

Abellard went to work on the knocker again. The sound of heels clacking against a parquet floor resounded from within.

"You're my Kevlar vest, understand? Whatever I say to do,

you do it. I don't say nothing, make like a fuckin' statue till I do. Understand?"

Monday didn't respond, eyes dully focused on the door. Her mind was spinning with possibilities of who might appear on the other side, and what might result. Could she entertain even a nanosecond's hope that Rusty would be the one who answered the door? If so, what would happen next?

"I asked you a question," Abellard hissed, jerking her arm a few degrees north. "Do you understand?"

"I understand," she said in a husky voice.

"Better hope so."

They heard the sound of a latch turning. The door opened two inches, held by a chain. Pierre's swarthy face filled the crack.

"Mr. Abellard. This is—"

The revolver's barrel found a spot in the gap between the door and the frame, pointed upward at Pierre's chin.

"Don't even think about slamming that door. These rounds are 125-grain, and they can all travel through wood."

34.

Rusty's fingertips touched cool metal. He was standing by the chamber door, performing a tactile examination of the hinges. They felt sturdy and well maintained, free of rust. No way to move the door from where it met the jamb.

He shuffled over to the right and pushed on that side, finding less than an inch of wiggle room between the door and the wall. Just enough space to work his fingers through the gap and reach the padlock on the outside. The hasp it hung on was thick and securely drilled into the wall.

"I think trying to leave by force is a bad idea. Even if I manage to kick this open, it'll create too much noise."

"Let's take the risk and worry about it once we're outside."

"If it comes to that," he agreed. "You said you've tried the lock already?"

"Only about a hundred times."

"Combination or keyed?"

"Please," Marceline said, sounding offended. "You think a lousy combo lock would hold me this long?"

"Right. Should've known better than to ask."

That was true enough. Rusty retained a very clear recollection of Marceline's natural gift for the art of lock-picking. He'd seen it illustrated countless times during their formative years, when she worked as Prosper's onstage assistant while he acquired nuggets of rarified knowledge at an agonizingly slow pace under the older man's tutelage.

Back then, they used to communicate through a form of friendly competition. It became a kind of flirting. Who could master a certain illusion the fastest, and then teach it to the other with a teasing sense of superiority?

Prosper had shown some reluctance in instructing his young charge in even the basics of lock-picking until the moral gravity of the art was made clear. The only locks he was ever to spring open were those used in illusions performed of the corner of Royal and Dumaine. The first time Prosper caught Rusty using his newfound skills to enter someplace he wasn't invited would signal the termination of his apprenticeship.

With those rules established, Rusty had avidly taken up the study of opening all manner of locks. He got good at it quickly, but mastery only came with constant practice. For Marceline, it was a matter of effortless touch. She could coax pins and tumblers into movement through the force of sheer will, it sometimes seemed to a lovestruck young Rusty Diamond.

"This isn't promising," he muttered, reaching through the gap to measure the padlock's make and size. "Feels like a Master. Something from the ProSeries, I'd guess."

"Come on," Marceline said, mildly amused despite herself. "I'm sure you can do better than that."

Rusty continued his sightless inspection, fingers moving assuredly.

"Two-inch brass body to prevent corrosion, good idea with the humidity around here. And, let's see…a two and a half-inch shackle. Hardened boron alloy. Nine millimeters thick, if I had to wager."

"Now you're just showing off."

"Hardly," Rusty said, rubbing his hands briskly against his jeans to remove any sweat. "Showing off would be getting the damn thing open."

He leaned in close and went to work. For several minutes, it was nothing short of infuriating. His fingers felt as deprived of their sensory perception as his eyes, fumbling over the lock like the appendages of some drunken oaf. Skinning his knuckles repeatedly against the sharp corners of the gate's bars, he barely registered the pain. All he could feel was the clumsy uselessness of his hands, which incensed him.

"Damn it!" he roared after the fourth failed effort.

"Calm down and try this."

Rusty felt her place a thin, almost weightless strip of aluminum in his palm.

"I found it pretty worthless," she said. "But maybe you'll have better luck."

"You made a shim?"

"Bad one," she shrugged.

"How?"

"I asked for a Coke a few days ago when Mr. Hood brought my morning meal. No chance I'd get a bottle, but I figured a can might not be out of the question. Bingo. Next time he came up, I threw a fit. Said my water broke and I was going into labor."

Rusty was surprised to hear her laugh softly.

"Man, I made a *scene*. Knocking over the furniture, screaming blue murder. I don't think he bought it, but he forgot all about the can when he came back for the tray after I calmed down."

"That's the crafty girl I remember," Rusty said, pinching the aluminum shim between two fingers.

The shim slid easily into the gap where the shackle inserted into the lock's body. Rusty forced himself to go slowly, not wanting to bend the flimsy aluminum. He dug the tip in deeper, progressing by millimeters.

For a startled moment, he thought he had it. Then he felt the shim fold under the pressure.

"Fuck. It's too weak."

"Told you," she sighed. "Ready to try force?"

"Not quite," Rusty said, reaching down to pull off his left boot. He held it upright, heel toward the ceiling, and caught the folded wooden knife in his other hand as it fell free.

"Remember this old bugaboo?"

"You've got the Marrow Seeker?" Marceline asked, audibly incredulous. "Why the hell have you been holding out?"

"Didn't want to risk breaking off the tip. We might need it for other purposes than turning tumblers."

"Give me that," Marceline said, grabbing the knife. "You can't break Terrebonne teak, and you know it."

"Better safe than sorry."

"Pshh. If we don't bust this lock, we won't have any other purposes to worry about."

Rusty couldn't argue with that logic. He stepped away from the door, leaving her free access to work.

For the next minute Rusty stood motionless, listening to a series of small ticks and clacks as Marceline did her thing. She worked the tip of the Marrow Seeker's teak blade into the shackle's insertion point. She kept at it with a prodigy's touch, feeling the lock's inner pieces adjust by miniscule degrees.

"Goddamnit, Marcie. I can't believe it's been—"

"Quiet. Let me concentrate."

The shackle sprang free with a resonant snap. Rusty smiled at the sound.

"Haven't lost your touch, I see."

"Oh, you see, do you?" Marceline said, pressing the folded knife back in his hand.

"Poor choice of words. Don't rub it in."

Marceline pushed gingerly against the door, opening it by inches to prevent any betraying creaks.

"Looks like a landing here," she whispered. "Some stairs going down on the right."

"What else? You see any other way out?"

"It's dark down at the other end. I think there's a bannister."

"Let's check it out. They brought me up these stairs, might still be watching them."

Ten paces took them to the far end of the landing. A rickety bannister followed a second stairway down to the back of the carriage house. This whole side of the building had not received any of the refurbishment evident in the area around Marceline's chamber. A small rectangle of moonlight burned through a hole in the roof. The steps were slick with moss and lichen. No electric lamps offered guidance.

Marceline proceeded slowly down the staircase, aided only by another patch of moonglow coming from an open doorway at ground level. She held Rusty's hand tightly, warning him where one entire step had rotted away.

Finally, they reached bottom. There was only one door in sight, effectively limiting their options. Rusty figured if they got outside they could circle around until they arrived at the section of grounds where the old stone well was located. From there, even without vision, he'd have his bearings.

They were just stepping out the carriage house's moldering back door when they heard the sound. Part cry, part gurgle. It came from Rusty's immediate left.

Marceline froze.

"That was a person," she whispered.

"Where'd it come from?"

"Shh. There's a door to the left of where you're standing. Little window cut into it, like the one holding me."

A muffled, strangled sound came again. Unquestionably the sound of something in pain.

"Maybe it's someone who needs help," she said, releasing Rusty's hand.

"Can't worry about that now," he replied. He reached out, failing to make contact with her. "Marcie, for Christ's sake!"

"I'm right here," she answered, her voice coming from a few feet away.

She pulled open the barred Judas window and peered through. On the other side lay a chamber roughly the size of the one where she'd spent the past five days. This one was much darker, stone walls pressing in with the grim austerity of a prison cell.

A bare 80-watt bulb hung from a cable. Marceline's eyes were drawn to a dim thrashing on the floor. What she saw stole her breath. Even in the sepulchral light, she knew who she was looking at. The face was too horribly familiar to escape recognition.

Claude Sherman lay sprawled across a filthy pallet, his body strained into a highly unnatural position. Both wrists were chained to the wall above his lolling head. A ball gag filled his mouth, held in place by a Bungee cord wrapped around his head. He rolled and twitched, legs kicking feebly, on the edge of consciousness.

She'd seen this man dozens of times—most often at the casino, sometimes at Joseph Abellard's house in Vacherie, where Sherman had shown an unfailing knack for interrupting peaceful moments of the kind she used to share with Abellard before things turned sour. The last time she saw Claude Sherman, he was wearing a custodian's uniform at Bon Coeur.

Marceline gasped as she got a clearer look into the chamber. All the hair had been shorn from the right side of Sherman's head, exposing the pale flesh beneath. That entire half of his cropped skull was caked in blood, the ear dangling limply.

The uncut nails of Sherman's right hand were speckled red. Marceline realized with a fresh shudder the damage to his ear hadn't been inflicted by some sadistic torturer. Claude Sherman had attempted to claw it away himself, his reach constricted by the chains. His eyes darted upward, spotting her face framed in the Judas window. A moan fought to break free of the gag but came out only as a suffocated release of oxygen. He struggled to sit upright, eyes beseechingly fixed on hers. The chains went taut and he collapsed on the stained pallet.

Marceline couldn't know it, but Sherman had spent the last thirty-odd hours trying—first desperately, then with something far beyond simple desperation—to dislodge the insect that even now bristled and burrowed deep inside his Eustachian tube. The same mature half-inch earwig Anne Guillory had teased into his ear with the aid of a straw while he lay drugged by the *curare*-dosed tea.

Had he been conscious and unfettered in the early minutes after it crawled inside, Claude could have removed the bug as easily as knocking out water after a swim. But the *curare* rendered him insensible for over three hours. By the time he came to in this filthy chamber, hands shackled, the earwig had burrowed in far too deeply.

It would never remove itself, thanks to its genetic defect lovingly demonstrated to him in the conservatory. Guillory had found her last useful purpose for Claude Sherman, testing the impact of the old wives' tale when applied to a living subject.

VECTOR never had a chance to deploy such a tactic on a

high-profile target in the name of nature—and the earwig was never considered a viable weapon even in the developmental stage—so Claude would have to suffice. How long until madness took hold, until the allure of death's release overrode the survival instinct? Time would tell.

Marceline pushed the Judas window shut, overcome with revulsion. She felt Rusty's hands on her shoulders, shaking her.

"What the hell's in there?" he asked, and she realized he'd probably been asking it for some time before she heard the question.

She exhaled slowly, regaining a sense of equilibrium. Then she grabbed one of his hands and started guiding him through the doorway that led out of the carriage house.

"I'll tell you later," she whispered. "Don't ask me to tell you right now."

35.

Joseph Abellard backed Pierre Montord across the dimly lit hall, toward the great room. He held the gun waist-high and kept Monday in front of him, clenching her arm tightly. Without turning around, he pushed the front door shut with his foot. It swung on hinges in need of some oil, stopping an inch before closing all the way.

"Please put the gun down," Pierre said, hands raised in submission. "There's no need for it. We're prepared to go through with the exchange."

"Nah, we're way past that," Abellard said, feeling marginally more calm than he had outside. The fuzz in his head from the blows he'd been dealt in the Escalade had cleared. Moving freely with a loaded weapon in hand, he started to embrace the fact that he was in control of the situation.

"Get your ass in there where I can see you," he said, pointing to the great room.

Ninety-five percent of Abellard's attention was on Pierre, waiting for the first signal that would necessitate putting a bullet in him. The remaining five percent was devoted to spotting a sign of that motherfucker Diamond.

Without knowing Diamond's location in this big dark house, Abellard knew he was leaving himself somewhat vulnerable. Even with a gun, he couldn't rule out the possibility of being surprised again. All the more reason to get this done fast.

"Where's Professor Bitch?"

"She's not here," Pierre stammered, pausing a beat to glance toward the staircase.

"Bullshit. I want her down here, and then I want to see my woman. Both those things better happen pretty goddamn quick."

"If you're concerned about Miss Lavalle, let me assure you—"

"On the floor," Abellard told Pierre as they emerged from the hallway into the illumination of the great room. "Keep them hands up high."

Pierre did was he was told, lowering himself into a cross-legged position on a damask rug in the center of the room.

"Move an inch and you're dead," Abellard told Monday, shoving her into the nearest chair.

"There's no need for all this, Joseph."

Three heads turned at the sound of Guillory's voice. She stepped into the room behind them, having just descended from the second floor. Any surprise she may have felt at this scene was concealed from view.

"Good," Abellard said, keeping the gun on Pierre. "I was getting ready to air out your boy if you didn't turn up. Take a seat."

He gestured toward the same sofa where Guillory had sat less than an hour ago when dealing with the first hostile man to darken her door tonight.

"You certainly know how to complicate a simple transaction. Was it beyond your capacity to handle this without bringing a stranger to my home?"

With a glance at Monday she added, "Two strangers."

Abellard was feeling more in control with these people assembled in his frame of vision. He'd never seen any house staff other than Pierre on his previous trips here, but even if there was a maid hiding in some broom closet right now, he wasn't going to worry about it. He knew how far this property was located from any hick cop who might respond to a distress call.

"I know you got some kind of attachment to this pretty motherfucker," he said to Guillory, jerking his head toward Pierre. "But I get the feeling it runs a whole lot stronger the other way, so I ain't gonna bother threatening him."

The gun rotated away from the muscled manservant, putting Guillory directly in the line of fire.

"Don't point that at her!" Pierre bellowed.

"Here's how this works. I don't see my woman in sixty seconds, I shoot. You pull some bullshit, try to grab a weapon or do any fucking thing except what I just told you, I shoot. Sixty seconds."

"This is all so unnecessary," Guillory murmured.

Abellard stepped closer so the .38 hovered less than a foot from her temple.

"Make that fifty."

"I'll get her, just stay calm!" Pierre cried, face contorting, though Anne Guillory appeared only mildly fazed by the muzzle inches from her head.

"She's in the carriage house," Pierre continued, lurching to his feet. "I might need a little more time than you're giving me."

"Forty-nine. Forty-eight. Pretty soon I'm gonna start counting by five."

"This is crazy, just stop!"

"For God's sake, do as he says," Guillory barked, sounding more disgusted with Pierre than with the man holding the gun. "He won't do anything until he sees her."

"Don't bank on that, Professor Bitch. I might just unload and start looking for myself."

Pierre moved quickly to the end of the room, opening one of the French doors that led out onto the rear grounds.

"If anything happens to her, you'll never get what you want."

"You still here, motherfucker?"

Pierre disappeared out the door, pulling it shut.

A weighted silence fell over the room, so heavy that Monday could almost feel it pressing down on her shoulders. She was no longer aware of any pain radiating from the spot on her cheek where Abellard had buried the revolver's butt several minutes earlier. She knew that whole side of her face would hurt like thunder in the morning, but for the moment it was nothing more serious than a weak throb.

Monday was waiting for her chance to bolt. Her phone was in her jeans, but who was she going to call?

And where the hell was Rusty?

"While we wait," Guillory said, "maybe you'll consider something. Whatever anger you might be feeling toward me is best directed at yourself."

Abellard didn't respond. He'd abandoned his countdown, knowing the only person it had any effect on was no longer in the room.

"Did you think there would be no consequences for falling behind on our agreement? My clients are highly demanding, Joseph. The one thing they don't have is time."

"That ain't none of my concern."

"But it is. Your most recent delay cost me a client, in the most literal sense. A lady—her family name won't mean anything to you but it's well known amongst the wealthier strata—she'd been waiting—"

"You!" Abellard shouted, swinging his gun arm at Monday, who'd started inching off the chair in preparation to make a run for the hallway. "Sit the fuck down!"

Blood going cold, she eased back into the chair.

"As I was saying," Guillory continued, "my client waited as long as possible. Or rather, her daughter waited. It was the daughter who arranged the purchase. She'd been expecting a crop of viable cells for one last salvo against the Hodgkin's afflicting her mother. That delivery never came. The old woman died last night, you'll be saddened to learn. This isn't the kind of business where one can lure back disappointed clients with the promise of better treatment the next time around."

"Time's almost up," Abellard said, feeling just about ready to turn this place into a charnel house.

One of the French doors crashed open, making everyone jump. Pierre came charging into the room.

Monday's breath caught in her chest as she strained to see if anyone else was coming in behind him. Rusty? Marceline?

"She's gone," Pierre bleated to Guillory. "They're both gone!"

Monday braced herself for a reaction from Abellard, expecting an immediate explosion. He didn't say a word, but the thin fabric of composure he'd been maintaining was visibly tearing at the seams.

She saw the change come across his face, could almost hear the trigger being squeezed a fraction of a second before it happened.

"Don't!" Pierre screamed, but it was too late.

The gun went off, and Monday screamed too.

36.

It took them a few minutes to navigate around to the front of the carriage house. Marceline measured each step with caution. Sensing this was for his sake, Rusty urged her to pick up the pace. The pain in his head had receded to a tolerable level, feeling less like two burning spikes had been thrust into his eyes than an unusually intense migraine.

They soon found themselves on the same cobblestone pathway he'd walked before. Marceline led them toward the main house, seeking cover from any lights wherever possible.

"Let's hold up," she said, crouching behind the stone well and pulling him down with her. "We're behind a well."

"All right," he nodded, locating it within the mental snapshot he'd taken earlier. By honing in on individual details like the well and the copper lanterns, a fuller picture assembled in his mind's eye.

"There a magnolia tree up on the right," he said. "Fifteen feet or so?"

"Uh huh. I can smell it from here."

"That's our next checkpoint."

"Hold it."

Marceline lifted her head above the well's rim to scan the back of the house. She glimpsed a silhouetted figure pass by a pair of French doors on the ground floor. It may have been more than one person, she wasn't sure. Lace curtains behind the glass prevented a clear view.

"Good to go?" Rusty asked.

"I just saw someone in the house."

"Man or woman?"

"Couldn't tell. Let's hang for a minute."

Marceline kept her eyes on the French doors, waiting to see if the figure reappeared. Rusty ground his teeth and muttered with the frustration of being sightless until she told him to hush. After what seemed like a safe interval, she stood.

"Looks clear. Let's move."

Keeping low, they jogged hand in hand across the grass until the magnolia's leafy boughs offered a veil of protection.

"How far's the house now?" Rusty whispered.

"There's a porch about twenty feet in front of us. No lights, looks empty."

"We need to get to the driveway out front, but we can't risk going through the house."

"So what do we do, climb over it?"

"Might be fun to try if we had more time," Rusty said, once more calling upon his mental snapshot. "There should be a gap up ahead on the right, between the house and some hedges. See it?"

Marceline squinted into the darkness and shook her head.

"Not really, it's dark over there. Might be a little bit of space."

"Let's try it. If I'm wrong we'll try something else."

They rapidly closed the distance from the magnolia to the back corner of the house. Marceline flattened herself against the wall and peered in the direction he'd indicated.

A narrow path stretched between the west gallery porch and a high row of hedges along the property line, just as he'd described. It was covered almost entirely in darkness except for some faint moonglow. This side of the house featured fewer windows than the front or back, and none of them were lit.

"Goddamn," Marceline said, squeezing his hand. "I forgot how good you are at this."

"I'll hold off on taking any bows until we're out of here."

"Can't see how far it goes," she whispered. "Maybe all the way to the front."

"Let's find out. If we have to go over a wall, so be it."

Twenty paces down the tight thorny path brought them to

the front corner of the porch. As Rusty had predicted, a brick wall six feet in height connected the space between the porch and the hedges.

Marceline was ready to move herself over it with a swift two-handed vault. Rusty calmly reminded her she was five months pregnant. He insisted she use his cupped hands for leverage and begged her to take it slowly.

Once she was on the other side, Rusty followed. He didn't need his eyes to scramble up and over the wall with ease.

A faint glare appeared in his left field of vision, coming from a bright lamp above the front door. It was the first flicker he'd seen since his exposure to the plant residue. He thought he could barely discern the shape of the house's front facade.

Don't get too excited just yet, he cautioned himself. *Could be a trick of the brain, easy.*

Marceline took his hand and they walked a few paces toward the front door, which stood open an inch or so.

"We're looking at the driveway, right?"

"Yeah," Marceline answered. "Straight ahead."

"Black Escalade parked there?"

She paused before replying, recognizing the vehicle.

"Is that Joseph's?"

"Don't worry, we're leaving him here. He won't be following without his keys."

"Where is he now?" she asked. Rusty didn't like the sound of that question.

"Cuffed to the wheel. Hopefully still unconscious."

"I don't see anyone in there. The driver's door is open."

Rusty silently cursed himself for not incapacitating Abellard more fully, even if that meant a lethal blow. But as he berated his own timidity, he still couldn't imagine himself taking the man's life in cold blood.

"Let's move fast," he said. "We need to get to the end of the driveway, and it's a decent walk."

"There's another car here," Monday said. "A silver Lincoln."

"*What?*" Rusty groaned, feeling his stomach drop like he was being pulled back into Barataria Bay all over again.

"It's parked in front of Joseph's."

"Jesus Christ."

"What's the matter?"

Goddamnit, Monday. Why didn't you keep your fucking post?

"Whose car is that, Rusty?"

He hesitated, unsure how Marceline would respond to learning the identity of his partner in this rescue operation.

"Your friend, Nurse Reed. She helped me track you down. Couldn't have done it without her."

"Monday?" Marceline asked, her incredulity clear as a bell. She grabbed Rusty's arm, not softly. "You got Monday mixed up in this?"

Rusty turned away from her, moving toward the door he couldn't see except in the dimmest of outlines. He threw himself against it, ready to kick it down, and the door yawned open.

Marceline reached out to grab him.

"Wait! How are you going to—"

Gunfire exploded from within the house, killing the question before she could finish asking it.

37.

Anne Guillory didn't scream when the bullet pierced her ribcage, but Pierre did. The agony in his voice sounded like he was the one who'd just absorbed a 125-grain hollow point round. He hurdled across the room, oblivious to placing himself in the path of another shot, and threw himself over Guillory even as she was crumpling to the floor.

Landing on top of her while trying to cushion the fall, he wrapped himself into a tight protective shield. He used his entire body to create the widest possible range of obstruction.

"Get up," Abellard ordered him. "Get the fuck up!"

Pierre didn't hear him, or made no sign of it. Guillory's breath was coming irregularly. The bullet had pierced her right lung, limiting respiratory function to a minimum. Pierre pressed his ear to her heart, then raised his head to face Abellard.

"I need to take her to a hospital!"

"Fuck that. On your feet."

Guillory released a pocket of suppressed air from some wounded place inside, sounding more surprised than injured. Pierre frantically placed his lips on hers and forced oxygen into her lungs.

"I said on your feet!"

"She's still alive. I need to get her help right now!"

"You ain't goin' nowhere till I see Marceline Lavalle."

A stunted breath caught deep in Guillory's diaphragm. She released a wet gurgling noise like a tire slowly deflating. A froth of pinkish blood appeared at the corners of her mouth. Pierre wiped it away and resumed his frenzied attempt at resuscitation.

"Where is she?!"

"The carriage house," Pierre moaned, glaring up at Abellard with tear-streaked eyes. "She was in the carriage house ten minutes ago, I swear it!"

"Show me."

"I need to get her to a hospital!"

"No one's leaving, so shut up about that. Do what I tell you or you're getting the next one."

"For God's sake!" Pierre pleaded. "You can have money, whatever you want. There's a safe upstairs with over six hundred thousand in it. Just let me help her!"

Watching it all happen, Monday raised herself from the chair by inches. Abellard stood at quarter profile to her, focused on the two people on the floor but not completely showing his back.

Monday knew too sudden a move was likely to attract his notice. The hallway opened up less than three yards from where she stood. If she could reach it, buying even a second or two of blockage from Abellard's firing range, she might be able to make it to the front door.

A broken exhalation escaped from Guillory's lips, followed by a pooling of blood that trickled down her cheek. Pierre Montord looked down at her, his face a mask of disbelief, and knew he'd just witnessed her final moment.

He buried his face in the pale flesh of Anne Guillory's neck. His shoulders heaved in a silent sob, quickly followed by another until he resembled a human oil derrick hopelessly pumping an empty deposit from which life would no longer flow.

"What's it gonna be, man?" Abellard said in a calmer tone, looking down at the two prone forms.

Pierre emitted a guttural cry and pitched himself off the floor. It was a suicide effort at best, a flying leap directly at an armed man. Abellard retreated with surprise but his finger closed on the trigger almost lazily.

The bullet caught Pierre in the neck, jerking his head back even as his brawny frame continued its forward momentum. His knees hit the floor first, upper torso following. Abellard backed away to avoid being struck by the falling body.

Ears ringing from the shot, Monday saw her chance and took it. She bolted over the arm of the chair and ran toward the hallway. Abellard caught her movement in his peripheral vision and swiveled. The revolver rose in his hand, four rounds still in the chamber.

"Stop!"

She took two more steps, accelerating. It wasn't enough. The hallway was still five paces away. Even if she got there, then what? The dividing wall would offer protection for only as long as it took Abellard to catch up with her. She'd never make it out the front door. Even if she banked a quick right and raced up the stairway, he'd shoot her down. There was no place to hide, but she didn't stop moving.

Abellard took aim as Monday dashed across the carpet. He didn't rush.

Guillory and Pierre had died too quickly. He couldn't even say with any certainty they'd suffered. This one would be different. This bitch had known Marcie all along, probably polluted her mind with bad ideas from the start. Hell, she was probably the one who convinced her to break off their relationship.

Abellard lowered the gun from where it was trained on the base of her skull to her lower back. He found the spot he wanted. Not enough satisfaction to be had from blowing a hole in her head. No. Make her feel it. Destroy her spine with one shot.

Monday's right foot rose from the floor as her left planted hard, pushing for maximum speed. Stretched into a sprinter's pose, extending as far as she could.

She'd heard Abellard yell at her to stop. She knew he wouldn't speak again. The next sound she heard would be a thunderous ignition of gunpowder propelling the bullet that killed her.

Eyes blurred, her mind flooded with adrenaline to a point where she didn't recognize the tall dark figure who'd emerged into the hallway from the front door. She knew him, but couldn't come up with his name for all the money in the world. Not just this second.

She saw his black-cloaked arm rise, in a similar motion to Abellard's when he'd lifted the gun. The arm came hammering forward in a downward arc, the hand opening.

Something flew from its grip, flying end over end. Her senses slowed by stress overload to I'm-going-to-die-right-now speed, Monday saw it coming straight at her, flashing in the murky light.

It was sharp, incredibly sharp.

The Marrow Seeker grazed past her head close enough to slice off a single curl of amber hair. The shorn lock twirled silently to the parquet at her feet. She lost sight of the wooden blade as it rocketed past, pinwheeling at the speed of a helicopter's rotor.

The knife continued its flight clear across the hall. All the way into the great room, where its razor-sharp tip embedded itself into the throat of an astonished Joseph Abellard, whose finger reflexively closed on the .38's trigger and released a round that missed Monday by less than a foot before disappearing into the paneled wall next to her.

All seemed suspended for a moment in the gunshot's fading reverberations. Then the revolver fell to the floor, and the man who'd fired it followed.

Abellard was dead before his face smacked against the damask rug. Monday didn't see it. She was still standing in a rigid posture of shock, unsure if she'd been shot in the back or carved by a flying blade.

She looked up at the tall, dark form filling the unlit space in front of her. With a burst of recognition, she knew who it was.

Of course. Who else would it be? And where the hell had he been all this time?

Rusty hadn't seen Abellard die either, but he wasn't seeing anything at all.

38.

Nobody said much on the return drive to New Orleans. Monday used her phone's GPS to traverse the lightless rural byways of Livingston Parish onto the eastbound I-10, cautiously steering the Navigator while Rusty and Marceline huddled in the back seat.

The trip passed largely without incident. They experienced no delays except for a five-car wreck outside Metarie that forced them to detour off the interstate for a mile before resuming the journey home.

Not until the high-rises of downtown NOLA came into view did an argument break out inside the Navigator. It had to do with where they should stop first, and it grew fairly heated before bubbling to a lukewarm resolution.

Monday insisted they go directly to an emergency clinic, so both Rusty and Marceline could get thoroughly checked out. She herself felt no need for medical aid. Her wounds were superficial. The gun butt's bruise on her face wouldn't be going away soon, but some vanishing cream would render her able to go about daily life without inviting stares. Her arm still screamed from Abellard's chickenwing, but that would heal. Monday knew an excellent holistic practitioner and yoga guru in Pirates Alley who would certainly have some remedies to offer.

Marceline flatly refused Monday's plan. Her top priority was getting to her father's house and letting him know she was still alive. To delay that revelation for even another hour was intolerable. They'd tried calling his landline several times from Monday's phone but got no answer. Prosper was probably riding the streetcar back home even as they sped toward the city.

Rusty backed up her wishes, insisting his eyes could withstand a little more time until receiving medical attention. He and Marceline claimed a majority vote on the matter. Monday grudgingly conceded, but only after Marceline agreed to a full examination the next day. Blood work, pelvic and cervical exams, ultrasound, everything. Though she seemed in good health and persisted in maintaining that she hadn't been ill-treated during her confinement, only a full evaluation could confirm no harm was done to her or the baby.

That issue settled, they turned to the larger topic of exactly how much of what happened tonight should be reported to the NOPD. This required no debate whatsoever—all three reached the same conclusion of their own accord.

There would be no police involvement. Period. Rusty's killing of Joseph Abellard ruled that out, now and forever. It was that simple. They never saw that house in Maurepas. Never heard of Anne Guillory. End of story.

No amount of careful explanation of all the mitigating circumstances would change the fact that he'd hurled a knife into a man's throat. Even if he found a sympathetic ear in Dan Hubbard, which was doubtful, charges would be pressed. Marceline would have to relive her ordeal by explaining it all to the police, quite possibly doing it again from the witness box.

What was the point? The people who deserved punishment had all gotten it. They wouldn't be coming back. Let them molder in that elegant room until weeds grew over the whole house and there was nothing but dust to tell the tale. If and when someone happened upon their remains, the Navigator's threesome had nothing to do with it.

For Rusty and Monday, this was an easy decision. Marceline found it more painful and complicated. Despite cutting Joseph Abellard out of her life over a month before with no intention of reconciling, she had history with the man from which she'd never be separated. Raising his child, his memory would stubbornly hover over her life in one way or another.

Marceline didn't hold any ill will toward Rusty for what

he'd done. She knew what would have happened if he'd acted a fraction of a second later. But she still had to grieve silently for Joseph Abellard. If not for the man he was, then for who she'd once hoped he could be.

As they crossed the New Orleans city line, Monday looked in the rearview and saw Rusty staring out the window at the passing streetlights, blinking furiously.

"Any better?" she asked.

He shrugged. He could just barely make out the odd flash, straining to discern something recognizable in the whirl of fuzzy patterns. He wasn't sure if he really saw any of it.

"I can't tell," he answered. "Maybe a little better."

"Can I ask you a question?" Monday said. "It's been on my mind ever since we pulled out of there."

"Sure."

"Did you have any idea where that knife was gonna land? I mean, in your...present condition?"

Hearing this, Marceline lifted her head from Rusty's shoulder where she'd been resting for a few minutes.

"I've been wondering about that too."

Rusty didn't reply right away. The mention of the knife made him reach into his pocket to make sure it was there. His fingers ran over the grooved wood of the Marrow Seeker, feeling sticky moisture that had to be Joseph Abellard's blood.

Everything that happened in the short span of time from when Abellard fell dead and the three of them drove away from the Guillory property remained somewhat unclear in his mind. It occurred to him that he didn't know who'd extracted the blade from the dead man's throat and returned it to his possession. Could have been either of the women in this vehicle.

"Rusty," Marceline said. "We asked you a question."

"Don't you ladies know a magician's not supposed to reveal his secrets?"

He smiled at the feel of her elbow nudging his ribs.

"I was once privy to *all* your secrets, magician. Hell, we learned most of them side by side."

"That we did," Rusty said softly. "That we did."

"I'm feeling a little left out," Monday chimed in from behind the wheel. "Since that knife came awfully close to my own noggin, I think I'm entitled to hear the truth. I promise not to tell a soul. Cross my heart and hope to die."

"Well," Rusty sighed, "somehow I just can't say no to you two."

"The truth," he continued after a contemplative pause, "is that I spent well over ten thousand hours working on my knife throwing skills. Miss Lavalle here can attest to that. As you must recall, Marcie, one of my reliable show-stoppers in Vegas was hurling blades at live targets while blindfolded. Over the course of more performances than I can count, I never missed."

"Very impressive," Monday said, hitting her blinker to merge into the exit lane for Esplanade. "But that wasn't the question."

"I'm providing background. See, when you throw a knife blindfolded—or, hell, any object—you can't just rely on the timed pattern of a rehearsed routine. In my stage act, we choreographed every last detail so that when I let a blade go, I knew exactly where the targets would be in their rotating pattern. We're talking Swiss watch levels of precision when it comes to timing. But that alone isn't enough stave off the possibility of something going wrong."

He left it there for a moment. Neither of the women spoke. Though sightless, Rusty could feel Monday's gaze on him in the mirror. The partial explanation he'd just provided, truthful as it was, couldn't help but open up a question in both their minds.

She's thinking about my confession to Prosper. She's wondering how someone with my kind of training could allow a trick to go wrong the way it did at Paul Ponti's house.

"Additional measures were needed," he continued, "to ensure I could throw a blind knife with confidence. I had to learn to create mental photographs using my other senses, sound and touch especially. Even without looking, I had to see the basic arrangement of people and objects in front of me. That's what I did tonight."

"OK," Monday said, sounding disappointed. "I guess that kind of answers the question."

"No, it doesn't," Marceline countered. "She asked if you knew where that knife was going to land when you threw it."

Rusty settled back into his seat as Monday steered onto Camp Street.

"Tonight," he finally said, "I needed a little luck."

• • •

The Navigator pulled to a stop at the curb in front of Prosper Lavalle's shotgun house. Across the street, Coliseum Park slumbered under the glow of towering sodium lamps. Not a single denizen was to be found on its manicured lawns, other than some squirrels foraging for nuts.

Arms entwined, the three of them hobbled across the cracked sidewalk and climbed a short set of stairs to the porch in front of Prosper's home. Rusty counted the steps, relying on the woman on each side of him for balance.

Marceline peered through the window adjacent to the door. A soft yellow light glowed from within.

Through a gap in the curtain, she saw her father dozing in his favorite chair. A lamp burned over his shoulder, illuminating the open book on his lap he'd been too tired to keep reading. Chin resting on his chest, his long legs stretched out to the center of a hooked rug at his feet.

"He's sleeping," she whispered, feeling her eyes fill. "I almost hate to wake him."

"Trust me," Monday said. "He won't mind."

"That's right," Rusty added. "He's probably dreaming of you right now. There's a key under the mat, I told him we'd be coming back tonight."

Monday lifted a corner of the aged rubber doormat and retrieved a house key. She slid it into the lock, turning it so softly the tumblers barely made a sound.

Halfway through the door, she turned. Monday and Rusty held their places on the porch.

"You're not coming in?"

"Nah," Rusty said with a shake of the head. He could

almost see her shape silhouetted in the glow from the living room, but it was little more than an indistinct blur. "You two should be alone."

"Definitely," Monday said before turning to Rusty. "And we need to get you checked out."

Marceline nodded. "Rusty, I…" The words faltered on her lips.

"Go inside," he said with a smile. "We'll talk tomorrow."

"You'll be in New Orleans awhile?"

"Yeah. I'm not sure how long, this town's a little too rough for me. But I'll stick around for a bit."

"Good."

She reached out to touch his cheek, then gently pulled the door closed.

Monday leaned forward to look through the open space in the window. Framed in the gap between the drapes, she saw Marceline lean down to tap her father's shoulder.

Prosper's eyes blinked open, adjusting to the light slowly and with effort. His face composed itself into a map of uncertainty quickly washed over by a flood of relief. Not happiness, or even gratitude. Not yet, those would come later. At this moment, the old man was simply overcome with relief.

Marceline kneeled down and let him embrace her. They held that pose, arms entwined, tears flowing in a conjoined stream.

"What am I not seeing?" Rusty whispered from his darkened spot on this same porch where he'd once sat for hours at a time, mastering basic illusions and trying to impress a teenaged Marceline with his budding skills.

Monday slid both arms around his waist, pulling him in tight.

"Exactly what you'd want to see. She's home."

39.

The better part of a week passed before Rusty felt more than middling confidence that his eyesight had returned to 20/20. Only a thorough vision test could determine that, but he didn't feel in any particular rush to get one. He could see well enough, and the prospect of learning he'd suffered even minor diminishment depressed him.

Everyone gets a little beat up along the way, the body breaks down in measurable degrees from hard use and the passage of time. Everything came with a price. If some weakened visual capacity was the required fee for Marceline's return to safety, he'd gladly pay.

After dropping her off at Prosper's house the night they drove home from Maurepas, Monday had taken him straight to the nearest walk-in urgent care center. A sleep-deprived clinician peppered Rusty with questions, clearly puzzled by his ailment. Rusty spun a marginally plausible story about visiting the City Park greenhouse and stupidly rubbing his eyes after picking up some rare tropical plants.

The clinician didn't appear to buy that explanation, but he did offer some encouraging information. The topical effects of the Excoecaria residue were highly unpleasant to the eyes but by no means permanent. Direct contact with the retina virtually guaranteed a period of sightlessness that might last up to a week, but careful maintenance of ocular hygiene should restore full sight with time.

Swabbing Rusty's eyes with saline solution and discharging him, the clinician offered a dubious piece of advice about being more careful when handling exotic plants in the future.

Monday waited in the lobby while he was being treated. They got back to her apartment a little after three A.M., both too exhausted to do anything but sleep the moment they fell into her bed. Waking late the next morning, they made up for it.

That afternoon Rusty returned the Navigator to Hertz, checked out of the Cornstalk Hotel, and moved his luggage into Monday's apartment. It was a short-term arrangement, and wordlessly agreed upon as such. They used the amiable pretext that Rusty should remain in New Orleans at least as long as it took for his vision to fully return. He'd not only save money by staying at Monday's place, but also benefit from sharing quarters with a nurse who could offer aid in the event of any unforeseen impediments to his recovery.

That was a wonderful ruse, all the more satisfying since neither of them believed it. Rusty's eyesight greatly improved within seventy-two hours of being poisoned, but they both agreed he should stick around a little longer to stave off a potential relapse.

He ended up staying almost three weeks, and it was a healing time in more ways than one. The breathless moments he shared with Monday only grew sweeter with repetition, but it was the opportunity to reconnect with Prosper and Marceline that Rusty valued most.

During the day, when both women where working at Bon Coeur (Monday had resumed her duties after receiving a clean bill of health), Rusty would loiter around the Quarter for hours, often popping into the Mystic Arts Emporium. Sometimes he'd just merge with the other tourists and shoppers, silently watching Prosper work his craft from the back of the crowd.

Marceline's return visibly rejuvenated the elder magician, spurring some of the most exquisitely rendered illusions Rusty had ever seen him perform. Once in a while, Prosper would invite him to assist with a particular trick, making a cryptic comment to the audience that this stranger might just know a thing or two about the mystic arts. On three occasions, a spectator asked Rusty if he was "that magician who used to play Vegas…you know, whatever happened to him?"

He demurred from directly answering those inquiries as politely as he could, then figured maybe it was better not to hang around the Emporium during peak hours. Instead, he would join Prosper and Marceline for dinner in the Quarter on nights when the old man decided to close up shop early. When Monday wasn't working at Temptations, they made it a foursome.

Rusty waited three full days after the events at Anne Guillory's house before deciding he couldn't put off calling Dan Hubbard any longer. He sensed it might look better to visit the Sixth Precinct in person, but didn't trust his eyesight completely and didn't want to answer any questions about it.

He thought long and hard about what to say and what to omit before placing the call. In the end he concluded a good lie—or an entire network of lies—was much like a good magic trick, in that it was best kept as simple as possible.

He told Hubbard the detective's instinct's had been right all along. Stressed out by the impending challenges of single motherhood and feeling unsure of her ability to meet them, Marceline Lavalle had taken an impromptu trip out west to visit a friend in Las Vegas. She'd gotten into a petty argument with Prosper and exacted revenge by not notifying him of her plans, a cruel ploy she'd come to regret. Father and daughter had since reconciled and she was now restored to her position at the Bon Coeur ward, at least until taking her planned maternity leave.

No crime, no foul play, just a mundane family dispute that turned a little ugly. It was certainly out of character for Marceline Lavalle to do a runner like that. But people act out of character all the time, as the detective himself had noted.

Hubbard remained silent for most of the phone call, grunting once or twice as Rusty wove his fabric of bullshit. The silence remained after Rusty stopped speaking, and a terrible moment passed when the subject of Joseph Abellard seemed sure to storm the conversation.

Had the casino boss been reported missing by his men at the Carnival, or someone else? Had officers from the Livingston Sheriff's Department discovered three bodies at a remote estate miles from the nearest marked road? (Four, if they looked in the carriage house and found what was left of Claude Sherman?) Was Hubbard holding his lip just long enough to let Rusty hang himself by saying too much?

The detective put those paranoid speculations to rest by clearing his throat and saying was he glad the girl turned up. To his credit, he resisted the urge to add anything along the lines of I-told-you-so.

Dan Hubbard wished him a safe flight home and ended the call. Rusty sat motionless for several minutes, allowing a cautious but growing realization to settle in.

It's over.

•••

"This is too much, Rusty."

"Nope. Not by a penny. I don't have any pay stubs, but trust me. It's a fair accounting."

Prosper set the envelope full of bills down on the table in his living room. He eased back into his favorite chair.

"I don't recall making out that well. Guess it's because the cost of living's so much higher out there."

"Don't forget," Rusty said with a nod to where Marceline sat on the couch. "Half of it's hers."

"She'll end up with a damn sight more than half. I won't spend a fraction of it in the time I got left."

"Way to keep the conversation cheery, Dad."

"You know what I mean," he replied, reaching over to pat her knee. "I just want to leave you with as much as possible, and it ain't like I got many extravagant desires at this point."

"It is a little overwhelming," Marceline said with a glance at the thick pile of hundreds. "Seeing so much in one lump. Drawing nurses pay for the last few years, I forgot what entertainment money looks like."

"My advice," Rusty said, "is to put a nice big chunk in a safe deposit box. Dip in as you need to. Diapers aren't cheap, or so I've heard. Take the rest and set up a trust for the kid. Hire a good estate lawyer so you don't get hosed on taxes."

Marceline looked at him and started to say something, but Rusty spoke first.

"No thanks needed. This is just a payment for services rendered, and long overdue at that."

"Still a wee bit presumptuous, aren't you?" she said with a grin. "That mentalism bit only goes so far, you know."

"Sorry. What were you going to say?"

"I was going to thank you, but not for the money."

"No need for that either. Just text me a picture from the maternity ward. I can't wait to get a look at the next great standard bearer of New Orleans magic."

"You'll be the first to get one."

Rusty opened his arms and she stepped into them. He let her go and turned to Prosper. The old man rose to his feet before Rusty could tell him not to.

A simple shake of the hand served as a parting gesture. Their eyes locked for a long moment of wordless communication. It was more than enough. Rusty made for the door, never a fan of extended goodbyes.

Later that evening, he and Monday enjoyed dinner for two at Jacques-Imo's. As they perused the dessert menu, he opened his mouth to tell her something he'd been avoiding for almost a week. She beat him to the punch, preemptively agreeing with what he was going to say. It was time for him to be heading back to Ocean Pines. He couldn't crash at her place indefinitely, that was never in the cards.

They were each anxious in their own way to get back to whatever passed for routine before they'd crossed paths. This unexpected chapter in whatever it was they shared had come to a close. If the future held anything for them, they would find out in due time. Rusty wasn't prepared to make any promises about relocating to New Orleans, any more than Monday was prepared to say she'd wait for him.

They both knew the score, why make a scene about it? Leaving the restaurant without ordering dessert, they shared one last fevered night together that took them clear through to the dawn.

Monday had an early shift at the ward so Rusty said he'd take a cab to the airport. She agreed, then changed her mind at the last minute. Getting a coworker to cover her shift, she drove him to Armstrong International, taking the interstate at slower speeds than he'd ever seen her follow.

They embraced in a temporary parking space at the departure level. Monday ended it, telling him to have a safe flight and then turning away before betraying too much with a look on her face.

There were no seats available in first class. Rusty got stuck in a window seat in row 28, which was fine. He told himself he was happy to be going home. Sleepy little Ocean Pines sounded like a tonic after a month in New Orleans.

The return flight was a lot less eventful than the one that brought him south, for which Rusty was grateful. Clear skies all the way. Not so much as a little hiccup of turbulence.

Best of all, he was able to see it. If not quite as clearly as he once might have, then close enough.

He didn't make much conversation with his seatmates on the flight back to Baltimore, content to simply look out the window. His eyes got irritated after prolonged exposure to sunlight, lined with angry veins well beyond the standard description of bloodshot. He wasn't too worried about that. The clinician had told him it might take months for the irritation to fully resolve.

He retrieved his dust-covered Lexus from the lot at BWI and made the familiar two hour drive. His favorite part of the journey, crossing over the Chesapeake Bay Bridge to reach Maryland's eastern shore, struck him with a surprisingly depressive wallop. The sense of content anticipation he'd felt about returning to Ocean Pines while on the plane suddenly vanished.

What was there to feel good about? Once again, he was crawling back to the place where he'd grown up but where he'd never totally felt at home. Returning here after after spending the last month in another place that was once home but somehow never would be again, at least not in the same way.

As he drove along Route 1 toward Ocean Pines, Rusty

reflected on a basic truth he'd somehow managed to avoid ever since that bleary dawn when he'd turned his back on Las Vegas and everything he'd built for himself out there.

He had no home.

Not Ocean Pines, comfortable as it was. Not New Orleans, despite the emotional bonds he'd formed there, both old and new. Certainly not Vegas, a place he was scared to even think about in any great detail.

How long could he keep hiding out here in coastal Maryland? Whiling away the days in his big rented house, seeing few people except for the occasional drink with his cop buddy Jim Biddison. Waiting for some kind of sign to arise, telling him he'd truly escaped the consequences of the past—or for some unseen ax to fall and bring the delayed punishment he'd long felt was due.

As he pulled his car into the pebbled driveway of 24 Echo Run, noticing the piles of leaves that had accumulated in his absence, Rusty just couldn't make himself feel like he'd returned to a place where he could stay much longer. Something had to give.

He let himself in and set his bags down in the front hallway. Then he walked through the empty house with the uneasy gait of a trespasser. Rusty didn't know exactly what had happened to make this place where he'd lived for over a year seem like it belonged to someone else. He didn't know if it was a lingering sense of disorientation from the utterly insane events in which he'd played a role in Louisiana, or if it would prove to be a more lasting phenomenon.

All he knew for sure was that things had changed. Marking time here in Ocean Pines and waiting for an indication of what to do next was no longer an option.

He knew what to do.

He had to go back to Vegas, and find out exactly what was waiting for him out there.